# THE ANGEL
# TREASON

*a novel*

by

## M.W. TALLEY

OCTOBER 30, 2017

theangeltreason.com

*This book is dedicated to my brother, Christopher Scott Talley, who died too soon. I miss you.*

Chapter One

Sandriel was sitting on the bed in his hotel room, staring blankly at the barrel of his pistol when his phone rang.

"Yes," he answered.

"This is Ramiel," a man on the other end said.

"And?"

"I know we haven't spoken in a while, but I need you to pick up my daughter."

"Right now?"

"Yes, right now."

"I haven't slept in four days," Sandriel said.

"Sandriel, I don't care. This is important to me. You're the only angel I can think of who I trust to get her back to me."

Sandriel looked back at the barrel of his pistol.

"Hello?" Ramiel asked. "Are you there?"

Sandriel put the pistol on the nightstand, and said, "Yes, I'm here."

"Are you okay?" Ramiel asked.

"I'm fine. Give me an address."

"I've already sent it, along with the details," Ramiel said.

Sandriel took the pistol from his nightstand and put it in his shoulder holster.

"I'll leave in a few minutes," he said, and then ended the call.

---

Miles away, in a small house in a once prosperous city in Michigan, a young woman named Amanda heard her mom's shrill voice that only seemed to hit those high notes when she had been drinking vodka. "Amanda! Get off your ass and get me some cigarettes."

Great, Amanda thought. My first day off in a week and I get to spend it buying cigarettes for my drunk mom.

"Okay, I'm off to the store," Amanda yelled. She paused for a moment, waiting for a reply, and didn't hear one.

As she walked to her car she noticed the flat tire almost immediately.

"God hates me," she muttered.

Just then she saw a silver Mercedes SUV speeding down her street, windows down and music blaring. She looked at the driver and thought: Looks like some stuck up rich kid in his daddy's car.

The Mercedes had almost passed her house when it suddenly screeched to a halt. Oh my God, Amanda thought. Why?

She realized he was yelling at her, but with his music so loud she couldn't make out what he was saying. After a few seconds, he shut off the music, jumped out of the car, and walked toward her at a startling, almost unnatural speed.

"Are you Amanda?" he asked. "Amanda Ingles? Ma'am, are you the Amanda Ingles who submitted a DNA test approximately four weeks ago?"

It took her a few seconds to grasp what he was saying. She wasn't sure if it was the barrage of questions he was asking; his strangely formal, rapid-fire speech; or the entire situation that was making her head swim.

"Yes . . . I am her," she said hesitantly.

"Good," he said. "While I apologize profusely for not having more time to explain myself, I must let you know that you are, at this very moment, in great danger. But lucky for you, the men who are looking for you were not as quick at finding you as I was."

"So, Ma'am," he said, in a polite southern accent. "It is in both of our best interests that we go inside and gather your things, and then you come with me so I can get you to safety."

He firmly grasped her by the arm and began walking toward the house.

"Wait a minute! What in the hell are you even talking about?" she asked as she pushed his hand away from her. "I don't know who you are, and there is no way I'm going anywhere with some fancy redneck who just tells me some story about people looking for me. I don't know how things work in West Virginia, or wherever you're from with that silly accent, but around here girls don't just run away with random people -- no matter how nice their cars are."

He paused, looking her over. "I do apologize, Ma'am, but I assure you I am no random guy, or kid, or whatever you think I am. I look young for my age," he said with a slight grin. "I'm a lifelong friend of your father's, and I was sent here to take you to him. That is all I can tell you concerning that for now. Trust me. I am here to help you."

"What? My dad? My dad left us. And you're here to save me? From what? Are you a cop or something?"

"No, I'm not a police officer -- far from it. I'm more like a messenger." He grinned again. "Is your mother home,

Amanda? Maybe she can explain to your satisfaction, but I cannot stress enough that time is of the essence and we need to move out quickly."

"I'll go inside and get her," she said. "But you're not setting foot in my house. Wait on the porch."

The man nodded, and Amanda heard him mutter something about the lack of hospitality in the North. As she went into the house, she yelled for her mom.

Amanda explained to her mom what had just happened. As she waited for her mom to comprehend -- quite a task for her in her current condition -- Amanda noticed the strange man on the porch was fidgeting with something under his suit jacket.

"So, Mom, can you please tell me what is going on?" Amanda asked. She realized that her mother was also staring at the strange man on the porch, most likely trying to assess the situation through a haze of liquor-induced confusion. Either that or she was moments away from passing out. Amanda couldn't tell which one it was, having experienced the latter occurrence with increasing frequency over the last several years.

"Mom, snap out of it!" Amanda yelled as she shook her mother to attention.

"What are we going to do? Should we call the cops?" she asked. "I think he's crazy!"

Either the word "cops" or "crazy" seemed to draw the man's attention on the porch, Amanda noticed. He looked at them for a moment, then lit up what appeared to be a cigarette. "Gross! He's a smoker," she said aloud without thinking.

"Come with me," Amanda's mother said, grasping her hand and pulling her toward the door.

"What do you want with my daughter, stranger?" her mother asked. "And how do you know her father?"

The stranger looked at her mom, smiled slightly and said, "Do not forget to show hospitality to strangers, Ma'am, for by doing so some people have shown hospitality to angels without knowing it."

"Yeah, I know," Amanda's mother interrupted. "Hebrews 13:2."

"An impressive display, Ma'am," the man on the porch said. "I was also told by Amanda's father that, if I was so graced by your presence, to tell you he missed his Mimosa."

"Oh my god! What are you even talking about?" Amanda could not control her frustration. "Mimosa? The drink? Well, that figures. Is this some kind of joke? Will someone please explain what's happening?"

Amanda looked at her mom waiting for a reply, but realized her mom looked totally dumbfounded . . . as if placed in a trance by what the man had said.

"No, Amanda not the drink . . . Mimosa, the silk plant . . . the Persian silk plant. Only your dad called me that. You should go with him. He is a friend of your Dad. Trust him."

"What? Just like that? I tell you there is some strange guy who is talking about people coming after me and you want me to just run away with him?"

"Miss Amanda," the man said, with a southern drawl that she felt was beginning to drive her insane, "I'll explain on the way. But we need to get you . . . you specifically, far away from this address as soon as possible. Now, please if you would gather your things so we can exit these premises, it would be greatly appreciated."

"Just go," her mom said. "I don't have time to deal with whatever you or your dad has gotten involved in anyway." After a moment of startled clarity, her mom appeared confused again.

"But I haven't done anything!"

"If you didn't do anything then why are all these people looking for you?" asked her mom, clearly feeling the effects of the half empty gallon of cheap vodka sitting on the counter. Amanda knew the cycle. Her mom had already started to enter the blackout phase and it wouldn't be long before she passed out. She had probably already forgotten what they were talking about.

Amanda felt the tears welling up in her eyes and told the well-dressed stranger to give her a minute. The man looked at her sympathetically, turned his eyes back toward the street, and said in a consoling tone, "Of course . . . I'm sorry for all of this." It was as if he understood exactly what she was feeling. "I'll be in the car."

"Okay. I'll be quick," she replied.

"Just get the essentials," he said, still scanning the road. "I have enough money to buy any clothes or anything else you may need. I'll just feel a lot better when we put some distance between us and this place."

"You don't seem very worried," Amanda said, noticing his coolness.

"Well . . . lucky for you we got your information before they did, but I'm not one to take any chances. It could be minutes or it could be days before they figure out who you are. But, anyway, I'm good at what I do. Grab your things. I'll be in the car."

What the hell did he mean by that? Who "I" am. And who is this "they"? Amanda thought as she grabbed a few plastic grocery bags. As she looked her bedroom over she realized there were so few things that really meant anything to her. Her half-broken laptop, purse, makeup, brush, bathroom supplies, and a ring a boy had given her when she went on a class trip to Washington, D. C. That was all she could think of bringing. She wasn't sure what to think as she looked around the house. Would she be back? She felt as if she were dreaming. She wasn't positive if she was or not, and even less sure if it was a good or bad dream.

On her way through the living room, she paused for a long look at her mother, who was now completely passed out on the couch. It was one of the few times when it was quiet in the house . . . when she was passed out.

Amanda thought about leaving a note, knowing her mom wouldn't remember all that had occurred, but she decided not to. She didn't think her mom deserved one. She knew she might regret not leaving that note one day, leaving her mom to wonder what had happened, but at that moment she didn't care. She felt she was on her own now and had to look out for herself.

On her way through the kitchen she hated so much, the one her mom made her clean twice a day whether it needed it or not, she grabbed one last thing -- the largest knife she could find.

"A girl can never be too careful," she said, feeling a sudden sense of empowerment for the first time in her 18 years on this earth.

When she got outside she saw the SUV was still running, but was surprised to see the young-looking well-dressed stranger holding the door open for her. No guy had ever done that for her, she realized. After he took the grocery bags full of her belongings from her and placed them in the trunk, she realized she had started twirling her hair between her thumb and index finger. A nervous habit she knew she did around certain guys. She stopped immediately as he got into the driver's seat. Maybe he was just trying to hurry her along.

She began to speak but was suddenly aware of the interior of the vehicle. She had never been in a Mercedes before, and was shocked at the extravagance. All the leather and polished wood seemed unnecessary but strangely comforting. It was so quiet compared to the cars she was used to riding in. The silence was broken by the man, whose relaxed demeanor was betrayed only by bright blue eyes that constantly darted between the rearview mirror and the road ahead.

"Amanda, I do believe we are safe for the present, and I'm sure your head is swimming. Feel free to take a nap, if you are tired. I will wake you when we arrive at the hotel."

"Are you freaking serious?" Amanda said, with a sarcastic look on her face. "I don't know who you are, you basically told me I was going to be abducted, and it looks like you are the one doing the abducting. You seem to know my dad somehow, who left me and my mom when I was three, I might add. That's only the tip of the iceberg when it comes to all the questions I have going around in my head right now. I don't even know your name for God's sake."

He nodded her way, still focused on the mirrors. "It will be a lot for you to take in."

"After what just happened I'm pretty sure I can take it in," Amanda retorted.

The man just smiled. "Well, Ma'am, we'll see. It's a long drive. Ask away."

"First of all, what's up with the accent, and all the ma'am stuff? You sound like the guys in some movie about Gettysburg I had to watch in history class."

"Ah, yes, the War of Northern Aggression. Well, I've spent a good many year in the south. Virginia specifically. I suppose I grew rather fond of their way of speaking and picked it up at some point."

"Do you miss it? Virginia, I mean."

"Sometimes, I miss it I suppose, but I'm used to moving around and not becoming attached to places or people."

"I've moved around a lot, too," Amanda said, forgetting about her predicament for a moment. "I think it's because we've moved around so much that we make a point not to become attached. That's just what I think, at least. I could be wrong, I guess. Everyone's different."

"Yes, that makes sense. Do you think we'll always be like that, Amanda? Never wanting to be too attached to others?"

"I hope not," Amanda replied.

"Yes, Amanda, I hope not as well. Do you want to listen to some music?"

"I just listen to Lana Del Rey, mostly."

He played with the stereo, until he found some music he thought she would like.

Amanda thought maybe his accent wasn't so bad after all. She liked the slow overly pronounced way he said her name. She realized she was playing with her hair again, and stopped immediately, again

"So, you still haven't told me your name."

"I was given with the name Sandriel," he replied with a grin. "I go by Sander now."

"That's different. Is it a family name?"

"Not exactly," he said grinning once again. "Just the one God gave me."

That was an odd answer, Amanda thought. She wanted to know more about his personal life but didn't want to pry.

Why couldn't I have met this guy under different circumstances? He seems to be truly interested in what I think. No guy had ever taken the time to ask me what I thought about anything before, no matter how trivial the question. It didn't really matter. No guy like this one would be interested in me anyway. He's cute and obviously has money. Me? I'm just a Plain Jane, like Mom always tells me.

"Something wrong, Amanda?" he asked.

"No, why? Never mind that. . . I just . . . I just have a lot going on in my mind right now."

"Understandably so, Amanda. It's been a very unusual day for you, to say the least. Try to get some rest. I'll wake you when we are there."

"At the hotel?"

"Yes, not too much longer," he said softly. "Get some rest dear." His eyes still danced between the road and the rearview mirror.

I like the way Sander calls me 'dear', she thought. As she leaned back and closed her eyes, she felt the tiny hairs on her arms stand up as a cozy chill flowed over her body, and she drifted into sleep.

Amanda suddenly felt the hard grip of Sander squeezing her knee. "Are we there?" she asked groggily.

"Now, don't panic but we are being followed," Sander said.

"Wait, what? By who?"

"I'll explain that later. This car is bulletproof," Sander said softly, trying to keep Amanda from panicking. "What I need you to do is crawl into the back floorboard and lie down."

"What? Why? I thought you said the car was bulletproof."

"Because in order to shoot the people following us I will need to have my window down, since I can't shoot through the bullet-resistant glass, and I am not too keen on any of their stray bullets possibly hitting you. That's why," Sander said calmly. "Now do it fast; it should be over quickly."

Amanda unbuckled her seat belt and awkwardly squeezed between the two front seats making her way into the rear floorboard. No matter how much she crouched she didn't feel like she could make herself get low enough.

Sander reached onto the back seat and pulled what felt to Amanda like a heavy jacket over her head and back. "This is insane," she whispered.

She couldn't see a thing but heard the unmistakable sound of two heavy metal clicks, the feeling of the SUV braking and then heard a series of muffled thuds, followed by Sander cursing under his breath.

As she felt the SUV accelerate she could still hear Sander cursing.

"Are you okay?" Amanda asked. There was no response. She realized she was shaking as she pulled the heavy vest from over her head. "Are you okay?" she whispered again, still too afraid to look up.

She felt the car decelerate, then come to a complete stop. What was happening?

"It's over, Amanda. You can get back up front with me."

Amanda felt relief pass through her body at the sound of his voice. As she arose, he got out of the SUV with what looked to her like a long pistol or small machine gun still in hand. He opened the passenger door, and helped her to her feet. Amanda couldn't hold back her tears anymore. It had all been too much. The realization that this wasn't a game anymore -- that he wasn't just some guy there to sweep her off her feet and take her away from her boring life -- was all too real. She let the tears flow.

"When you didn't answer me and the car stopped I thought you were dead. I was waiting for it to crash . . . I was too afraid to move," she said in a shaky voice. "Did you kill them?"

"Yes, Ma'am, they're dead," he said softly, as he awkwardly put an arm around her. "I'm good at what I do."

She could tell her crying was making him uncomfortable and he didn't know how to respond, so she hugged him tightly, burying her head in his chest.

"Thank you, Sander, for saving me. I'm sorry for crying. I just . . . I didn't hear your voice and I thought the worst for a second. I was worried about you. I'm okay now."

"It's okay, but we better get back on the road," Sander said. As he pulled away from her embrace, he paused and looked her in the eyes, and said, "Thank you, too, Amanda."

"For what?" Amanda asked.

Sander looked shyly at the ground, avoiding eye contact, and said curtly, "For caring about me, too." Sander quickly composed himself, saying, "Come on, we have to go."

So, the southern gentleman has a soft side, Amanda thought as Sander opened her car door for her. As she caught a glimpse of her reflection in the window, she remembered her mother's words: *No guy will ever find you attractive.*

Lost in thought, Amanda realized Sander had said something.

"Your cell phone," he repeated. "You'll have to get rid of it now. It's how they found us so quickly."

"What? How do you know?"

"It's how I would have tracked you if I were looking for you."

"Then why didn't you have me throw it out in the first place?" she asked, staring at him in disbelief.

"I had to know . . ."

"Had to know what?" she interrupted, feeling both confused and perturbed by his nonchalant attitude.

"I wanted to know exactly who they were going to send after you," he said. "I recognized the driver, but the other one was new, I think. A novice. He never pulled his gun, if he even had one."

"Wait. So you wanted someone to try to kill us? You are insane. Is my dad in the mafia or something? Nothing is making sense."

"No, not the mafia. Your dad is a powerful man. You would make quite the bargaining chip is the way I see it. To his adversaries, you would be worth a lot more alive than dead. Thus, the lack of shooting on their end, I suppose, but then again, I didn't exactly give them the chance. Don't worry, you were never in any real harm. Like I said, I'm good at what I do. I just wanted to see what we were up against."

Amanda stared at him, feeling numb, still waiting to wake up from this strange savage dream at any moment. She pinched herself through her jeans pocket. Nope, I'm not dreaming, she thought. I can't believe this is really happening.

"Now your cell phone, my dear," he said. "Can I have it, so we aren't interrupted by any more unpleasant distractions?"

Still staring at him, she handed him her phone without saying a word.

"I'm going to duct-tape your phone to one of the trucks here at the next exit. It should buy us some peace and quiet for a while and throw anyone else off our trail . . . Then we can get back to playing fifty questions."

More like fifty million questions, Amanda thought.

"If you need to freshen up, or are hungry or anything, you can do all of that when we stop," he said.

"I'm fine," Amanda said. "I feel like I'm about to pass out. Please don't wake me up to any more gun fights if you don't mind . . . I'll go ahead and thank you in advance."

"Yes Ma'am, I'll let you sleep through the next gun fight, if those are your orders," he said, smiling.

Chapter Two

"We're here, "Sander whispered. "Wake up, Amanda. We're here."

Amanda yawned, looked at Sander, squatting beside her open car door, then at the two well-dressed men standing several yards behind them, then back at Sander's face. Being so close to him, for once, she noticed the fierceness in his eyes. Maybe he is older than he looks, after all, she thought.

"Who are they?" she asked, nodding her head at the men.

Sander turned to see who she was talking about. "Ah, yes Ma'am. They're just the valets. I tipped them, but I'm going to leave the SUV here. A bulletproof Mercedes tends to bring up a lot of unwanted attention, believe it or not," he said in a sarcastic tone. "And valets are going to gossip no matter how much I tip them."

"Of course," Amanda said, thinking: I wonder if it's that obvious that I've never stayed anywhere that had valets before.

"I took the liberty of booking the room while you were sleeping. I'll get our things and we can go inside," Sander said, as he made his way to the back of the SUV.

"Is my mom going to be okay?" Amanda asked.

"Yes, nothing will happen to your mom. She's a civilian, and worth nothing to them, or our organization for that matter. It's you they wanted . . . But I think I sent a pretty strong message that you were not going to be harmed or taken, when I killed the two men who made the mistake of following us earlier."

"I would say you did," Amanda said, nodding her head in agreement as she walked to the entrance of the hotel.

"Mr. Johnson!" a man with a baggage cart yelled. "Can I take those to your room for you?" he asked, motioning with his head at the luggage Sander was carrying.

"I'm good, but thank you anyway," Sander replied.

"Mr. Johnson?" Amanda asked. "Your name is Sander Johnson?"

"No," Sander said in a quiet voice. "Johnson is the name I travel under, sometimes. Second-most used surname in America, so a little easier to go unrecognized. I could go by Smith, I guess, but even if your real name is Smith, when you give that name to people, it always sounds like you're lying or trying to hide your real identity . . . At least it does to me." He smiled and realized Amanda was looking around dumbstruck.

"What is the name of this place?" she asked, spinning around, taking it all in.

"It's the Brown," Sander replied. "The Brown Hotel. We can go somewhere else if you're unhappy with it . . . But I can assure you -- we are safe here. This is my turf."

"No, no it's gorgeous. It's perfect. It just looks more like a museum or a palace, not like any hotel I've ever stayed in," she said, still looking around. "Did you say *The* Brown Hotel? Like in *The Great Gatsby?*"

"Well aren't you a surprisingly well read young woman," Sander said with a smile.

"It was my favorite book in high school," Amanda said confidently. Smiling, she added, "It was better than the movie."

Sander couldn't help but laugh. "Anyway yes, this is it . . . The Brown Hotel from *The Great Gatsby.*"

"So, you have a romantic side, do you?" Amanda asked.

Sander seemed to ignore Amanda's question as they entered the elevator and he handed her what looked like a credit card.

"This is the card to our room suite. It's on the top floor, and the only way to get to the top floor is if you put this card in here when you press the floor number. Got it?" he asked. "Sorry if I'm telling you things you already know. I just want to make sure you have a basic idea of what's going on. I have no idea what must be going on in that head of yours at this point."

As they exited the elevator and walked toward their suite, Amanda noticed an attractive blonde woman around her age approaching them.

"Hello!" the woman said, staring at Sander and practically ignoring Amanda. "My name is Jenny and I'm the concierge for this floor. If you need directions or anything at all just let me know. If you don't see me out here or in the lounge, my number is by the phone in your suite. Can I possibly get you something to drink?"

Noticing the concierge ignoring Amanda, Sander looked at Amanda and said, "Would you like anything, my dear?"

"No, I'm okay," Amanda said softly, looking at the floor.

"Okay then, I'll be here if you need me," the concierge said in a bubbly voice that made Amanda's blood boil.

No matter what I do, I will never be as beautiful as that concierge, Amanda thought, and she bet Sander thought that, too.

Sensing Amanda's mood, Sander said, "My dear, let's see our suite."

Amanda smiled a fake smile. It was the most beautiful room Amanda had ever been in. It was as big as her house, she thought.

"I need to put some things away," Sander said as he took off his suit jacket, revealing two holstered pistols. "The room service menu should be on the counter. Go ahead and order whatever you want. Order me something, too; you can decide. I'll be sleeping in this room since it's closer to the door, and the other one is yours, of course."

Amanda ordered room service for the first time in her life and waited for Sander. She still had so many questions for him. She wondered where this journey was going to take her. She heard a lot of metal-clicking sounds coming from Sander's room. Guns is what she was guessing. She pictured his suitcase full of nothing but guns and preppy clothes and laughed.

Sander finally walked out of his room, this time without his two holsters, she noticed, but he was carrying something that looked like an Uzi from the movies she had seen. Her heart skipped a beat. Perhaps he was there to kill her, after all, she suddenly thought. Surely he would have done it before now when they were on that empty interstate forever, or when she was sleeping.

He saw the way she was looking at him, and immediately asked, "Have you ever fired a gun, Amanda?"

"No," she replied.

"Well, I don't think you will ever have to, but I'm going to show you how, just in case," he said with a serious look on his face.

"Is that an Uzi?"

"No, Amanda, this is an MP7, but you're kind of close. Kind of." He grinned slightly, handing her the weapon. "Don't worry; it's not loaded."

It was the first time she had held any kind of gun and was surprised at how light it was. Almost like a toy. She held the MP7 and aimed it at her reflection in the mirror with both hands. He stood behind her and guided her hand to a switch behind the trigger.

"When the switch is up all the way, it's on safe so you can't fire it," he said, guiding her hand down. "When it's in the middle, it's in single fire, and when it's at the bottom it's fully automatic, so you are going to basically spray bullets."

There was something about holding the weapon and having him so close to her that was making her head swim, in a good way.

"In your case, if you ever must fire this thing, flip the switch all the way down, point it and pull the trigger until they are dead. Okay. It's as simple as that. Switch all the way down, and let them have it. If there ever does come a time you must fire this gun, aim for their chest unless they are right up on you because your hands will probably be shaking."

I wonder if he can feel my body shaking, Amanda thought and giggled at how immature she felt at the moment.

Just then there was a knock at the door, then another. Amanda noticed the serious look on Sander's face, as if a million thoughts were racing through his mind at once.

"I think it's room service," Amanda said.

"Oh, yes. Sorry. Holding the weapon and everything . . . Got my mind wandering, I suppose."

Maybe he did feel me trembling after all, Amanda thought.

As he walked to the door she saw him pull his shirt tail over the pistol he had stuck in the back of his pants. He had no idea how sexy she thought he was right now, and it made her laugh again.

Sander looked through the peephole, then talked to the person at the door like he was familiar with them, and returned with their meal.

"Cheeseburgers and wine," Sander said smiling. "Interesting choice. Are you even old enough to drink?"

"No, I'm not. But you are, and I had never heard of most of the other stuff on the menu," Amanda said.

"I didn't mean to sound pretentious; I was being serious. I love their cheeseburgers. That's all I order whenever I'm here."

"You're just saying that to make me feel better. That's all right, at least you're being sweet. How long have you been coming here?"

"I stay here whenever I'm in Louisville. I guess I've been coming here since about the '30's."

"Thirty?" Amanda said smiling. "You look maybe 25 years old. 30 tops."

"No, I meant the 1930's. I suppose there is something I've been meaning to tell you. I'm a fallen angel."

Amanda laughed.

Sander's expression didn't change.

"Oh my God, you're serious! That's it. You're crazy, aren't you?" Amanda said, her eyes darting toward the telephone.

"Don't touch that phone please," Sander said. "I guess this is the only way I'm going to convince you."

Then Amanda saw the most amazing thing she had witnessed in her short life. The room lit up in a bright auburn glow as what appeared to be wings came out of Sander's back. They were shaped like the wings of an eagle, but appeared to be on fire. Burning like red flames that caused her to squint as she tried to comprehend what she was seeing. It was beautiful, and terrifying at the same time.

"Don't worry, Amanda; my wings can't burn you. They are basically just light, and quite useless now, anyway. I can't fly anymore. The only thing my wings do for me presently is remind me of a time I'd rather forget," Sander said mournfully. "Do you believe me now? I tell you the truth when I say I am an angel. My name is Sandriel, one of the fallen angels expelled from Heaven, and you are the daughter of one."

And then the wings disappeared from Sander's back as if they had never been there.

Amanda sat there, mouth partially open, in dead silence for what seemed like an eternity, pondering, and questioning everything she thought she knew about life. About the world. She had so many questions she literally didn't know where to begin.

Finally, it was the lost, sad look on Sander's face that brought her mind back to focus. "Are you my guardian angel?" Amanda asked.

"For the moment," Sander said, still looking at the floor. "But not in the sense you are thinking. God didn't appoint me to look after you, if that's what you mean."

"Do it again . . . your wings," Amanda said walking up to Sander.

"I'd prefer not to. They remind me of when I was someone else, someone who did things I'm not especially proud of . . . someone you wouldn't have liked."

He could tell by the wide-eyed expression on Amanda's face that she probably hadn't heard a word he had said. He extended his wings once again.

Amanda flinched, staring at him in awe.

She reached slowly toward one of the wings and then jerked her hand back. "Wow!" Amanda said as she waved her hand through the wings. "They are nothing but light. Almost like a hologram or something," she added. "But you can feel a slight vibration when you touch them. This is amazing!" she said as she continued to wave her hand back and forth through Sander's wings.

Sander grinned slightly, finding Amanda's childlike fascination and innocence amusing. He put his wings away.

"Does it hurt when your wings come out? "Amanda asked.

Sander thought for a second, and replied, "No, there's no physical pain."

"I don't know what to say," Sander said looking back at the floor. "I could tell you my story but it would literally take a mortal's lifetime to hear. I apologize for not being more forthcoming when we first met. But under the circumstances, I thought that hearing there was a real possibility of you being kidnapped would be difficult enough for you to comprehend, much less the fact that fallen angels exist, that I exist. It's been so long since I've exposed my true self to a human that I've forgotten where to begin. I can't think of a simple way to explain what I am to you. It's true that the fallen angels all followed Lucifer at one time, but even angels can be aware of the mistakes they have made in the past and do their best to correct them . . ."

"Oh ... my ... god! You're really a freaking angel," Amanda said with a huge smile on her face.

Sander laughed. "Thank you for lightening the mood."

"You looked a little sad. I was just trying to change that."

"It worked," Sander said with a shy grin.

"This is madness! I do have a lot of questions, though. One doesn't get to spend the night in a hotel room with an actual angel very often."

"Fallen angel, I'm not exactly an angel anymore, more of an ex-angel I suppose. That is a more simplistic way to describe what I am. We rebelled, along with Lucifer, because we believed he was right and we wanted what you have, what humans have: free will. So we fought many bloody battles against our brothers . . . our fellow angels, and God banished us, the rebellious, to earth . . ."

Amanda interrupted, "So God is real?" she pondered that for a few moments. "I mean . . . I've always believed, but you talk about him like he's just some guy you used to know."

"Yes Amanda, I assure you he is real," Sander said. "More powerful that you can believe. We tested that, and lost."

"And the devil?" Amanda asked.

"He's real as well Amanda," Sander said. "Having had thousands of years to think about this, I realize it was when God created you humans that the trouble really began. Up until then, Lucifer was God's favorite angel, and everything, at least to me, seemed right in Heaven. It was when God created man -- and we basically became messengers, following God's will -- that the problems began arising. We saw humans could follow God's will if they wanted to, but they didn't have to. He gave humans a choice that we never had. So, we began questioning God, his plan, his intentions."

"Eventually we had enough of this perceived double standard, and with Lucifer as our general we rebelled against God and his loyal angels. We went to war with him against God's angel army. Looking back now, I realize we were insane to believe we could win an all-out war against God. Even we were deceived by the great deceiver himself, Lucifer."

"Even after we lost the war in Heaven and were banished to Earth, Lucifer deceived us, convincing us we had somehow triumphed by gaining our free will. To tell you the truth, during our first centuries on Earth we took over completely, married human women, and were treated like gods. We did many unspeakable, wicked things under Lucifer's banner. Eventually God had enough of the way we corrupted you humans, his precious creation, and he decided to start over. He flooded the planet, sending most of us to the abyss."

Sander realized Amanda was looking at him spellbound.

"I apologize. I have a habit of rambling . . ."

"No, no, no," Amanda said excitedly. "Keep going. What happened after the flood?"

"Ah, yes, well after the Great Flood, those of the fallen angels who remained were in two camps. There was a group who believed we should remain loyal to Lucifer because he did, after all, help us in obtaining our free will. And, there was another group of us who thought following Lucifer was the most idiotic decision we could have made at that point . . ."

Sander paused for a moment, appearing to be deep in thought, and then continued, "Because, God had just shown us who was in charge when He flooded pretty much the entirety of the Earth. So, if we followed Lucifer again and we started corrupting and having our way with humans the way we had in the past, who was to say He wouldn't flood the place again? Eventually, most of the fallen angels who were left chose a side, and that is basically how the two great houses that exist today were formed -- House Lucifer and House Ramiel -- your father being the head of House Ramiel. Sorry, that is a rather concise history lesson about us, but we don't really have all year to go through the complete story of fallen angels. I'm sure they will tell you more when we get to the House Ramiel compound.

"So, you're saying my dad is the leader of a group of fallen angels? This is crazy," Amanda said, eyebrows furrowed in concentration. "So what does that make me?"

"It makes you the daughter of a very powerful fallen angel."

"So, I'm not a princess or anything?"

"No, unfortunately not," Sander said, as he noticed a look of disappointment sweep across Amanda's face.

"I'm not special?"

"Did you not hear a word I just told you? You have the blood of one of the most powerful fallen angels on this earth running through your veins. Of course, you're special. Not only that, but you, pretty lady, have the most handsome fallen angel currently on this earth here to protect you. If that doesn't make you special, I surely do not know what does."

Amanda couldn't help but laugh.

"You know how to make a lady smile," Amanda said.

"Thank you my dear. I've had thousands of years of practice," Sander replied, purposely overdoing his smooth southern accent.

"Amanda, your father shapes empires! You are a very special girl indeed. One I am glad to have met, by the way . . ."

He paused, "And this is coming from someone who has literally met millions of people."

Amanda could feel herself blushing.

"I have some more questions."

Sander nodded.

"If I'm part angel, do I have any super powers?"

Sander started to speak and then paused in thought for a moment.

"Not in the way I believe you are thinking. I've noticed throughout the centuries that some half-bloods, rather, most half-bloods, display the most curious traits. Some are exceedingly strong, some unusually gifted in the arts. Our blood seems to affect each of them," he corrected himself, "of *you*, in its own individual way, and I suppose some go through their lives without realizing their full potential."

Sander glanced at her and didn't see the look of disappointment he expected, instead she appeared to be studying his face.

"Are all angels, I mean fallen angels, pretty boys?" she asked, smiling.

Grinning, he said, "No, we don't all look alike. There are angels who look like every race of humans, you'll see when we get to one of the House Ramiel compounds. I've always looked like this. This is the way God created me. We don't age physically. We appear the way God created us, until the end of days, or we die."

"Wait," Amanda interrupted. "Until you die? How long do you live?"

"Well, we need food and water like you, just not as much. I've gone months without either. In Heaven, we didn't need such things, but when we were exiled, along with our free will came the new feelings of hunger and thirst. But given food and water, I suppose, we can live forever."

Sander thought for a moment. "Basically, anything that can kill a human can kill us. We can just take a lot more of it."

"Here," Sander said as he stood up and walked to his room.

He returned holding a knife. He handed the knife to Amanda, while rolling up his shirt sleeve.

"Now, cut my arm."

"I'm not cutting your arm."

He took the knife back, and Amanda watched, intrigued, as he proceeded to cut his arm. Fascinated, she watched the wound close almost as quickly as he was cutting it.

"Amazing!" Amanda said, still staring. "What other super powers do you have?"

"I don't know why you insist on calling them super powers," he said. "But compared to humans, we are stronger, faster and better-looking." He laughed. "I'm kidding about the better-looking part. For example, if I must take on ten men in a fight, I won't hesitate. If there are twenty or more I might get a little worried," he said smiling. "But then again, I have trained for combat for centuries, and not all the fallen angels have. Not all of the fallen have fought in as many wars as I have. On equal terms, men have killed some of us before. Not very often, but through history it has happened. So, we are by no means one of the super heroes you are thinking of."

"This is the most interesting conversation I've had with anyone in my life!" Amanda blurted out. "I feel like I should be writing it down."

"No, I'm glad you're not. The less people know about our existence the better. It's easier to control humans when they don't realize who is controlling them, Amanda. We learned that a millennium ago. Besides, I have been keeping a record of my personal exploits for thousands of years in a cave in Persia. I'll take you there after things have calmed down between the houses and I feel it's safe again."

"Oh, are you asking me on a date?" Amanda asked.

"Yes, it's a date, if you're interested; but first we need to get you to your father safely."

"I'll think about it . . . the date, I mean," Amanda said smiling.

As Amanda heated their now cold cheeseburgers in the microwave, she felt Sander staring at her. It made her uneasy. Feeling self-conscious, she asked awkwardly, "If House Lucifer and House Ramiel are enemies, does that make House Ramiel the good guys?"

There was silence.

Then Sander stammered, "Um, yes, sorry I didn't catch that. You reminded me of someone I used to know, for a second there."

"Did you love her?" Amanda asked jokingly.

"Yes, more than she ever knew," Sander replied with a far-off stare, as if still deep in thought.

The reply caught Amanda off guard.

"What was her name?"

"It's not important," Sander said, clearing his throat. "You said something about House Ramiel being good, I believe?"

"Yeah," Amanda said. "I take it House Lucifer is pretty evil, because, well because they are called House freaking Lucifer, for Christ's sake. They should think about hiring a new PR person or a name change or something."

Sander couldn't contain himself and laughed hysterically. "Yes," he said. "If House Lucifer were to ever go public, I think a name change might be in order."

"How about House Amanda?" Sander asked.

"Nope, too plain. Like me," Amanda said as she shrugged. "I like House Sandriel better. It has more of a regal sound to it."

"I don't know," Sander said. "I think 'House Amanda' is more beautiful than you realize."

Sander stood at attention and, as if making an announcement, he said in a stern voice, "I am Sandriel, proud servant, and loyal soldier of House Amanda! All who stand against us shall perish by the sword! Long live House Amanda!"

"For a bad-ass fallen angel, you're kind of immature," Amanda said, smiling.

"I do my best, My Lady," Sander said, grinning as he bowed to her. "It's getting late. You should probably be getting to bed. You have a big day, or should I say a big new life, ahead of you."

"You haven't answered even half of the questions I have," said Amanda.

Sander looked down at the ground. "We have tomorrow for questions. You need to get some rest. Don't worry, I'm not going anywhere," Sander said.

He pulled something from his pocket and inserted it into the MP7 he was showing her how to fire earlier.

"Now it's loaded," he said, as he pulled a lever in the back and flipped the switch behind the trigger to the top position. "Remember what I said about firing it?"

"Flip the switch all the way down and squeeze the trigger," Amanda replied.

"Perfect." He walked into her bedroom and put the weapon on her night stand. "I'll leave this here for the night. I just thought you might feel safer with it around."

"I feel safer with you around," Amanda said. "Sleep in here with me."

Sander looked like he was thinking, then proceeded to walk into his room and returned with four pillows and a blanket. He put them on the floor by her bed. When he noticed the way she was looking at him, he said, "What? I like a lot of pillows."

"It's not that," she said, nodding her head from side to side. "Reading women's minds isn't one of your super powers, apparently."

"No, Amanda, I guess it isn't."

Amanda thought, I'm seriously spending the night in a hotel room with a freaking fallen angel who happens to be a gentleman. She laughed aloud at the entire situation and the madness the day had brought.

When she got in the bathroom, Amanda realized she didn't have anything to change into. She stripped down to her bra and panties and looked at herself in mirror. Not horrible, I guess, she thought as she checked herself out. Something about being around Sander made her feel beautiful, and gave her a confidence she had never felt before. She sucked her belly in and arched her back, pushing her chest out. Now if I can hold this position. She exhaled, giggled, and with her best posture she opened the door and walked out of the bathroom.

Sander was already lying on the floor by the bed watching the news on TV, multiple guns on the night stand nearest him, and the MP7 on the other.

"Oh wow," Sander said as he turned to look at Amanda. "You're beautiful."

"I think you're lying but thank you. That just made my night," she said as she jumped into bed and got under the covers.

"I feel safe now."

"Good," he said smiling. After a minute or so he added, "You know when you asked me earlier if I thought House Ramiel was good? The truth is I think that we are all evil. Every last one of us. There are things that all of the fallen have done that should never be . . . forgiven."

He glanced up on the bed and realized she was already sleeping. "Sweet dreams, little Amanda . . . I hope one day you realize how beautiful you really are," he whispered as he closed his eyes.

Chapter Three

"Good morning," Sander said.

"What time is it?" Amanda asked, standing at the bedroom door.

"A little after noon."

"Oh, sorry. I sleep when I'm stressed. I guess you noticed that yesterday."

"It's normal. There's no rush. I ordered breakfast earlier; there's still some on the counter. Or you can order room service again if you're hungry."

Instead, Amanda just sat down and stared at him, watching him clean his guns. She noticed how perfect his dark gray suit fit him, and how his black shirt looked as if it had just been pressed.

Feeling her stare, Sander said, "I thought we would do some shopping today, so you didn't have to prance around all day in your undies."

Smiling, but ignoring his comment, Amanda asked, "Do you have a girlfriend?"

"No Ma'am, not presently," he said, smirking.

She doubted that. "Have you ever been married?"

"Yes, but it was a while ago."

He had stopped cleaning his pistol, and was looking blankly at the table.

"I'm sorry. I shouldn't have asked."

"It's okay . . . um," he cleared his throat. "I don't talk about things like that enough, I suppose. It's probably not healthy holding things in. Anyway, her name was Sarah, and she died of Spanish flu while I was overseas during the Great War . . . 1918. So like I said, it's been a while."

Amanda wished she hadn't asked. She saw his eyes were filmed over with tears, but he was fighting any show of emotion.

"So, when do you want to go shopping?" she asked, to change the subject.

"Anytime you're ready."

As Amanda dressed, she thought things weren't so bad now after all. In fact, she thought she was happier, and felt freer, than she ever had in her life. To make it all that much better, she literally had a guardian angel! One she could touch and feel, and one she wanted to smother with kisses every time she looked at him. She caught herself laughing aloud. Okay, Amanda, she said to herself, you're acting like a little school girl with a crush. So, stop it! But the truth is she didn't want to stop it. He was charming and handsome, and she never wanted him to leave her.

"Amanda, are you all right?" Sander yelled.

"Yes, why?"

"No reason, just usually when you aren't sleeping you're asking me a million questions, and you were quiet, so I was worried."

"Very funny," Amanda said.

I was being serious, Sander said to himself.

"I'm ready," Amanda said, jumping toward Sander, doing her best impression of the bubbly blonde concierge on their floor, who she thought Sander might be interested in.

"As lovely as ever. Let's go buy you lots of stuff."

Amanda knew for a fact that absolutely no guy had ever said that to her before. She got goosebumps.

As they exited the elevator and entered the hotel lobby, Sander noticed Amanda looking up at the ceiling. "Beautiful, isn't it?"

"Yes. It's perfect. The detail of the gold inlay on the ceiling is amazing. I hadn't noticed it yesterday."

"They don't build many places like this anymore," he said, as he pressed his palm on a cold marble column.

"I really do feel like I'm in *The Great Gatsby*."

"I guess that makes me a gangster, and you a girl cheating on her husband."

"There was so much more to it than that," Amanda said, pretending to be angry. "Besides, I hate to break it to you, Sander, but from what I've seen, you actually *are* kind of a gangster!"

"Well, kind of, maybe . . . but with as many wars as I've fought in, I prefer the title *soldier* – 'Once a soldier always a soldier!'"

"Gatsby fought in World War I, too," Amanda said.

"Yes, I had forgotten. Enough about Gatsby and Daisy. This is Sander and Amanda's place, now."

Amanda hugged him. "That comment just made my day! Sander and Amanda's place it is!"

"Is the mall okay?" Sander asked as they made their way to the SUV. "Just makes more sense, since we can get pretty much everything you'll need there. It's up to you, though."

"Yes," Amanda said, realizing she wouldn't have known the names of any expensive stores, anyway. She was expecting Wal-Mart.

"Great. One second," Sander said as he jogged over to the valet standing outside and handed him what appeared to Amanda to be a small wad of money.

"Let's go," he said as he held the door for her.

Amanda wondered why he would give a valet a wad of money, but didn't want to pry. She could tell Sander was the kind of guy who did what he had to do to get what he wanted, and he wasn't the type to explain himself unless he felt like it.

Amanda noticed Sander seemed more relaxed today as he drove. She had no doubt that he was carrying at least one gun, but his eyes weren't constantly on the rearview mirror like they were yesterday.

"How many wars have you fought in, soldier boy?" Amanda asked.

"Oh, it's question time, is it?" Sander said smiling. "More than I can or care to remember, to answer your question. I haven't fought in a war for a country since World War II, but I was in every major American war before that. I've always fought for America, if that's what you were wondering . . . I fought for Virginia during the Civil War," he said nonchalantly. "I also fought in the Crusades, as much of a mess as those turned out to be." He stopped to think. "However, I guess the Crusades did help cement some of our banking interests through the Templars." He paused. "Honestly, it's probably easier for you to name a war you know about, and for me to answer yes or no, than for me to name them all."

He noticed Amanda was looking at him with a questioning look on her face. "You fought for Virginia during the Civil War?" she finally asked.

"Yes, I told you I had lived in Virginia for a while."

"Yeah, but that was before I knew you were thousands of years old or whatever."

"Amanda," he said grinning, "I rebelled against the Lord God Almighty himself. I figured at the time, that rebelling against my country was only the logical progression."

She laughed. "That was kind of funny. I won't judge you. I'm sure you had your reasons."

"If you're talking about slavery, well I can assure you: for me that war wasn't about slavery. It was about a Yankee that killed my friend. If my friend had been a Northerner and had been killed by a Confederate, then I would have fought for the North. Angels don't care about a human's skin color; a human is a human. Anyway, for a soldier sometimes fighting for your friends is why you are fighting in the first place. Sometimes war is as simple as that. Politicians are the cowards who tie their wars to agendas! They are the ones to be blamed! Not the soldiers!"

"You're cute when you get worked up."

Sander laughed. "Yes, I was getting kind of serious. Sorry. I've honestly made so many mistakes in my life that it hurts when I think about them sometimes."

"I understand. Everyone has things they don't like talking about, and with everything you've been through, I can't begin to wrap my head around the number of things you must try to erase from your mind."

"Remember when I was explaining how fallen angels can die?" Sander asked. "Well . . . more fallen angels have died at their own hands than any human's."

"That's sad," Amanda said, not sure exactly what to say to that, but hoping Sander would never think of doing such a thing.

"Well, anyway, enough of that. Today is your day, Princess, so let's blow some money."

As they went from store to store in the mall, Amanda couldn't get over how easily Sander spent his money. It was like: 'Just pick out whatever you want.' By the time they entered the seventh store she was positive he wasn't looking at any of the price tags. She felt like a queen, and even though some of the girls working in the stores treated her like she was beneath them, it didn't bother her too much, because Sander made every attempt to show them she was with him. The way the girls were looking at him, however, made it a little hard for her to believe he didn't have a girlfriend.

As Amanda was trying on shoes, she realized a short curly haired blonde had caught Sander's attention.

"Sander!" she said. "How do they look?" Amanda spun around.

Sander grinned. "Perfect!"

I might be falling in love with his mischievous little smile, she thought.

"I think I recognized someone," he said. "We should probably get going after we pay for those."

"An ex-girlfriend?" Amanda asked with a little attitude.

"No, nothing like that," he said, as he walked with her to pay for her shoes. "It's probably nothing."

Even though he said that it was nothing, Amanda noticed he kept looking around the store, the way he had when he was checking the rearview mirror yesterday.

"Are all the girls in Louisville models or something, or is this where you angels come to breed? The girls here are gorgeous. All of them," Amanda said, trying to get Sander's attention.

That made Sander smile. "Yes, there are a lot of pretty women here, I suppose, but I'm with the prettiest one."

"You're kind of hot, too," he said to the cashier who was listening in on their conversation.

Amanda hit his chest, laughing.

On the way to the car, Amanda grabbed his hand to see what would happen. He just smiled. Walking hand-in-hand, she looked at him, wishing this moment would last forever. She wished he felt the same way for her as she felt for him.

After Sander opened her door for her she spun around, facing him, with her nose almost touching his. Is he going to kiss me, she thought. He slowly leaned closer. As she smiled, she heard a sharp crack, and blood appeared on Sander's left sleeve.

She saw the expression on his face drop. Before she even had time to think, he shoved her hard enough to push her into the car's seat and saw him drop as he slammed the Mercedes door. She heard two more cracks as she peeped her head up, and saw the blur of Sander sprinting across the parking lot toward a car. It was terrifying and amazing to watch. No living thing could possibly move as fast as he did. She watched in horror as Sander pulled a man from the car, yelling something at him as he squeezed the man's throat. She saw the man saying something, but couldn't hear a thing while she was in the safety of the bulletproof SUV. When the man stopped talking, Amanda saw Sander put his hands on either side of the man's head and make a quick jerking motion. Sander let go and the man dropped, lifeless.

Sander put his hand on the pistol under his jacket, scanning the parking lot as he walked calmly back to the SUV. He walked directly to the driver's side and opened the door.

As he started the Mercedes, he asked, "Are you okay, Amanda?"

"Yes," she said softly.

As he drove away he said, "I'm sorry you had to see that."

"It's fine," she replied, staring at him doe-eyed.

"I know who it was. There's something I need to do. All right?"

"All right," Amanda said, still stunned by what just happened.

It was dead silence on the drive to the hotel. Sander had a fierce look on his face, Amanda thought. Even though the anger couldn't stop his face from looking innocent, it was his eyes that betrayed him. Like the eyes of a wolf, it was the rage in them that made them so terribly beautiful.

When they got to the hotel, Sander got her things out of the SUV and carried them briskly to the elevator. Amanda followed close behind. Sander hit the up button and held the elevator door open, placing her things inside. Still holding the door, he handed her the key card to their suite.

"The concierge will help you take all of your things into our suite. Lock the door and don't answer it for anyone. I'll be back in under a half hour." He reached into the elevator, inserted the card for their floor, and hit the clubhouse floor button.

"Sander, don't!" Amanda said as the doors closed.

As the elevator went up, Amanda collapsed.

When the doors opened, the concierge saw Amanda sitting on the floor with her head in her hands.

"Oh, honey, are you okay?" the concierge asked.

Amanda just looked at her and nodded.

"Look, sweetie, I'm going to bring all those bags to your suite for you. Okay?" The concierge helped Amanda up.

Amanda nodded.

Amanda grabbed a couple of the bags, while the concierge carried the rest into the suite.

"Honey, if you need a drink or anything, I'll be right outside."

"Thank you," Amanda said, in a hushed voice.

"Please God," Amanda said, kneeling on the cold hardwood floor of the hotel suite. "Forgive me of all my sins. I don't pray often, and I'm not a very good person, but please let Sander be all right. I know you know him, and no matter what he's done, please look out for him. I need him. Please don't let anything happen to him, God. I'm begging you. Please look out for him."

As Amanda prayed, Sander was just reaching the address he had received from the man in the mall parking lot. When Sander got out of his car he popped the back of the SUV, and pulled out an MP7 A1, much like the one he had left in the hotel room for Amanda. He cocked it and put it on single fire. As he approached the door he looked to either side and, not seeing anyone, proceeded to knock on the door. When no one answered, Sander kicked the door open. There were six people sitting in the living room, all staring at the strangely young-looking man in the grey suit holding a weapon.

A woman about Amanda's age, sitting in a recliner, yelled, "What the hell?"

Other than the cold clicking of the suppressed MP7 A1, her question was the last thing anyone in that house ever heard.

Fifteen minutes later, Amanda heard a knock at the door and rushed to the peephole, praying it was Sander.

"Please, God. Please, God. Please, God," Amanda repeated as she looked.

"Oh, my God," she said as a sigh of relief escaped her.

She flung open the door and threw herself on Sander. "Don't ever leave me again!" she said as she squeezed him, never wanting to let go.

"I'm sorry," he whispered into Amanda's ear, as he hugged her back.

"Don't be sorry, Sander. You were only protecting me."

"Yeah," Sander said softly, even though he was almost positive it was him they were trying to kill this time. There were a lot of people who would benefit from his death, he knew. He should have left someone in that house alive, at least long enough to question. Stupid, he thought. He knew better, but something about them nearly harming Amanda had awakened a part of him he thought he had buried years ago.

"I'm just glad you're okay, Amanda," Sander said.

As she pulled away to look at him, her eyes went from his face to his blood-stained left arm. "Oh, my God! Your arm! You need to get to a doctor!"

"No, I'll be fine. It's healed up already," he said, touching his arm and flinching slightly. "Almost healed up," he corrected himself. "The bullet went right through."

"Oh," she said, staring at his arm. "I forgot." She gently pulled the stained gray suit sleeve away from his wounded arm, as Sander noted the concern on her face.

"I was so scared," Amanda said. "I felt so helpless without you around. Promise me right now that you won't leave me again."

"I shouldn't have. Just the thought of you being hurt . . . I snapped. I should have walked you up here, at least. I'm so sorry."

"Where did you go after you dropped me off here?"

"The man in the parking lot gave me a name and an address. I went to . . ." Sander paused. "I went to get revenge."

"Did you kill them?"

"Yes," Sander said looking at the floor. "All of them." He felt the need to explain for some reason. "If I hadn't they might have come at us again. I honestly don't know. It could have been a hit on me or them trying to get you. I have no idea. But they're all dead."

"How many were there?"

"Nine," Sander said still looking at the floor. "Six in the living room, and three in the back."

"That's nine less people we have to worry about hurting us."

Her comment surprised him, and Sander looked up at Amanda, who was slightly rubbing her chin as if deep in thought.

"What's it like -- killing someone?" Amanda asked.

That caught Sander even more off guard. "I guess . . ." He hesitated. "I guess it's different for everyone. Like today, when it happened I was glad they were dead, but in the back of my mind, now, I wish there had been another way. They were just following orders. I had no right to take their lives, really. They didn't deserve to die any more than I do. It's hard to explain. It's different every time. I'm sure I'll have a different answer the next time it happens."

"Do you see them in your dreams? The people you've killed? You always hear people saying that in movies . . . Wait. Actually, do angels even dream?"

"Sometimes you see them. There have been so many, actually, and yes, unfortunately angels do dream. Why are you so interested in killing all of a sudden?"

"I've never met anyone who's killed someone before. I was curious."

"It's nothing I'm proud of," Sander said looking down at the floor again.

"Oh, don't look like that," Amanda said, lifting Sander's chin up. "All I know is if I had been with anyone else today, I would be dead right now. But I'm not, and I have *you* to thank for that. You're my guardian angel."

Sander finally smiled slightly. "You're a very strong girl, Amanda. The last few days must have been completely crazy for you."

"You think?" Amanda said, sarcastically. "There isn't even a word for how the last few days have been for me. If I was back home, I would be working a double shift waiting tables right now." She smiled. "Instead I'm in a hotel room in Louisville with some crazy fallen angel who used to hang out with Lucifer. Not only that, but that crazy angel saved me from getting shot earlier, after he bought me a bunch of clothes." Amanda broke out laughing. "Yes, I would say that things being crazy for me is the understatement of the freaking year!"

Sander laughed along with Amanda. "What?" he said, smiling. "You really think I'm crazy?"

Amanda was still laughing. "Yes! Think about it. You go running around, buying everything you want, shooting people like it's no big deal. Hell, you got shot in the arm earlier, and you're all like . . . 'Oh, it will heal itself.'" And to top it all off, you're talking about taking me to see my dad, who's the boss of a bunch of angels. So yes, if that doesn't make you crazy then I don't know what does," Amanda said, laughing so hard she was almost crying. "This whole situation is crazy, but I like you, so I think I'll let you stick around."

"Well then," Sander said, "I'm glad that at least you find me likeable."

"Yeah, you're all right," Amanda said smiling. "Crazy, but likeable . . . and slightly charming."

"Yes, you're all right, too, I suppose," Sander said. "Likeable, and kind of hot . . . for a human."

"Really?" Amanda asked. "You really think so? Don't lie. Since I appointed you my guardian angel, I command you to tell me the truth."

"Yeah, definitely. Mortal girls like you are what got angels like me in trouble in the first place. Genesis 6:2: 'The sons of God saw that the daughters of man were attractive. And they took as their wives any they chose.' I'm not sure who convinced you that you were unattractive, but take my word for it -- you are beautiful."

"You just made my day again, Sandriel."

As Sander looked at Amanda, he hoped she really did believe him when he told her she was beautiful. He could tell someone had convinced her that she wasn't, and it bothered him that such a wonderful, innocent being could look in the mirror and see herself any way other than the way he saw her, the way God created her. Perfect.

"Are we still safe here at the hotel?" Amanda asked.

"Yes, I made some calls on the way here," Sander said. "This is probably the safest place for us at the moment. Unless I hear something, we'll most likely be leaving tomorrow."

"I'll order room service since we're staying in."

"There's a restaurant downstairs if you would rather…," Sander started before he was interrupted by a knock at the door.

Amanda, startled, stared at him.

"It's nothing. I'm sure," he said. "I have this hotel on lock down."

After looking through the peephole, just in case, he opened the door.

"Well hello, Sir," the concierge at the door said. "I just wanted to check on you and your wife and make sure y'all were doing okay. I thought I'd just give you this -- free of charge, on the house. After all you've been through today, I thought it might help make the day a little better." She handed Sander a bottle of wine.

"Ah, yes. That's so kind of you," Sander said. "She is feeling a lot better, and so am I. Thank you very much, Jenny, and here, because of your thoughtfulness, this is for you." Sander reached in his pocket and handed her a $50 bill.

"Oh, you did not have to do that. Thank you so very much. If you need anything, you know where to find me."

"Yes Ma'am. You have a wonderful evening, and thanks again," Sander said as he closed the door.

Sander looked back at Amanda, who was on the phone making faces at him.

When she hung up, Sander said, "That was the concierge."

"Yeah, I know. She has a crush on you."

"What? How can you tell?"

"Apparently, guys, even angels, are clueless when it comes to women. The way she looks at you, touches her hair, keeps smiling. I can just tell."

"Interesting. I better write this down." He started laughing.

"Funny," Amanda said smiling. "I ordered room service."

"Good. I had told the concierge, Jenny, we were in a car wreck when I saw her earlier, by the way, to explain the blood on my jacket and you being a little off. She gave us this bottle of wine, and was just checking to see if we were doing all right."

"Told you she had a crush on you," Amanda smirked.

"No, it's just a nice hotel. She was just checking on us, nothing more. Anyway, it occurred to me that I should probably explain more about House Ramiel, and answer any other questions you might have, since we are going be seeing your dad soon."

Amanda sat on the couch looking at the bottle of wine Sander placed on the glass table in front of her. "What's your position in House Ramiel? You also never told me how you feel about them. Are they good, evil, or what? What exactly do they even do?"

"I thought I told you . . . You may have been asleep," Sander said. "House Ramiel basically runs things. It's so much bigger than I think you can conceive -- the power the two Main Houses have. They literally run the world. They have been around since the beginning of time, and have basically shaped history as you know it. When I say history as you know it, that's exactly what I mean, because the history you know is not how history really happened *per se*. You only know exactly what they want you to know, Amanda. The news, what you hear on the radio . . . They are the ones who decide what is broadcast. Think of it like this. If you think the White House governs America, House Ramiel and House Lucifer govern the White House and every other government of any consequence on this planet. House Ramiel and House Lucifer govern the world. They pull the strings; think of them as the puppet masters."

"What? I was still thinking they were more like shady drug dealers or something. You make them sound like the Illuminati."

"I wasn't even sure you had heard of the Illuminati," Sander said. "But yes, if you have any idea about what people think the Illuminati are, then you have an idea of what House Ramiel and House Lucifer are."

"The puppet masters. This is insane; I can't believe it's all real. Why do you say 'they,' instead of 'we'? I thought you were part of House Ramiel."

"Well, that's a little complicated . . . I'm more of an 'associate' of House Ramiel. When the two Great Houses formed so long ago, I originally sided with you father's house, but I went through a period of time when I wasn't sure I even wanted to live anymore . . . After the second War of the Houses, I went my own way. I suppose that's why I'm self-sufficient now. I don't really need either of the houses' help, and they know it. But recently, a little over a century ago, I rejoined House Ramiel. I still do my own thing, and don't take any orders from any house, but my loyalty lies with your father, for now."

"Forever the rebel," Amanda said.

Sander laughed. "Indeed."

"You never answered my question about House Ramiel. Are they good or evil?"

"That's such a difficult question to answer," Sander said. "It's much like asking a Democrat if a Republican is good or bad, or vice versa. As for the two Great Houses, there are good and bad members of both organizations, as far as I'm concerned. I'll let you make your own decision about them. They both have done good and bad things over the thousands of years of their existence, depending on how you look at it."

Sander stopped and thought for a moment. "For instance, if there isn't enough food in a country, and everyone is going to die of starvation, is it good or bad if you introduce a virus that randomly kills 30 million people so that at least some of the population may live? Those are the kinds of decisions they make. Whether that is good or bad is up to you."

"I think I understand now," Amanda said.

"In the greater scheme of things, I still think we, the fallen angels, are evil though, when I reflect on all we have done over the years. Sometimes, I think the world would be so much better off without us," Sander said.

"Don't say such things, Sander! I've known you for like two days, and I think the world of you. Two days ago, I felt ugly and unwanted, but around you I feel beautiful."

"You are beautiful, Amanda," Sander said.

"You might not be able to read my mind, but you have the strange ability to make me blush on command," Amanda said. "You haven't told me what my dad was like. Is he young-looking like you; is he a nice man?"

There was a knock at the door.

"Think your order is here," Sander said. "Don't get up. I'll get it."

As Sander walked to the door, Amanda watched him reach behind his back to make sure his pistol was there. What a crazy life he's lived, she thought. She realized her life was going to keep getting more interesting, too. She thought she could handle it, but it would be so much better with Sander around to protect her. She wondered if the other fallen angels were anything like him.

"Cheeseburgers and wine again," Sander laughed. "We certainly have plenty of wine."

"Can you even get drunk?" Amanda asked.

"Yes, I can. It takes a lot more to get me drunk than most mortals though. I stopped drinking ages ago. Over the years, I've realized I have two weakness, and drinking is one of them. I just don't like how I am when I've been drinking. I'm not myself, so I've become a teetotaler, I suppose."

"Interesting. What's your other weakness?" Amanda asked. "Women?"

Sander smiled mischievously.

"Ha! I knew it!" Amanda said, laughing. "So, do you abstain from women, too?"

"No, not really, but sometimes I wish I did. You see, when you can live forever, and you fall in love with someone who can't, you watch them age, you watch them get weak, and suffer, and there is usually nothing you can do about it. It's painful seeing that happen to someone you care about."

"I see," Amanda said, frowning.

Sander looked at her for a moment. "Well, I'm not sure if your father would want me to be telling you this but I suppose you would have found out about it eventually . . . While human doctors have their Hippocratic Oath -- that is supposed to keep them following certain ethical standards and in the process, basically keeps them, well most of them, from experimenting on humans -- certain fallen angels have absolutely no problem using humans as 'guinea pigs'. This has resulted in a lot of unusual discoveries, among other things . . . ."

Sander thought for a second. "Anyway, several hundred years ago, we discovered that if a half-blood, such as yourself, is given a blood transfusion with the blood of a pure fallen angel, then that half-blood will be able to live forever, like us. Some think that House Lucifer may have been experimenting on this procedure long before that. None of the half-bloods who have gone through the process have ever died from natural means, but they don't exhibit our exceptional speed or strength, either. I figure you would have found out about the 'blood ritual' eventually. You were bound to meet some of these 'immortals' at one of House Ramiel's compounds, anyway. That's what we call the half-bloods who have gone through the process, by the way: immortals."

Sander could see the wheels already turning in Amanda's head.

"Oh, my God! So I could live forever?" Amanda asked.

"Well, you are Ramiel's daughter. I'm sure you'll be given the opportunity," Sander said.

"What, why didn't you tell me this earlier?" Amanda asked. "What's the down side; there has to be a down side to this. What, do I have to drink blood for the rest of my life? Does it turn me into a vampire or something?"

Sander laughed. "No you don't become a vampire. I've often thought maybe that's how the vampire myths started, though -- fallen angels experimenting on humans, making some of them immortal with their blood."

"So, no downsides," Amanda said.

"Well, some fallen angels might say having to live forever is a downside. Also, you are going to appear the same age you are when you have the transfusion done, literally forever. So, if you want to look 30 forever, wait until you're 30. See what I mean?"

"Yes, I understand. I don't think I would want to look the way I do now forever."

"Trust me. Any girl would love to look like you do," Sander said with a smile. "Amanda, someone told you that you weren't pretty and you believed them for some reason . . .

You can go through life believing the liar who told you that you weren't pretty, or you can believe me when I tell you that you are. I have seen Nefertiti and Helen of Troy with my own eyes, and take my word for it when I say you are just as pretty as any of them."

"Thank you, Sander."

"I never met Cleopatra, but from what I've heard, you're probably just as pretty as her, too," he said smiling. "I'm just trying to make you feel better about yourself, I suppose."

"You're hysterical, and thank you. I don't know -- I guess I just need to be reminded, after years of being put down . . . I thank you for everything. I probably sound like an insecure little kid, and I apologize if that's how I seem."

"You don't have to apologize to me. I'm probably the most immature of the fallen angels you will meet." He laughed. "Most of them don't really associate with humans as much as I do, other than their servants, maids, and the like, so a lot of them seem a little pretentious, and stuffy. You'll find out soon enough."

"It's kind of late," Amanda said. "I should probably get some rest. Thank you for all the clothes and shoes and everything else you bought me. I appreciate you saving my life again today, too."

"Anytime," Sander said, as he peeked in Amanda's bedroom. "Just making sure your MP7 is where it should be."

"You know I won't feel safe unless you sleep in there with me."

"I just didn't want to overstep my bounds or anything. I wasn't sure if you wanted some privacy."

"No. My guardian angel needs to be with me at all times."

"Yes, Ma'am, as you wish."

As Amanda was changing in the bathroom, Sander sat on the floor going through his nightly ritual of checking that his two Glock 19's were clean, functional, and fully loaded, a bullet in each chamber. He was glad Amanda was feeling more confident about herself, and he wondered if she would really go through with the blood transfusion one day.

Amanda walked out of the bathroom, wearing a black lace slip that made her completely stunning, Sander thought.

"Stop staring! You're making me self-conscious." She smiled, as she jumped into her bed.

"I'm sorry. I didn't even realize I was."

"I feel like you're my servant with you sleeping on the floor like that." Amanda laughed. "Good night, Sandriel."

"I've slept in a lot worse places," Sander said, smiling. "Usually, as long as there aren't bullets flying around or artillery fire going over my head, I'm not too picky."

She took one last look at him lying there on the floor, ready to protect her at a moment's notice. Such a gentleman, Amanda thought, and then she closed her eyes and drifted off to sleep as if all was right with the world, and to her that night, it was.

Chapter Four

When Amanda awoke, she heard Sander in the other room, the sound of metal on metal undoubtedly coming from one of the guns that never seemed to leave his side.

"Hello," Amanda said. She noticed Sander was wearing a dark blue suit today, looking impeccable as usual. Breakfast was sitting untouched on the counter. He always seemed to be one step ahead of the game. She wondered if the other fallen angels were like him.

"Good morning, young lady," Sander said as he put together one of his pistols. "There's some breakfast over there," he pointed, "if you're hungry."

"Thank you."

"We'll be heading to the House Ramiel compound today. We'll finally get you to your dad."

He noticed the smile disappear from Amanda's face. "Nervous?"

"Yes, "Amanda said, nodding her head.

"You shouldn't be. It's safe there. House Ramiel has compounds all over the world. This is one of the most secure, and your dad has as much security as the President, if that makes you feel any better."

"It's not the security. I feel safer with you than anyone I ever met. It's meeting him that makes me nervous, and disappointing him, and meeting all the new people. That's what makes me nervous. I picture all these rich people walking around in their fancy clothes, looking perfect all the time, kind of like you. I think I'll be out of place."

"It's not a bunch of beautiful people . . . There are some sloppy looking fallen angels." He laughed. "I'm sorry I shouldn't say such mean things, I'm just trying to make you feel better." He was smiling. "As far as looks, there are all kinds there: humans, immortals, fallen angels. A lot of security, especially when your dad is there. This compound in particular has always reminded me of a smaller, more modern Buckingham Palace, if that makes any sense. There's a lot of ceremony and unnecessary pomp and circumstance. At least there used to be. It's been a while since I've stayed there."

"I'm still nervous."

Amanda had the loneliest look on her face, Sander thought. He purposely tried his best not to become overly caring or emotional, especially when it came to humans, but there was something different about this one.

"If you want, I can stick around there for a few days I suppose," Sander said. "Until we figure out your dad's plans . . . or you get sick of me."

"You were planning on leaving?"

"Yes. Your dad sent me to pick you up and get you to him safely . . . as a favor. I still have my businesses to run, money to make. For all I knew you could have turned out to be some annoying girl who I couldn't stand . . . It turned out that you weren't some annoying girl at all, quite the opposite." He paused, trying not to grin.

"Yes. Please at least stay there as long as you can."

"I promise, I will. I haven't even spoken to your dad in a few days, so there's no telling what's been going on with House Ramiel. Lately it seems like there's always some new crisis arising, or upstart to put down, so he might need me around longer. I suppose we shall see."

"Thank you, Sander. I know you're a busy, important person. I just feel safe with you."

"You don't have to explain yourself to me. Being the new person sucks. I know how it is." He smiled.

"I'll go get dressed and get my stuff," Amanda said.

"Remind me to send someone out to get you a suitcase when we get to the compound. Sorry, that wasn't very thoughtful of me. I should have brought one yesterday. I'd give you mine, but walking around with a bag full of guns looks suspicious." Sander laughed.

Amanda laughed too, picturing the look on their bubbly concierge's face if she saw her walking with a grocery bag full of pistols and MP7's.

As Sander finished cleaning up and putting away the rest of his things, he thought about Amanda. How her smile seemed to brighten up the room and how seeing that lonely helpless look on her face earlier had torn him apart. He needed to get his head straight. He couldn't afford to let his emotions get the best of him. Women, like drugs and alcohol, always eventually brought pain.

"Sander! What are you thinking about, Mister?"

"You. Oh my, Amanda! You look immaculate."

"Thank you!" she said, spinning around in her new yellow dress. "I've never worn a $600 dress before."

"I've never worn a $600 dress before, either," Sander said laughing.

"You're hilarious!" Amanda laughed.

"I have worn a kilt," Sander said, rubbing his chin. "I suppose that's close . . . I don't think it was worth $600 though. Anyway, we should get going if you're ready."

"One minute," she said looking around. "I never want to forget this moment. I wish I had my phone; I would take some pictures."

"We'll get you a new one of those today. Here, you can use mine if you want."

Amanda grabbed his phone, going room to room taking pictures of the suite.

"Okay," she said, running up to him. "Smile, pretty boy." She put her head next to his and took a picture of them. "Wow, your eyes look intense," she said as she looked at the phone. "Here, let's take a couple more; I was making a weird face in that one." Amanda took six more pictures, scrolling through each one slowly, scrutinizing their faces in the pictures. "OK. I like this one."

Sander just smiled. "Yes, that one's good."

"I wish I could send these to the people at work! Oh my god; they would be so jealous. I'm ready to go when you are," she said as she picked up her bags.

"No need. I'll have Jenny get someone to take them to our car," Sander said as he walked to the club floor lobby a few feet away.

Moments later the valet entered. Amanda recognized him as the tall stocky kid to whom Sander had given a wad of money the other day.

"Mr. Johnson, how was your stay?" he asked as he loaded the luggage cart.

"Exceptional as usual," Sander said.

"Good to hear. I can get those for you if you want, Mrs. Johnson," he said pointing to her bags.

Amanda's face lit up with a huge smile at being called Mrs. Johnson. "Thank you."

"Mr. Johnson, um," the valet stuttered slightly, "can I speak to you privately for a second? It's about your Mercedes you wanted me to watch."

"It's fine; you can say whatever it is around Mrs. Johnson," Sander said, grinning ever so slightly.

"Oh, um, there was a guy walking around your Mercedes about an hour ago. He didn't touch it or anything but he was walking around it and he was eyeballing it pretty hard. He might have just been checking it out; it's a nice ride. But he walked off pretty fast when he saw me looking at him."

"Thank you," Sander said looking at the valet's nametag. "Thank you, Dennis. What did he look like? Were you able to get a good look at him, by any chance?"

"Better, Sir. I got some pics of him." He pulled his phone out.

"Smart man," Sander said as he crooked his neck, studying each one as the valet scrolled through them.

"I don't recognize him," Sander said. "Can you send those to me if you don't mind?"

"Yes sir," the valet said.

As the valet was sending Sander the pictures, Amanda wondered if she could do what Sander did for a living. She still didn't understand exactly what he did, but it seemed like he had to always be one step ahead, like he could never relax.

"Thanks, Dennis," Sander said handing the valet seven hundred-dollar bills from a huge roll of money he pulled from his jacket pocket. "Keep my number by the way. I might have some more work for you down the road. That was very smart of you to take those pictures. I'm always looking for intelligent people to work for me."

"Thanks so much, sir," the valet said. "That'd be great! You have a wonderful day! You have a wonderful day, too, Mrs. Johnson!" he said, nodding toward Amanda. "I'll rush these down to your Mercedes immediately."

"Thanks Dennis," Sander said, looking at the pictures on his phone.

"Could be nothing," Sander said to Amanda. "Well, are you ready, Mrs. Johnson?"

"Ha . . . Mrs. Johnson!" Amanda said. "I almost cracked up when he called me that!"

Amanda saw Sander leave a hundred-dollar bill on each bed for the housekeeper and then tip the concierge $300 on the way to the lobby. She could not believe the way he threw money around. If she had had any doubt about how wealthy these fallen angels were, those doubts were definitely gone now.

When they got to the Mercedes the valet was waiting for them. After loading the bags and luggage, and while Sander inspected the SUV, Amanda made a point to say goodbye to Dennis, the valet, so he would call her Mrs. Johnson again.

"I'm getting nervous," Amanda said as they got on I-65 South.

"Don't be nervous. I told you I'll be there with you. Hopefully it will be a nice uneventful drive. It will give us some time to chat."

"Yeah I guess we haven't really had time to chat. It's been the craziest, strangest, most wonderful, confusing two days of my freaking life." She laughed. "Oh, you know, you still haven't told me what my dad is like. What's he look like?"

"Your dad's a good guy in my opinion. Honestly, I've always thought he looked at me as his adopted son or something." Sander laughed. "Seriously, he's always giving me advice, trying to keep me out of trouble. He means well. He's also a very good leader, a fair leader. You don't stay in power for as long as he has if you aren't. Unlike House Lucifer, which has gone through multiple leaders due to internal power struggles and assassinations, your dad has overseen House Ramiel since the beginning.

"Good. I was worried he'd be some kind of tyrant or something. I've been doing some thinking and I was like: The only type of person that could keep Sander in line would have to be a tyrant," Amanda said, laughing.

"Very funny," Sander said, smiling. "I follow him out of respect, not fear. As far as how he looks, well, in Heaven there is a hierarchy of angels and the higher your rank, the older you look. Your dad was one of the Seraphim, and looks older than me. So yeah, not all fallen angels look my age. Originally both houses were strict about keeping the same ranks in the houses as we had when we were in Heaven. With all the wars, fighting, and suicides over the years, though, there really just aren't enough fallen angels left on earth to worry about ranks. We know what each of us are good at, and we do our part to survive. I mean -- I know every fallen angel who is left on this earth, not necessarily by name . . . I'm bad with names." He laughed. "But I would definitely recognize them. That's how few of us there are left."

"I'm still a little nervous. I was wondering: why did my dad . . ."

Sander interrupted her, looking in his rearview mirror, "What the . . . I think that cop behind us is going to pull us over."

Amanda turned and looked at the police car behind them. "Were you speeding?"

"Just barely," Sander said as the police officer turned his lights on.

"What about all the guns?" Amanda asked excitedly.

"We'll be fine," Sander said, pausing. "Let me do all the talking."

"I agree," Amanda said nervously.

As the police officer approached the SUV, Sander rolled his window down and put both hands on the wheel.

"License and registration," the police officer said.

Sander slowly handed him his wallet, and said, "There's a phone number in front of my license, you might want to call that, and my registration is in my glove compartment. I have two pistols in there, a bag full of weapons in the back, an MP7 behind each seat, and two pistols on myself. I am licensed to carry all of them."

The police officer looked at the many licenses in his wallet.

"One minute," said the police officer, looking at Sander strangely.

When the police officer went back to his car, Amanda said, "Oh, my God! My heart is racing."

Sander smiled. "You'll be fine; you're doing great, Amanda."

Amanda sat as still as a statue, too nervous to move, as Sander watched the police officer in the rearview mirror for several minutes.

"Here he comes," Sander said.

"Here's your wallet sir," the police officer said. "Son, you know some important people; I've never had anything like that happen before." He shook his head. "You're free to go."

"Yes, officer, I suppose I do," Sander said. "Have a good day."

"Yes sir, you too," the police officer said, standing there looking at Sander curiously.

Sander rolled his window up and drove away.

"I think that was probably one of the coolest things I've ever seen in my life!" Amanda said, laughing and dancing a little in her seat.

"We run the world." Sander grinned mischievously.

"Oh, my God! I thought we were going to jail," Amanda said. "With all of the guns in here."

"That phone number is kind of a 'get me out of jail card'," Sander said. "Basically, his boss's boss's boss." Sander smiled. "You'll be given one, too. Just don't go crazy with it and start robbing banks and stuff like that," Sander said, laughing at the thought of Amanda robbing a bank. "There's only so much trouble it can get you out of."

"I never really had any intention of robbing a bank, but now that you mention it, it sounds kind of exciting," Amanda said jokingly.

"Oh dear, I've created a monster," Sander said, purposely overdoing his southern accent. "We'll be at the compound soon."

As they drove along the country roads, Amanda was flabbergasted by all the open land. Miles and miles of land, barbed-wire fences, and what looked to her like corn fields. She was so used to the city that she was surprised places like this still existed. Sure, she had seen places like this in movies and on television, but to see it with her own eyes, it felt to her as if she had gone through a time portal.

"Looks like we are out in the middle of nowhere," Amanda said.

"We are, kind of," Sander said. "But, actually we're less than an hour away from Nashville. A few of the better protected

House Ramiel compounds throughout the world are in secluded areas like this. It's safer that way."

As they made a sharp turn down an old gravel road they approached a large, ornate black metal gate.

Sander looked at her and said, "This is it."

Several seconds later the gate opened.

Amanda looked at the tall trees as they drove down a newly paved two-lane driveway for what seemed like an eternity when Amanda suddenly said, "Oh, my lord!"

She saw a building that reminded her of the White House, as they exited the forest and drove by several mansions with huge yards.

"This is insane," Amanda said. "How does a place like this even exist? It's all so beautiful."

"Yes, it is," Sander said, looking at her. "Very beautiful indeed."

He pulled in front of one of the many mansions that sat on either side of the main drive leading to the building that Amanda thought looked like the White House.

"This is Tabrill's home when he's at the compound. Tabrill is a fallen angel also, and this is where I was told to take you," Sander said.

Amanda looked up at the mansion, then at the sports cars in the driveway, with foreign names she had never heard of. The elegance of her surroundings made her feel small and out of place.

"Are you coming with me?" Amanda asked.

"Of course," Sander said. "Hopefully, Tabrill's wife is here. She's a human; you'll like her. She doesn't have enough of our blood in her for her to become one of the immortals, but Tabrill loves her," Sander said, as if deep in thought. "It's a little sad, actually. Anyway, let's go introduce you."

"Okay," Amanda said nervously.

As they approached the door Amanda grabbed Sander's hand, squeezing it tightly.

As Sander went to ring the doorbell, it was flung open. A very pretty woman, who Amanda guessed was between 45 and 50 years old, looked at them both and smiled.

"Well hello, Denise," Sander said, bowing slightly with a big smile on his face.

"Sandriel!" Denise said. "Get your troublemaking butt in this house!" Denise laughed. She then looked at Amanda and said, "Oh, my lord. You are too adorable! Look at you! Come here and give me a hug." She wrapped her arms around Amanda. "Girl you are precious!" Denise said, stepping away to get a better look at Amanda.

"Sorry," Denise said. "I let my Southern hospitality get in the way of introductions. My name's Denise, and you must be Miss Amanda. You'll be staying here with me, if that's fine with you. I'll show you the ropes, answer any questions, and keep you away from troublemakers, like this boy Sandriel." She grinned at both of them.

Amanda smiled. "Yes Ma'am, that sounds great. It's very nice to meet you."

"Oh, don't be so formal. I can't get over how adorable you are," Denise said. "Well, you two come on in. I'll fix you something to eat. I'll send the help out to get your things."

As they followed Denise inside, Sander glanced at Amanda, who was looking at him smiling. He was glad Denise was there, she was a sweet woman, and she would hopefully make Amanda feel more at home.

As Denise pulled a pie out of the refrigerator and placed it in the oven, Amanda sat down at the round, oddly plain, wooden kitchen table that seemed out of place in the richly decorated house.

"Sandriel, before you sit down, be a gentleman and fix that pretty young girl something to drink, please," Denise said.

"Ah, yes Ma'am. Where are my manners?" Sander said, smiling. "What would you like Amanda?"

"Water's fine," Amanda said.

"Oh, don't be shy," Denise said. "Sandriel, reach up there, second cabinet from the left, and pour that girl a little Southern Comfort. Loosens the nerves a little when you're somewhere new," she said, turning and winking at Amanda. "Pour me a little too, if you don't mind. It's been a long day."

As Sander finished fixing their drinks, Tabrill entered the kitchen. Sander handed Amanda her drink and nodded at Tabrill. "Tabrill, this is Amanda."

"My pleasure, Amanda," Tabrill said.

So, all fallen angels don't look like Sander, after all, Amanda thought. Tabrill appeared to be African and looked to be about 50 years old, very slim but muscular. She looked him over, and like Sander said, she didn't think she could tell him apart from any other human. She didn't notice an accent of any kind, but he did have very intense eyes -- nothing too out of the ordinary, but there was definitely something a little different about fallen angels' eyes.

"Security told me when you were at the gate," Tabrill said. "Sorry I took so long; I had some things to take care of. I'm glad you both made it here safely."

Tabrill seemed like a very serious person, Amanda thought.

"If there is anything you need, let me or Denise know," Tabrill said to Amanda. Turning his attention to Sander he said, "Meetings are over for the day. Ramiel should be at the Main House, whenever you and Amanda are ready."

Sander nodded.

"Well, if you'll forgive me, I have more business to attend to," Tabrill said. "It was a pleasure to meet you, Amanda." He walked over and shook Amanda's hand and then walked over to Denise who was tapping her cheek as if motioning for a kiss. He kissed Denise and then left the room.

"Same old Tabrill," Sander said. "Always so busy."

Denise laughed. "So, how was your trip, Amanda?"

"Interesting would be one word for it," Amanda said.

"I can only imagine." Denise shook her head. "I remember when Tabrill told me he was a fallen angel. Girl, would you believe I fainted? I kid you not; I fell flat on my face." She laughed. "It's a lot to handle. They're nice people though, for the most part. We'll talk more about it when Sandriel isn't around."

"You know I can hear you?" Sander said, smiling. "I mean I'm sitting right here."

Denise laughed. "How have you and Sander been getting along? I've done my best to turn him into a proper Southern gentleman. He's got the accent down pretty good; I'm not so sure about the rest."

"He was a complete gentleman," Amanda said, looking at him. "He even slept on the floor in my room."

"Sandriel," Denise said, "You should have been sleeping on the floor outside that girl's room, not in it."

"No, I asked him to," Amanda said. "All the guns, the shooting. Everything was happening so fast, I don't know how much it showed, but I was terrified. He made me feel safe."

"Oh my dear, you're going to have to tell me about the shootings, bless your heart," Denise said as she gave them both some pie. "I was just playing about sleeping outside your bedroom. Sandriel's one of the good ones. I don't know about you, Amanda, but I could use a refill." She looked at Sander and pointed to the bottle of Southern Comfort. "Go on, eat your pie and drink your drink, your daddy is probably anxious to meet you . . . And don't be nervous, Amanda. Your daddy is one of the good ones, too."

After they finished eating and Amanda finished her drink, Sander and Amanda took the short drive to the Main House.

"This place is spectacular! I don't have the words to describe it," Amanda said after they climbed the stairs and stood outside the huge metal doors. "Are you sure I look all right?" she asked Sander.

Sander looked her over, then stopped at her eyes, saying, "You look perfect."

"How about me?" Sander asked. "How do I look?"

"Aw, you look great," Amanda said, reaching up and fixing the part of his hair. "There, that's better."

Sander smiled. "Ready?"

"I guess so."

Sander opened one of the large, heavy doors for her. As they walked in, Amanda saw the interior was even more extravagant than the outside. She was almost breathless at all the marble and paintings everywhere. There was even a red carpet that led from the entrance to the grand staircase in the center of the lobby. This place looked like a palace from a movie. She felt as if her head was spinning as she looked at all the well-dressed men and women walking about. She noticed a lot of them were looking at her curiously as they walked by and it made her feel self-conscious.

A man with an earpiece and a weapon hanging from his shoulder smiled and hugged Sander. The way tough guys hug, Amanda thought . . . barely touching, just patting each other on the back.

"Been too long, Sandriel," the man with the earpiece said.

"Have you seen Ramiel?" Sander asked.

"One second and I'll find out where he is."

The man spoke into the cuff of his shirt, Amanda noticed, and then put his finger over his ear, like security did when she watched the President on TV, she thought.

"If you'll follow me, I'll take you to him," he said.

Amanda felt her heart begin to race.

They went up the carpeted stairs, Amanda keeping one hand on Sander's arm and one hand on the cold white marble banister to steady herself.

They then came to an elevator where the man with the earpiece looked into something that seemed to scan his eye, then there was a beep, and the doors opened.

"After you," the man said as he ushered them in.

He hit the top floor button and they were there faster than it seemed they should have been, Amanda thought, as the doors opened up to a small lobby with a woman sitting at a front desk.

"Hello Sander," she said. "He's been expecting you both. I'll page him and let him know you're here." Amanda noticed the secretary was the first person at the compound to call him Sander instead of Sandriel, but didn't dwell on it, becoming increasingly nervous about seeing her dad.

The secretary looked at her computer. "He'll see you now." She stood up.

"I know the way," Sander said. The secretary said, "Of course," and sat back down, looking at Sander.

As they entered the office a gray-haired, lightly tanned man, slightly taller than Sander, looked them both over, smiling. He buttoned his black suit jacket as he approached them and with small tears in his eyes looked at Amanda and said, "I'm so sorry."

Amanda broke down in tears, not returning his embrace.

"I'll be outside," Sander said softly, feeling awkward at the displays of emotion.

Still hugging her, Ramiel said, "Please forgive me. I should have been there. I should have brought you with me in the first place."

Amanda pushed Ramiel away. She couldn't speak for a moment. Then she was crying uncontrollably, not sure if she wanted to hit him or hold him.

Finally, she was able to say something. "Why?" she asked. "Why?" Her cheeks were wet from tears.

"I don't know," he said. "I wanted nothing more than to protect you. At the time, I thought . . . ." He hesitated. "I thought the further you were from me the safer you would be, the happier you would be. I was so wrong. If there's anything -- absolutely anything -- I can do to make it up to you, please let me know."

Amanda stared at him, tears still slowly dropping from her face onto her yellow dress. "You can't just buy out of not being there for 18 years. You left me!" She felt numb.

Ramiel looked at her admiringly. "You've grown up to be a very strong and beautiful young woman. You have no idea how much it hurts me that I wasn't there to raise you. But you're with me now, and I can only hope you choose to stay."

Amanda tried to calm herself. Be an adult, Amanda. Be strong, she thought.

"Part of me understands why you left and part of me probably never will," Amanda said. "But I'm not going to let what you did interfere with my happiness."

"At least let me try to make up for it."

"We can be adults about this, and try to make a new start," Amanda said looking down. "But I can't promise I will ever forgive you."

"All I'm asking for is a chance."

"I'll at least give you that chance."

"Well . . . if we are starting over, can a father have a hug from his daughter?"

"Yes, Dad. I've missed you." She hugged him, crying again.

"Know that I never stopped loving you, Amanda," he said tearfully. "Welcome home."

Sander was pacing the floor outside the office practicing drill commands. "Squad Easy. Squad Will Advance. Right Turn . . . Squad Will Advance. About Turn," he said to himself as he went through the motions, when Amanda peeped her head out of the door.

"You can come in now," she said.

Sander smiled awkwardly. "Are you okay?"

"Yes. I'm fine now."

As Sander entered Ramiel's office, he saw Ramiel now had a remorseful look on his face.

"Thank you for getting Amanda back to me unharmed," Ramiel said.

"Not a problem," Sander said, still feeling the emotion in the air. "She's a strong girl. You should be proud to call her your daughter."

"I am," Ramiel said, gathering himself. "I truly am."

"I don't know what to say, honestly," Sander said, trying to change the mood. "It's got to be rough . . . for both of you, but you're together now, and under the circumstances we need to focus and figure out a way to put House Lucifer back in their place, because I can tell from the increased security around this place that something's up."

"I'm holding a council about that tomorrow; I'll need you there, Sander," Ramiel said. "For the time being, I'm going to need you around House Ramiel permanently. I know you like to do your own thing, but we need your help now more than we have in years."

Ramiel noticed Amanda sitting on a nearby burgundy leather chair listening intently.

"Amanda, Sander has always been . . . How should I put it?" Ramiel said. "A rebel amongst rebels."

Sander smiled. "I'll take that as a compliment."

"I'm honestly glad to have you back, old friend. There's no other angel I trust more. I've gone ahead and had your old house set up with food and everything else you'll need."

Sander nodded.

"I take it you've had a chance to meet Tabrill and Denise, Amanda? I hope their furnishings are to your liking."

"Yes, their house is beautiful . . ." Amanda said, hesitating. "I don't know if it's against your protocol or whatever, but is there any way I could stay at Sander's house, instead. I just kind of know him better. I feel safe around him. I mean he's already saved my life twice."

Ramiel looked at Sander curiously. "Yes," Ramiel said. "I heard reports about some of the happenings on your way here. I'm glad you were with Sander. I trust him, that's why I sent him, and I knew he would get you to me safely if anyone could. As far as protocols, you're an adult Amanda. We have no such protocols . . . Even if we did, Sander does whatever he wants, anyway." He laughed, still looking at Sander who was smiling at Amanda. He noticed Amanda returning Sander's gaze.

"I feel you looking at me Ramiel," Sander said. "We've known each other since the beginning, and I assure you I've been nothing but a gentleman. Anyway, are your IT guys still in the same place? I have some pictures I need them to run for me."

"You can have Lucy, the secretary, send them to them," Ramiel said. "Anything important?"

"Probably nothing," Sander said. "Just some guy looking at my Mercedes a little longer than he should have back at The Brown Hotel."

"Here," Sander said, flipping to the picture, and handing his phone to Ramiel. "Recognize him? Here are a few pictures of him, actually."

Ramiel scrolled through the pictures, studying them, then mistakenly scrolled to one Amanda had taken of her and Sander. He looked at it for a moment, noticing the happy look in Amanda's eyes, then scrolled back at to the man looking at Sander's Mercedes. "No, he doesn't seem to look familiar."

"Yeah, it's probably nothing," Sander said. "I'll be back in a few, it will give you two a chance to talk."

After Sander left the room, there was an uneasy silence for a moment, then Ramiel spoke to Amanda, "Sander is a good man, and like I told him, I trust him more than I trust any of the other fallen, but like all of us Sander has flaws. He is prone to being rebellious in nature, I've come to realize over the years. He really isn't one to settle down for too long, if you know what I mean."

"I know what you're hinting at, I think," Amanda said. "But I'm not some wide-eyed, naive little girl, either."

"He can be rather charming."

"Yes, I've noticed."

"I'm not putting him down at all," Ramiel said. "Sandriel has always been loyal to me and my house, but I notice things. I notice the way you look at each other, and you're my daughter, and I just don't want you to get hurt."

"Thank you for caring. Does he have a girlfriend?"

"Not that I know of. It's had to have been at least a century since he was married," Ramiel said. "She died of the Spanish flu . . ."

"Yes, he told me."

"Did he now? Interesting," Ramiel said, as he seemed to be thinking. "Now may not be the right time to ask . . . but maybe there is never really a right time to ask . . . Your mother? Is she still drinking?"

"Yes."

"I see." Ramiel looked hurt by her answer. Morose again, looking at the floor.

There were two knocks at the door, and Sander walked in.

"You two still talking about me?" Sander asked, smiling.

"No. We're done," Amanda said.

"Wait. Were you really talking about me?" Sander asked.

Amanda looked at Ramiel, and they both started laughing.

"I knew it," Sander said grinning, "It better have been good things. You know I can tell when you're lying, Ramiel."

Sander looked at Amanda. "That's another thing; never lie to a fallen angel. We can't read your mind, but there are certain ticks and mannerisms that give you away when you aren't telling the truth, and over the years we've perfected the ability to tell when you're lying."

"Yes. Well, I unfortunately have more work to do, but Amanda, I truly am *so* happy to have you back here with me," Ramiel said, as he walked toward Amanda and kissed her on the cheek.

". . . And you, Sander," Ramiel said. "You just stay out of trouble." He laughed. "Remember: council meeting tomorrow morning -- 8 a.m."

"Good to see you, too," Sander said, pretending to be angry.

"Seriously though I've missed you, old friend," Ramiel gave him a strong hug.

"I know what you mean. Good to be back," Sander said.

Sander held the door for Amanda, then looked back and nodded at Ramiel, who nodded back.

"Any word on those pictures?" Sander asked as he passed the secretary.

"Nothing yet. I can tell them it's urgent if you want," the secretary said.

"Its fine. I'll just check in the morning," Sander said.

After taking the elevator down, the door opened and Amanda was surprised at how many people were in the lobby.

"This is insane," she said. "This whole compound is like a little city hidden away from the rest of the world."

"Yeah, it is kind of crazy," Sander said. "What's crazier is there are dozens of these places throughout the world. They aren't all as busy as this one. Most of the staff travels to whichever compound your dad goes to."

"Do they all know?" she whispered to Sander. "That you're fallen angels?"

"It's not exactly on the application, or put out there openly, but they know."

"Why doesn't it get out there?" she asked. "To the rest of the world."

"Oh, trust me. It gets out, and when it does, people and their families have a habit of disappearing, being found dead from a heroin overdose, or shooting themselves twice in the back of the head, if you catch my drift. Besides, these people are paid vast amounts of money, and don't want to lose a powerful job like this. Even when it does happen to get out on occasion, it's too incredible for most of the public to believe anyway. I mean, you're here, seeing it with your own eyes and I bet there's a part of you that doesn't believe it. Worst case, you can always pay off the media to bury the story."

"You're right. Part of me doesn't believe it," Amanda said. "I've been pinching myself every few hours for the last three days to make sure I'm not dreaming. By the way, I just noticed everyone keeps staring at me."

"Yes, Amanda you are the new topic of gossip around here. Don't feel too bad. They gossip about me a lot, too. Like your dad said earlier, I do my own thing. So if I'm not around for a year or two, by the time I do eventually get back the rumors about me have grown to unimaginable levels. So please do me a favor, and don't put too much weight on what you're going to hear these people telling you about me."

"I won't."

"Unless it's good, then it's the absolute truth," Sander said smiling.

Amanda laughed. "So what are the rumors about me?"

"Let's see," Sander said. "You see those ladies huddled in the corner to the left over there who look like accountants? They are probably saying, 'That's the notorious Sandriel. I heard he's a fallen archangel, and put a love spell on that poor pretty girl in the yellow dress, and made her his slave." He laughed. "I'm just kidding. I haven't heard any rumors yet, but I'm sure there are some."

Amanda laughed, and the group of girls they had been looking at all turned and looked at her and Sander.

"Oh, my God. I think they really were talking about us," Amanda said laughing.

"Yeah, I think they were, too."

Amanda saw Sander wave at them, and the women all quickly turned and started talking to each other again.

"No, don't wave," Amanda said, laughing. "You just made it worse. Let's go get some fresh air." She grabbed Sander's hand and led him outside.

"Well, you just grabbed my hand and led me out of the Main House in front of everyone. That just started another rumor." Sander laughed.

"Oh no! I probably did! I have to be more careful. No offense. I know we seem to be getting along great and everything, but there is no way I am staying at your house tonight," she said, laughing. "I can't imagine the rumors."

"Yeah I know. I was going to advise against it. I already have this undeserved reputation as some kind of playboy or something, when I guarantee not a single person has seen me with a girl since . . ." He paused and looked down. "Well, since I was married almost a hundred years ago."

"It's because you're kind of cute and charming. That's why."

"What's this 'kind of cute' nonsense?" Sander said. "I'm very cute."

Amanda laughed. "You're pretty funny, too."

Sander smiled.

"So, are most of the people here human?" Amanda asked. "And this might be a stupid question, but where are all the female fallen angels."

"As far as most of the people being human, most of them are. The typical workers that any head of government would need," Sander said. "You see all those guys with weapons over there? Almost all of them are immortals. They've gone through the blood transfusion. Pretty much anyone you see with a weapon is an immortal, except the fallen angels of course -- we just tend to be more discreet."

Sander pulled his jacket open, revealing his double shoulder holster and two pistols. "As far as female angels, there is no such thing. No female angels are even mentioned in the Bible or Qur'an . . . Humans seem to always overlook that fact when they find out about us for some reason."

"I see."

"Actually, would you like a weapon? It just occurred to me . . ."

"No thank you. That's why I keep you around. You're my protection."

"Ah, I see," Sander said, smiling.

Suddenly a large man with shoulder length dreadlocks yelled, "Do my eyes deceive me or do I see Sandriel the great, scourge of the west, straight-up gangster!"

Sander turned, smiling. "Maurice!"

One of the guys with a weapon -- it looked like the MP7 Sander had given her -- was running up to them.

The man slowed and then strutted toward Sander and they punched fists.

"What are you doing here, man?" Maurice asked Sander. "First, they start beefing up security, and then I see the great Sandriel. That's when I know things are about to get real." He laughed. "When you're in town things usually start getting deadly."

Maurice glanced at Amanda. "I thought we were close, Sandriel. You're not gonna introduce me to your fine little lady friend here?"

Sander smiled. "Amanda, this is my friend Maurice. We've been in a lot of battles together throughout the years. Maurice, this is Amanda. Ramiel's daughter."

Maurice threw his hands in the air. "Ramiel's daughter! You serious? Uh-oh, hands off."

Amanda laughed. "It's nice to meet you."

Maurice got a very serious look on his face. "I'm sorry about that comment. I didn't mean any disrespect, Ma'am."

Sander didn't say anything; curious what Amanda would say.

"It's fine, no disrespect taken," Amanda said. "I took it as a compliment."

"Wow, we have the Boss's daughter here with Sandriel! Maybe things are about to get real," Maurice said. "Me and some of the boys were over here telling war stories, if you want to come over for a minute, Sandriel. I know some of the new guys would like to meet you in the flesh, after all the things they've heard about you."

"Yeah, I'll be over in a minute," Sandriel said.

"All right man. Damn! It's good to see you. I'm ready to kill some of those House Lucifer cucks."

Maurice jogged back over to the rest of the immortals.

"That guy's funny," Amanda said, smiling.

"Yeah, he's a good guy. He's one of Tabrill's sons. Maurice has had kind of a rough life. He grew up on the streets, basically. He used to be a cocaine dealer down in Miami, apparently, before he joined the Marines and eventually House Ramiel.

"Do you want to come over with me and meet some of the immortals? It gets boring only hanging with me, I suppose."

"Sure," Amanda said. "And it never gets boring hanging with you, by the way."

As they approached the group of men, they stopped talking.

Maurice said to the group, "Everybody, this is Amanda, the boss's daughter, and this right here is Sandriel, who needs no introduction. I was going to tell them the story about when I was kidnapped. Have you heard this one, Ma'am?" he asked, looking at Amanda.

"No," Amanda said.

"All right, Ma'am, this is a good one," Maurice said. "Listen up, boys. I had just joined House Ramiel, and I mean just joined. I was fresh. So, I'm minding my own business walking down the street one day in South Beach checking out some ladies and . . . BAM! . . . A van comes rushing up out of nowhere. A bunch of punks throw me in a van. Next thing I know, I've been kidnapped!

"So, they got me locked in the closet for days. I'm hungry. Ain't had nothing to eat. They keep telling me they're going to kill me if House Ramiel don't pay 'em, and I'm like: 'What the hell does that have to do with you not feeding me? If you're gonna kidnap somebody as least feed them something. Get me something off the dollar menu. I ain't picky.'

"Then, day four comes, and still nothing. So, I'm sleeping in this dark-ass closet and what do I hear? I hear BAM! BAM! BAM! BANG! BANG! That's what the hell I hear. I'm like:

'Aww yes, House Ramiel sent in the cavalry.' I'm thinking they sent an army to save yours truly. House Ramiel don't play. So, I'm hearing gunfire, people screaming, people crying, begging for mercy . . . I hear 'No, no, don't shoot me please'," and then BANG! So, I'm in the closet yelling 'That's what you get for not feeding me! House Ramiel don't take no prisoners!'" Finally, the gunfire stops, and I'm like: Oh man, the House Ramiel army has saved me!' and when that closet door opens, you know what I see? I said, you know what I see?"

The men nodded. "What I see when that door opens, is this pretty white boy right here!" he said, pointing to Sander. Sander smiled, slightly nodding.

"I see Sandriel standing there by himself with his face covered in my kidnapper's blood," Maurice continued. "That's it . . . just Sandriel! I'm still looking for the army that saved me. I look to my left, no army. I look to my right, no army.

"Sandriel came up in that place by himself and killed ten men like it wasn't nothing. Hardcore! And you know what the best part was? This bad ass white boy did it all wearing a three-piece suit! A freaking three-piece suit!" Maurice laughed. "If that isn't gangster, I don't know what is!"

Everyone looked at Sandriel.

Sander, feeling their stares said, "That reminds me, Maurice; you owe me a suit. Those bloodstains still haven't come out."

"Oh no!" Maurice said. "I told you Sandriel was the real deal. Gangster. I swore right then and there on that day: I was rolling with whoever Sandriel is rolling with. I don't care. I'm loyal to Sandriel for life."

"Here. I'll give you this suit I have on," Maurice said, pretending to take off his suit. "For real man, I owe you. You new guys follow Sandriel's lead and you'll be all right. Anyway, I'll holler at you later," he said to Sander. "We got a patrol in 10 minutes, but I'll see you around."

"Yeah man. Take care, Maurice," Sander said, as he nodded to the rest of the immortals.

"Did that really happen, you little 'gangster'?" Amanda asked as they walked toward his SUV.

Sander nodded, "Yes." he said, hesitating. "I didn't realize they hadn't fed him . . . I would have picked him up some food on my way there, if I had known."

"Oh, my God. That's hilarious. It seems like you have their loyalty."

"Yeah, I do. But they need to watch that kind of talk. They need to be loyal to House Ramiel, not to me. Some people around here could take his loyalty to me the wrong way."

"I see your point. Want to head back to Denise's place with me? I should probably head back."

"Yes, of course."

As they drove down the street to Tabrill and Denise's, Amanda looked at Sander. She was starting to get a sense of the power he held in her father's organization, and how dangerous his life was.

"Well, we're here," Sander said, laughing at the short trip. "That was pretty lazy of me; we could have walked. I'm pretty sure my car would have been safe where it was parked. Just habit, I suppose."

"Yeah," Amanda said. "I doubt anyone is looking to steal the great Sandriel's car around here," she said, laughing.

"The great Sandriel," Sander said laughing. "I like that. Start calling me that from now on."

"In your dreams," Amanda said with a smile. "A lot of these people kind of put you on a pedestal, but I think I've seen the real Sander a few times."

"Really?" Sander asked curiously. "And what is the real Sander like?"

"I think the real Sander is kind, protective, caring, and more sentimental than he likes to let on," Amanda said.

Sander thought for a moment. "And what do you think when you hear the stories about the people I've killed?" He looked at her inquisitively.

Amanda didn't hesitate. "I think you use violence when it's necessary to help or protect people you care about."

"I wish that was true," Sander said, eyes shifting down. "I've done some very horrible things in my life, unfortunately . . . unforgivable things."

"Well, you've been a gentleman to me, and that's all that matters as far as I'm concerned," Amanda said. "Now, let's go inside. We've been sitting in this parked car for a while and I don't want any of these people starting more rumors about me and you," she said as she laughed.

Denise answered the door. "Well look who it is! Miss Amanda and Sander! Honey," she yelled back at the dining room, "Amanda and Sandriel are here. You two go to the dining room. Sandriel knows where it is," she said looking at Amanda. "And I'll have the help bring you out something to eat."

"Thank you, Ma'am," Sander said, smiling politely.

Amanda followed Sander down an ornately decorated hallway into a lavish dining room. She followed Sander's lead and sat beside him at the long wooden table. She noticed Tabrill stand up and then sit back down after she did. She wasn't used to such manners. She thought it was strange that, so far, the most mannered men she had met on this earth happened to be angels who were expelled from Heaven.

"I hope you've had a pleasant afternoon, Amanda," Tabrill said.

"Yes, it's been great," she said. "Everything here is so beautiful. We just finished talking to your son, Maurice."

"Oh, yes Maurice," Tabrill said smiling as he nodded. "He's a little rough around the edges, but he's a good boy."

"He's funny," Amanda said. "He was telling us a story about him and Sander."

"Oh, really?" Tabrill said. "Which one?"

"When he was kidnapped."

"Yes. That was a scary time. Maurice and I both owe Sandriel a debt of gratitude for that."

Denise entered the room and Sander and Tabrill both stood until Denise sat down.

"How are you, Miss Amanda?" Denise asked as two maids walked in and put a steak in front of each of them.

"Honestly," Amanda said, "I'm not used to such manners, the way these two stood before you sat down." Amanda laughed.

"I've got these two trained, girl," Denise said. "Sandriel wasn't always like that. He used to be a ruffian."

"That's not true," Sander said, grinning. "I've always been a complete gentleman."

"In your own mind maybe," Denise said, then turned her attention to Amanda, looking at the steak in front of her.

"Oh, you aren't a vegetarian, are you? I can get you something else if you'd like."

"No, this is perfect," Amanda said.

"I want you to feel at home here," Denise said, then looked at Sander. "I hear you are going to be staying at the compound for a while."

"Word travels fast around here," Sander said. "Any other rumors?"

"Well you know how we ladies like to gossip." Denise laughed. "There might be one or two rumors going on about you."

"I'm not even sure I want to know," Sander said.

"I do," Amanda said, smiling.

"Oh, I'll tell you everything you want to know about that boy when he's not around," Denise said.

"Okay," Amanda said, smiling. "I can't wait."

"I think I'm going to start drinking again," Sander said.

Everyone laughed.

"So, what is it -- the rumor?" Sander asked.

"Well," Denise said, "of course everyone is curious about Miss Amanda here, and there is a rumor that you might be a little sweet on her." Denise looked at Sander as he glanced at Amanda who was looking at him smiling.

"Interesting," Sander said. "You girls gossip too much."

Denise laughed. "Sander, are you blushing?"

"No," Sander said, laughing. "They're just saying that because I'm the only one they see her with. It's nothing."

"If you say so," Denise said, smiling.

"I never said it before," Tabrill said. "But the real reason all of us on the council are glad you're here, Sander, is so our wives have someone new to gossip about."

"That's probably true," Denise said.

"Speaking of the council," Tabrill said, "Ramiel wants you and me to meet him before the meeting in the morning. He said he had some things to discuss with us before the other members arrived."

Sander nodded. A few moments later his phone rang.

"Sorry Denise," he said, grinning as she saw her giving him a dirty look for having his phone on at the dinner table. "I have to take this."

Sander stood up. "Yes," he said into the phone. "Interesting." He paused, "Is he a human?" Sander listened for a few more moments, said "Thanks" and hung up.

Sander sat down. "Sorry about that."

"I'll let it slide this time. I know you're an important man," Denise said with a wink.

"Speaking of cell phones, your dad wanted me to give you this," Denise said, as she walked over and handed Amanda a new cell phone. "If you want a different one just let me know."

"Oh wow," Amanda said. "Thank you. It's perfect."

As Amanda looked at her new phone, Sander said," They finally got a hit on some pictures I gave them to check out." He looked at Amanda. "Remember that guy who was checking out my Mercedes at The Brown Hotel? It turns out he has ties to House Lucifer."

"How did he know you were in Louisville?" Tabrill asked.

"I have no clue," Sander said. "He didn't touch the Mercedes. It makes no sense to me. Either way, I'll get to the bottom of it. I've got a name."

"I heard you ask if he was human," Tabrill said. "Was he?"

"They don't know," Sander said. "He could be immortal. They don't have access to the guy's DNA."

"Wait a minute," Amanda said. "When you picked me up, you asked me if I had taken a DNA test."

"Yes," Sander said. "That's how we found you."

"I can probably explain it to Amanda," Tabrill said. "Amanda, recently House Lucifer has been gathering as many half-bloods around the world as they can. We'll discuss this more tomorrow at the council, Sander." He looked back at Amanda. "The only way we can determine if someone is a half-blood, with angel DNA, is through a DNA test. House Lucifer came up with the idea to make getting a DNA test something humans around the world would want to do, so they could find out about how many half-bloods there were running around in the world that we didn't already know about. We have people working at every known DNA-testing company. They tell us when someone comes up as a half-blood. When your name came up, we knew House Lucifer would eventually find out about you, and since we didn't want anything to happen to you, we convinced Sander to go bring you to us."

"Wow," Amanda said. "When I took that DNA test I was just curious if I was French or German or whatever."

Everyone laughed.

"Instead," Amanda continued, "this guy," pointing at Sander, "comes up to my house and almost gets me killed at few times. I'm never taking another DNA test again," she said, smiling. "I'm kidding," she said, looking at Sander. "I'm so glad I took it, because it led me to all of you."

"Cheers to that," Tabrill said, lifting his glass.

Everyone lifted their glasses, looking at Amanda and saying cheers.

"On that note, I think I'll be calling it a night everyone." Tabrill stood, looking at Amanda and bowing slightly. "It has been a pleasure to make your acquaintance, and it's an honor to have you as a guest in my home."

"Oh, thank you so much," Amanda said.

Tabrill turned his attention to Sander saying, "It's good to have you back Sandriel. House Ramiel needs you. I'll see you in the morning."

Tabrill walked over to Denise and kissed her goodnight. "I love you, honey."

"Good night, sugar," Denise said.

Such a lovely couple, Amanda thought.

Sander turned to Amanda. "You don't have anything in my Mercedes do you? I'm going to have it destroyed tonight. The valet said that guy didn't touch it, but I've learned you can never be too careful."

"I don't believe so."

"I'll double-check before I have them take it."

"What kind of car are you going to get now? Another Mercedes?"

"I was thinking about a Range Rover."

"Nice. What color?"

"I hadn't thought about it." He looked at Denise. "I'm thinking about getting a Range Rover, Denise. I can't decide on a color . . . What's your favorite color?

"Pink," Denise said.

Amanda almost spit up her water laughing.

"I am not driving around in a pink Range Rover," Sander said, smiling at the thought of driving around trying to act tough in a big pink Range Rover. "What is your favorite color, Amanda?"

"Purple," Amanda said, crying laughing.

"You two are killing me," Sander said, shaking his head and grinning. "Someone go wake up Tabrill and ask him what his favorite color is, and if he says pink or purple, I'm going to disappear for another few years."

Denise laughed.

Denise said, "Sandriel, I think you would look very handsome driving around in a pink Range Rover." She laughed. "Now that would start some gossip."

"Yes, I believe it would," Sander said, smiling. "Black it is. I'm getting a black bulletproof Range Rover. Thank you for your help, ladies."

"Always here to help," Denise said.

"Yellow is actually my favorite color," Amanda said. "You in a purple Range Rover seemed funnier."

Sander nodded his head. "I'm still going with black."

"Will you be staying in the same house you used to live in while you're here Sander?" Denise asked.

"Yes, but I haven't been there yet. I'm not even sure if Ramiel's had the staff fix it up for me yet." He glanced at Amanda. "For the sake of Amanda's reputation, I'll probably stay at my house tonight. So you girls don't have so much to gossip about."

"Oh, don't be silly," Denise said. "I've already had the help set up the guest room next to Amanda's and they brought in your things earlier . . . I'm sure she'll feel more comfortable with someone she knows staying here. Besides, I'm the one who starts half the gossip in this place, anyway."

Sander looked at Amanda, who was smiling at him.

"Thanks, Denise," Sander said. He glanced at his watch. "I'll go check the Mercedes to see if you left anything in there, Amanda."

Sander got all of his weapons out of the Mercedes and walked back into the dining room. "I didn't see anything of yours Amanda, just these," he said, holding an armful of various weapons, his pockets stuffed with pistols.

"Dear lord," Denise said, looking at all the weapons he was holding. "I swear I still pray for you, boy. Someone needs to."

"You're just wasting your time praying for me," Sander said. "Anyway, thank you for dinner, and everything. I'm going to get some rest. Good night, ladies." He glanced at Amanda, smiled and made his way to the stairs.

"Third room on the right," Denise said.

"Good night, Sander," Amanda said. She looked at Denise and asked, "Can I help clean up or anything?"

"Oh no dear. I'm not going to let you lift a finger while you're staying in this house. Besides, I have maids for that."

"Oh," Amanda said, thinking about her home, and how she had always been the maid. "I'm not used to maids. It'll take some time to get used to that. I'm not used to any of this."

She spread her arms wide. "It's like a dream. I'm afraid I'll wake up and it will be over."

"You are too precious. Ramiel is very lucky to have you as a daughter. I know I would be. If you need anything you let me know, and I mean that."

"Thank you. If there's anything I can do to help you out around here, let me know. I should probably get to bed too, so I don't sleep all day."

"Girl, you sleep as long as you want. Follow me. I'll show you to your room."

When they got to where Amanda would be staying, Denise said, "This will be your room. I hope you like it."

Amanda looked around at all the marble, deeply polished wood, and a huge, amazingly detailed sunrise painting by the window. "It's beautiful. Fit for a princess."

"And now it has one. If you need anything you can either hit this button . . ." she said, pointing to an intercom on the wall. "And ask one of our attendants, or feel free to wander down to the kitchen if you like. I want you to think of this as your house, too."

"Thank you. You've been so kind."

"You're welcome. Good night, honey," Denise said.

"Good night," Amanda said.

Amanda walked to the closet and saw her clothes had already been put away for her. The closet was larger than her bedroom at her Mom's house.

She dressed for bed and laid down, admiring the large painting once again, and then glanced at the floor to the right side of her bed where Sander would have been sleeping if they had been at the hotel. She closed her eyes and prayed that when she woke up, she would be exactly where she was, and this all hadn't been a dream.

Chapter Five

After getting dressed in a brown tweed three-piece suit, white shirt and navy tie, Sander put a shoulder holster over his vest and made his way to the kitchen. He saw Tabrill was already up, smoking a cigarette and chatting with the butler. Not wanting to interrupt, he glanced at Tabrill, and motioned for a cigarette, waving two fingers in front of his thin lips. Tabrill tossed him the pack. As Sander lit it, he wondered why he made a point to try not to smoke around Amanda. He had remembered overhearing her say something about smoking being gross, but it wasn't like him to change his habits to please someone else. Very out of character, he thought.

"Ready?" Tabrill asked.

"Yep," Sander said, still waking up.

As they backed out of the garage in Tabrill's white BMW, Sander noticed they had already taken his Mercedes away to be destroyed. He wondered how long it would take for them to deliver his new SUV.

When they got to the Main House and were walking up to the entrance, they passed a group of immortals, who stopped talking as they walked by. They all nodded to Sander, a few of them saying, "Sir," out of respect. Sander nodded back. A tall, lanky security officer opened the door for him and Tabrill.

The security officer looked at him and said, "Good to have you back with us, Sandriel." Sander nodded once again, looking at all of the humans rushing around doing their daily tasks. Most of them avoided eye contact, but one attractive black-haired girl returned his glance and smiled at him. She looked familiar, Sander thought. He had known her; he just couldn't remember how. He smiled back and continued with Tabrill to the elevator.

 Tabrill put his eye next to a scanner, and the elevator door opened. When they exited the elevator, they walked to a large conference room with a long wooden table surrounded by large-backed chairs. Like any modern conference room, except with a medieval touch, Sander thought. Ramiel was sitting at the head of table, going through paperwork. He stood to greet them both.

"I'm glad to see both of you," Ramiel said. "I wanted you here before everyone else because I have received some troubling news." He paused. "It appears we have a traitor amongst us. I have confirmed that Aiden has been leaking information to House Lucifer."

"Aiden?" Sander asked.

"Zekiel's boy," Tabrill said. "This is troubling. Does Zekiel know?"

"No," Ramiel said. "Or at least he doesn't know that I know."

"Has this Aiden gone through the blood ritual?" Sander asked.

"No, I haven't allowed it yet, but it will begin to arouse suspicion if I put it off any longer. That's why we need to decide how to handle this, today."

"Why'd he do it?" Sander asked. "It can't be money or power; his dad is on the council. He has to have pretty much everything he wants."

"Not everything . . ." Ramiel said. "Aiden is apparently in love with one of Draysus's daughters." He looked at Sander.

Sander, felt Ramiel's gaze. "Which one?"

"Nikoletta."

"I hate to break it to Aiden, but Nikoletta isn't exactly known for her chastity," Sander said.

"She does have quite the reputation," Tabrill said. "What's he thinking?"

"First love, maybe," Ramiel said. "Love makes men do unwise things. Even good men."

"We have quite the situation here," Tabrill said. "A council member's son in love with one of the head House Lucifer's daughters, and he is feeding them information about us."

"That's not our only problem," Ramiel said. "I have the feeling Zekiel knows about it, and might possibly be giving his son some of the information that he is giving House Lucifer. Our informants have told me things that Aiden simply would not know, but a council member would. We'll discuss it more after the council meeting. I just wanted you both to be aware of the situation."

Sander was deep in thought.

Several minutes later the other ten council members, all fallen angels, arrived and made their way to the council room, greeting each other.

"Gentlemen, now that everyone is here, let's take our seats and begin," Ramiel said.

Ramiel sat at the head of the table, while everyone else took their seats, six chairs on either side.

"Gentlemen, I'm glad everyone could make it. I'm sure some have heard various rumors about why I brought you here today, so let's forego the formalities and get to the point. House Lucifer has been gathering up as many half-bloods as they can and is putting them through the blood ritual at an incredible rate. Originally, as you all know, the blood ritual was used mainly to keep our loved ones with us, hopefully for as long as we are on this earth. House Lucifer is using it to create an army.

"It doesn't seem like a huge issue," said a wiry long-haired angel named Maalik, who appeared to be of Asian descent. "Almost all of our own sons eventually fight for us as immortals. Sure, House Lucifer may have increased numbers, but an immortal is nothing more than a human who can hypothetically live forever. They don't have our speed or strength . . ."

"Fighting an immortal who has been training in combat every day for 200 years is a hell of a lot harder than fighting any human," Sander said.

Corinthus, an angel of European appearance with close-cropped white hair, interrupted, "The rumor is House Lucifer has also set up several harems at their compounds."

"Good points," Ramiel said. "Also, it's true they have set up harems where they are getting as many women pregnant as possible to have more half-bloods to then put through the blood ritual, and eventually having more immortal soldiers to fight for them."

"What about the treaties?" Tabrill asked.

"Apparently, they thought they could get away with it without us knowing," Ramiel said. "They aren't aware of the number of informants we have inside their organization." He briefly looked at Zekiel.

"Or, they think we're weak and won't do anything about it," Maalik said.

"That's also a possibility I have thought about, Maalik, and that's why we are going to do something about it," Ramiel said.

"It seems kind of smart what they are doing," said Anthus, a large powerful-looking angel, whose light-blue eyes and long blond hair gave him the appearance of a Viking. "Maybe we should be doing the same thing."

Sander said, "Absolutely not."

"Oh really, Sandriel," Corinthus said snidely. "I thought you, of all people, would be for us having a harem."

"You believe too many of the rumors you hear, Corinthus," Sander said smiling. "If you insult me again, we'll be settling it the old way."

"I, um, I apologize," Corinthus said. "Forgive me, I meant nothing by it."

"Honestly, gentleman, I'm sure we all would love to have a harem. I mean who wouldn't?" Ramiel said, laughing to break the tension.

The men laughed.

"When I said absolutely not," Sander said, "I meant we can't just start playing God again, and start making everyone immortal. What is wrong with House Lucifer? Have they forgotten about the Great Flood? Every one of us here was at the Tower of Babel. We know what God is capable of doing when we anger Him."

"Exactly," Ramiel said. "We must send House Lucifer a message."

"What kind of message?" Zekiel asked. "Diplomatic?"

"No," Ramiel said. "Something stronger. They have to be reminded that they are not free to break treaties on a whim, and their secret breeding program has been going on under our noses for the last five years. They made the first move, we will be making the last one. I intend to wipe out about half a company of House Lucifer's soldiers to send a message. They will greatly outnumber us, if we let them continue this program of theirs."

"It could start a war," Corinthus said. "Do we want to risk that? Tensions have been mounting, and this could potentially lead to the end of all of us."

"We've been at war with them one way or another since the Great Flood," Tabrill said.

"If it leads to a final battle between us, then maybe we should get it over with," Sander said.

"I say we attack," Maalik said.

"I agree," Anthus said. "If it is Armageddon they want then it is Armageddon we will give them! While they believe Lucifer will lead them to victory, risking angering God by allowing this breeding program of theirs to continue is much more risky than going to all-out war with House Lucifer. The breeding program of theirs must be stopped no matter the cost."

"Are we all in agreement, then?" Ramiel asked as he looked around the table and saw various nods. "Anyone disagree?" No one said anything. "Good. I'll go over the details with our soldiers. That's all; meeting adjourned."

As everyone left the council room after saying their goodbyes, only Sander, Tabrill, and Ramiel remained.

"Let's head to my office," Ramiel said.

After Ramiel closed his office door, he said, "Well, now that that is over, how do you think we should go about this? I would have asked the council, but with Zekiel there, it's too much of a risk, but I would appreciate any input either of you have. From the intel I received, there are two secluded compounds where House Lucifer is training large numbers of half-bloods as they wait to go through the blood ritual.

The room was quiet as they thought.

"I have an idea," Tabrill said. "A way to find out if Zekiel is as much of a traitor as his son, and to wipe out some of House Ramiel's soldiers in the process."

"Okay, lets' hear it," Ramiel said. "If Sandriel promises not to challenge me to a duel." He laughed. "I thought, Sandriel hasn't been in a council meeting in years, and he's going to challenge Corinthus to a duel."

 Tabrill and Sander laughed.

"You both know I've never liked that guy," Sander said. "He's wanted to be head of House Ramiel since the beginning."

"I know," Ramiel said. "I keep him on the council to have someone who thinks differently than I do . . . perhaps that and some sentimentality."

"Well, I'm not as sentimental," Sander said.

"I've never liked him either, Sandriel," Tabrill said. "But back to my plan. I think Ramiel should let Zekiel know exactly where and when we are going to hit House Lucifer. Let him know a time as well, and make sure he knows what direction we will be coming from. We can use helicopters, nothing too big, without the general public knowing about it, since you said it was secluded. If he tells House Lucifer our plan, then we should know about where they plan to ambush us. The thing is, we aren't going to follow the plan we tell Zekiel at all. We'll have an idea of about where House Lucifer would want to be if they are setting us up. We fly in with a few A/MH-6 Little Birds with 50-calibers and rocket pods or whatever's needed, I'll let someone else do the logistics, and wipe them out. Have the police and media in the area informed that the nearest military bases will be doing some training exercises that night. If word gets leaked to House Lucifer, it doesn't matter, since they'll be expecting us anyway.

"Yeah, that could work," Sander said thinking. "And if it's not a setup, we still wipe them out. That's a good plan, Tabrill. I'm going along on this one. If it's a setup, and something goes wrong, they'll have a better chance of getting back alive if I'm there. House Lucifer might have a few fallen angels there. A lot of our immortals have never fought a fallen angel before."

"I like the plan. But I don't like you going with them, Sandriel," Ramiel said.

"They'll need me. Your boys will most likely be going," Sander said, looking at Tabrill.

"Yes, I know," Tabrill thought while rubbing his chin. "I'd feel better if Sandriel was there with my boys."

"Okay then, Sandriel. Wait for my call. I'll summon Zekiel immediately. Tabrill, go inform the immortals."

"When are we doing this?" Sander asked.

"Tonight," Ramiel said. "Our immortals have been training for something like this for weeks, and we have the Little Birds we need. Is that a problem?"

"No, just a little surprised." Sander smiled. "Let's get to it!"

"Sander, keep your phone nearby," Ramiel said as he walked to his desk and pressed a button. He told the secretary to have Zekiel come to his office immediately.

Sander and Tabrill left Ramiel's office.

"I guess I'll see you a little later this afternoon, then," Tabrill said as he shook hands with Sander and headed to meet with the immortals.

Sander walked over to the secretary's desk and turned on his phone as he waited for her to return. Scrolling through his missed texts he smiled as he saw one that said: *Hey, this is Amanda. I wondered if you wanted to meet for lunch.* It was 10:30; he texted her back: *Yes, but unfortunately I don't have a car.*

*Can you talk?*

*Yes Ma'am.*

He answered the phone when it rang. "Well, hello, Miss Amanda." He realized he was smiling.

"Sander!" she said. "Ramiel . . ," she paused, "My dad had a car and all kinds of gifts waiting for me at Denise's when I woke up this morning!"

"Oh nice," Sander said. "What kind of car? Do you like it?" He glanced at Zekiel as he walked briskly by him toward Ramiel's office.

"I do! "Amanda said. "It's a white BMW X5 M. I don't know if it's bulletproof, though. I don't know how to tell."

"Shoot the windshield," Sander said, laughing. "Just kidding; don't do that. Do the windows go down?"

"Yes. I think so. I haven't tried. Your window went down and yours was bulletproof."

"I like my front windows to be bullet-resistant, not completely bulletproof . . . so I can roll them down. I like to shoot back."

"Yeah, I've noticed." Amanda laughed. "Do you want to meet for lunch?"

"Of course. Can you meet me here at the Main House? They have a cafeteria area that's decent."

"Yeah, that sounds good."

"Do you remember how to get here?"

"Yes. Drive straight until I get to the building that looks like the White House," she said sarcastically.

"Yeah. Sorry, I wasn't thinking. I'll wait out front for you."

"See you soon. Bye."

"Bye."

"Hello, Lucy," Sander said, as he turned to the secretary.

"Hi, Sander." She smiled.

"I told them to get me a Range Rover last night. Any word when it will get here?"

She looked at her computer, and said, "It should be here in about an hour."

"Thanks, can you tell them to drop it off at Tabrill's when it gets here?"

She typed something. "Done."

"Thanks, Lucy," he grinned.

"Anytime," she said, smiling.

As Sander went down to the lobby, he thought about the mission they would be going on later, and how long it had been since he'd been on a military operation for House Ramiel. It felt good. It was hard to explain, but there was a different feeling he got after fighting other soldiers, as opposed to gangsters. There was more honor involved fighting against a fellow soldier.

Amanda pulled up to the front of the Main House in her new BMW, and Sander got in.

"Hello," Amanda said. "Do you like it?"

"Yes," he said, looking around. "Very nice. Maybe I should have gotten one of these instead."

"The windows don't go down after all," Amanda said. "How am I supposed to shoot back?" she said with a serious look on her face.

Sander looked at her, surprised by the comment.

"I'm kidding," Amanda said after a few moments.

"You had me worried there for a moment. I thought you'd been hanging out with me too much. Maybe I was a bad influence."

"No, not at all. I missed you at breakfast. After having you around constantly for the last few days and all we have been through, it feels strange when you aren't around."

"Yes, I know what you mean," Sander said, thinking. "I was getting used to it, too. It's been nice   having you there."

"So . . . where should I park?"

"Well, you're Ramiel's daughter, so I'm pretty sure you could drive into the middle of the lobby and everyone would be too afraid to say anything." He laughed. "But most people park around back."

After being waved through several checkpoints and entering the lobby of the Main House, Amanda said, "Here they go with the stares, again."

Sander noticed that, as many people walked by, they did a double-take at Amanda.

"They're just curious about the boss's daughter. They stare at me like that, too. I would say you get used to it, but it would be a lie . . . You never really get used to it . . . I suppose you just learn to ignore them."

"Well, if they stare at you, too, then both of us together must be quite the spectacle."

Sander smiled. "Indeed."

"Let them stare," Amanda said taking Sander's hand, grinning. "Let's start some rumors."

"I like your style," Sander said, as he led her to the cafeteria area.

When they entered the eating area, it didn't look like any cafeteria Amanda had ever seen. It was dimly lit and reminded her of some fancy restaurant you would see on television. Somewhere you would go on a romantic date, she thought. Definitely not a cafeteria.

Amanda noticed a hostess standing by the entrance, to whom Sander nodded as he led her past. They walked through the maze of tables and booths, as people stared at them both, past an enormous buffet to another hostess standing outside a large set of closed wooden doors. She said, "Will it just be you two today, Sandriel?"

"Yes, Ma'am."

The hostess opened the doors to another eating area, this one smaller but similarly decorated. They were led to a small round table, where Sander stood until Amanda sat down.

Amanda was looking at a large chandelier, wondering how much one of those would even cost, when Sander asked, "Is this okay? It's not too bad of a place."

"Yes, it is perfect Sander."

As she looked at the menu, she said, "This is easily the nicest cafeteria I've ever been in. What are you going to get?"

"Cheeseburger and wine," he said, laughing with her, referring to what she had ordered at The Brown Hotel. "Actually, I was going to get a cheeseburger and no wine. How about you?"

Just then the waiter approached them, introduced himself, and asked what they would be having.

"Seafood salad and a sweet tea," Amanda said.

"Cheeseburger and water," said Sander.

After the waiter took their orders, Sander put his phone on the table. "I know it's bad manners having my phone out, but I have a mission later tonight, and your dad will be calling sometime."

The smile on Amanda's face quickly turned into one of concern. "A mission? Will it be dangerous?"

Sander nodded. "Yes," he said, glancing down.

"How long will you be gone?"

"I should be back tomorrow."

"Be careful. Promise me right now that you'll be careful."

"I promise, Amanda."

"Why do you have to go?" Amanda asked heatedly. "Let them take someone else."

"They need me there."

"Maybe I need you . . ," she stopped herself. "Just promise you'll be careful."

As she began to speak, out of the corner of her eye she saw two blonde girls walking toward them. "Who are they?" she asked Sander, nodding toward the girls.

Sander looked and then smiled. "I know them. They're cool. You'll like them."

He stood as they approached. "Well, hello ladies," Sander said, smiling.

"Hi, Sander," the skinny blonde with short hair said.

"We didn't come over to talk to you," the long-haired blonde said looking at Sander. "So, get over yourself!" She laughed. "I'm kidding," she said, turning her attention to Amanda. "We came to meet the talk of the town."

"I thought *I* was the talk of the town," Sander said.

"Don't flatter yourself," the long-haired blonde said, smiling at Sander. "Anyhow, I'm Jessalyn, and you must be Amanda. It's so nice to finally meet you," she said as she shook Amanda's hand.

"Nice to meet you, too," Amanda said.

"Oh, I love your hair," Jessalyn said.

"Hi, I'm Dimitra," the short-haired blonde said, shaking Amanda's hand.

"Hi, Dimitra," Amanda said.

"I'm sure you're getting tired of everyone coming up and bothering you, being the new girl. We just wanted to introduce ourselves," Jessalyn said.

"No, actually you two are the first," Amanda said. "It's mostly just stares."

"Really?" Dimitra asked.

"Yeah," Amanda said. "Everyone just kind of looks at me like I don't belong or something."

"Well, we'll have to put an end to that," Jessalyn said looking around. "There are a lot of stuck-up people around here. They've known each other forever . . . literally forever," she laughed. "Here, let's exchange phone numbers. You'll have to come over and hang out sometime. I'm having a little cocktail party soon, if you're interested."

"Yeah, that sounds fun," Amanda said.

After the three girls exchanged numbers, Sander said, "What? Nobody wants my number?"

"I told you to stop flattering yourself," Jessalyn said, laughing. Then she looked at Amanda. "I'm kidding. Sander's a good guy. It was nice to meet you . . . and I'll call you sometime."

"It was nice to meet you both, too." Amanda waved as Jessalyn and Dimitra left.

"I guess there are some people here who do more than stare," Amanda said to Sander.

"Yeah, you'll like them. They are Anthus's girls. Anthus is a council member and fallen angel. I've known those two girls forever. Both are immortals."

"Have you ever dated them?"

Sander grinned. "No . . . Well, no, not really. It's a long story. They're just friends. Anyway, Jessalyn is married to an immortal and I believe Dimitra is engaged to one. So . . . how is your seafood salad?"

Amanda cracked up laughing. "Sander, you are absolutely horrible at trying to change the subject."

Sander just grinned, blushing a little.

"But you're kind of cute when you're nervous, so I'll let it slide."

Sander's phone rang. He glanced at it, saying, "It's your dad."

"Hello . . . yes . . . I'll be there shortly," he said, as a serious expression came over his face.

"I hate to end our lunch early, but I need to run by immortal headquarters," Sander said. He looked at her barely eaten food. "Do you want to get that to go? Or stay and finish it? I can walk over there; it's not far."

"No, silly. I wasn't even hungry. I had just eaten breakfast," Amanda smiled, saying, "I'll drive."

"Thank you."

He stood up and left a $100 bill on the table.

As Amanda followed Sander through the cafeteria, she took his hand saying, "Rumor time," and they both laughed.

When they got to the immortal headquarters a few blocks down the road from the Main House, Amanda said, "Please be careful, Sander."

"We're not leaving yet," Sander said, going over some things on his phone's screen. "I'll try to see you before we go tonight."

Amanda smiled. "Good."

"Do you know how to get back to Denise's?"

"Yes, everything around here is easy to find. We were going to sit around and talk about you."

"Ah, my favorite subject," Sander said smiling. "Text me when you get there, so I know you're safe."

"I will," Amanda said, thinking that was sweet of him. She had never had a guy worry about her safety or happiness so much before. Sander was so much more caring and kind than he wanted others to think he was. She watched him as he entered the immortal headquarters. A heavily armed man at the door saluted him as Sander entered. He walked by several desks as he made his way back to the conference room, noting the smell of boot polish and starch that seemed to linger in the air of military facilities.

"There's the man!" Maurice said as Sander entered the room.

Sander nodded.

Tabrill and his sons, Maurice and Craig, along with three other men Sander recognized from previous missions, were standing around a large map that had been spread on a metal table.

Sander said, "I guess you heard. "They know we're coming." Everyone in the room nodded with solemn looks on their faces.

"Yes," one of the immortals named John said. "We're going in heavier than we originally planned."

"Good," Sander said. "What do they think we are coming in with? How many do they expect us to have?"

A skinny, dark-haired man named McDermott with black/grey hair spoke up, "That is the only good thing about this mission." He looked at Sander and then pointed to the map. "They expect us to be coming in light through here, on foot. They think we are only sending in a couple of squads that will come up through this pass from the south to blow up the barracks while they are sleeping. So, we have come to the agreement that if they took the bait and are looking to jump those two squads they would be set up at the north of the pass." He pointed to a location on the map. "With men also set up on either side on these high points here and here." Pointing again to two hills on either side of the pass.

"Does House Lucifer have any fallen angels stationed there?" Sander asked.

"We couldn't get any confirmation on that. That's why we decided to go in heavy. McDermott said. "Plus it's good you're coming with us, if there does happen to be any."

"We're not worried about any fallen angels! We have the most hardcore fallen angel on earth with us," Maurice said.

"I appreciate your faith in me, but you guys know as well as I do, that sometimes even the best plans fall apart when the bullets start flying. We should be fine though as long as they believe we are coming in on foot."

"That's what I think, too, Sir," an immortal named Jefe said. "We are going to be coming in from the north with 6 MH-6 Little Birds. We'll do drop offs at these three locations." He pointed at the locations on the map . . . "With 4 AH-6 Little Birds coming in behind them and hitting their main force that should be grouped up here. We also will have 2 extra Little Birds holding back, just in case. Hopefully the men on the MH-6's will just be mopping up any stragglers."

"All right; sounds good," Sander said. "Is the plan still to fly out at 2300 hours?"

"Yes, for now . . . It will take about an hour to fly out there," Jefe said. He looked around the table. "Make sure all your men are here at 2100, ready to go."

"What about here. With us sending out so many men, who is guarding this compound? We can't just leave it unprotected," Sander said.

Tabrill smiled, knowing why Sander was so suddenly concerned with the wellbeing of the inhabitants of the compound. One inhabitant in particular.

"We had 75 reinforcements arrive today," McDermott said.

"OK; good job," Sander said. "I'll see you boys soon."

"Hooah!" McDermott said.

"Tabrill can you give me a lift back to your place after I grab some fatigues and a weapon or two?"

"Sure, I'll be waiting in the parking lot," Tabrill said.

Sander walked out carrying a black duffel bag, and what looked like a katana to Tabrill.

When Sander got into Tabrill's SUV, Tabrill lit up a cigarette, looked at Sander and asked, "Do you think you'll need the katana?"

"I hope not, but if there's another fallen angel there, I might."

"Do you want one of these before we get to my place? I noticed you don't smoke around Amanda, by the way," Tabrill said with a grin.

"What?" Sander asked. "Is it that obvious? Yeah, give me one of those." He lit one of the cigarettes. "I just don't smoke around her because it's bad for humans. It doesn't affect us . . . I'm just being nice, is all."

"No, I don't think it's all that obvious. When you know someone as long as I've known you, you know exactly what they are thinking after a while."

"You're right. And I know exactly what you are thinking right now, so just shut up and drive."

They both started laughing.

"You can keep the pack. You'll probably need them later tonight." Tabrill said. "And good luck on the mission, Sander. I've known you too long to see something happen to you now. Are you nervous at all? I know I would be, especially now that they know you are coming."

"Honestly, I don't know what I feel. I'm not sure if its nerves or what. I mean I've done things like this thousands of times. I've been feeling anxious lately . . . Probably nothing. I'll just be glad when it's over."

"Well you do have a pretty new girl in your life that you seem to get along with, from what I have witnessed. It's been awhile, hasn't it? . . . Maybe it's the new emotions making you anxious."

"When you say it out loud like that, it sounds so stupid," Sander said, laughing.

"Yeah, but it's true. You haven't had a real girlfriend in almost a century, and Amanda is a very pretty young woman . . ."

"I mean . . . I'll admit I've thought about it, if that's what you want to hear. Who knows what life will bring? I can't think about things like that right now, anyway. I need to stay focused for tonight's mission. Do me a favor and don't tell Denise you said anything to me about Amanda. You know I think the world of your wife, but we both know she gossips."

"No, I won't -- don't worry. It was good to have a real conversation with you again, after all those years. Don't be disappearing on me anymore. I was seriously starting to think you might end it."

"Honestly, so was I . . . I thought about it but I didn't, and I don't feel like talking about that right now. Maybe another time."

"Well, I'm glad you didn't," Tabrill said. "Let's head inside, troublemaker." He smiled.

Sander walked up to his room and threw the duffle bag on the bed, laying the katana gently on the pillows. He looked through the duffle bag, laid the black camo fatigues out beside it, and did a quick inventory. He tried to think of anything else he might need for the night.

He called Lucy, Ramiel's secretary, to check on his Range Rover.

"Well, twice in one day! Aren't I the lucky girl?" Lucy said, as she answered the phone.

"Just checking on my Range Rover. I saw it wasn't here yet."

"It should be there within the hour," Lucy said.

"Thanks Lucy. Talk to you later," Sander said

"Bye, Sander," she said.

As he walked downstairs he heard Denise and Amanda chatting in the kitchen.

Sander nodded at the maid and made his way to see how Amanda and Denise were doing.

"Hello, little gossipers," Sander said, smiling.

"Well, you've had a busy day," Denise said.

"Not too bad," Sander said. He looked at Amanda. "I got to have a quick lunch with Amanda at least."

"Yes, I heard," Denise said.

"The day is about to get a whole lot busier. Well, the night at least; I guess you heard that, too?"

"Yes, and I'm going to fix you and the boys a nice big dinner before you head off. Please look out for my boys," Denise said.

"Yes, I'll keep them close to me," Sander said. "They'll be fine." He hoped he could keep his word, but he knew the reality of battle -- the unpredictability.

The butler entered the kitchen and looked at Sander. "Sir, your Range Rover has arrived."

"Thanks, Ill check it out in a bit," he said.

Sander's phone rang.

"Yes, Ramiel. I'll be there soon."

He looked at Denise and Amanda. "Sorry to have to leave after just getting here, but Ramiel needs to speak to me."

"It's OK," Denise said.

"Actually, do you want to come with me?" Sander said to Amanda.

"Sure." Her eyes lit up.

"Great. Sorry to steal her away from you like that, Denise."

Denise smiled at them. "Oh, don't be silly. You kids go have fun. Just make sure you're both back here for dinner or I'll be holding you accountable, Mr. Sandriel!" She laughed.

As they walked up to Sander's Range Rover, Amanda said, "I love how she calls you a kid."

"Yeah, I do, too. Sometimes I wonder if she realizes I'm many thousands of years older than her." He smiled. "Just kidding. She's a sweet lady, as I'm sure you've noticed. Tabrill got lucky finding her."

"It's sad that she can't become an immortal, too," Amanda said. She noticed Sander's frown.

"Yeah, I know. I wish they could find a way to make normal humans live forever, too. We've done experiments in the past but nothing has worked, at least nothing House Ramiel has tried. House Ramiel doesn't do those kinds of experiments on humans anymore. There was something too evil about it, I suppose, but I know House Lucifer still does. Maybe they will find a breakthrough one day. Between you and me, Amanda, I worry about Tabrill when Denise does eventually pass away. He loves her completely; I don't want him to do anything stupid. I've been on this world for thousands of years, but I don't have very many friends or people I can really talk to. He is one of the few real friends I have left."

"Well you can talk to me about anything – always," Amanda said. "I want you to remember that."

"Thank you, Amanda," Sander said, looking at the ground.

"Oh, I like your Range Rover!" Amanda said, wanting to change the subject.

"Yeah, it looks nice."

"I still would have gone with pink or purple."

Sander laughed.

He opened the door for her. As they drove toward the Main House, he rolled the front windows down as far as they would go and then back up, checking to see if they were bullet-resistant.

"Looks like the back windows are bulletproof," he said.

"All of mine are bulletproof," Amanda said. "None of my windows go down. I hope my air conditioning doesn't go out on a hot summer day."

That made Sander smile. "Yeah, your dad got you a bulletproof tank because he doesn't want any harm to come to you. I like that dress you're wearing, too. Is that one of the gifts your dad sent to you?"

"Yes. He called one of the maids and had her tell him my dress size. I guess it was thoughtful of him."

As they parked, Sander said, "He means well. He's just trying to make up for leaving you for so long. I can understand why you would hate him, too, though. But I see his point of wanting to keep you as far from him as possible for your safety."

"Sometimes I'm still furious at him and then, sometimes, I understand why he did what he did. He's like a stranger to me, though. I mean, he left when I was three. It's not like I exactly remember him . . . I guess I just have to give it time and get to know what kind of man my father really is."

"Well you met me -- that's something positive that's came out of all of this," Sander said laughing. "I'm joking."

"No, it's true. I really do believe God has a plan for everything that happens. His plan was for me to eventually meet you, I think."

"Do you really believe that?"

"Yes, I believe God has a plan for everyone and everything He created . . . even you, Sandriel. Now come on; let's go start some rumors!" She grabbed his hand, smiling.

Sander was laughing. "All the people who work here are going to be like, 'Here comes the hand-holding lunatics again.'"

"I know; it cracks me up. That's what they get for staring. They wanted rumors; we're giving them to them."

They both laughed as they entered the lobby.

The security officer held the door, smiling. "Hello, Sander and Amanda."

"They're starting to recognize you," Sander said.

"Yeah, probably as the girl who's always holding Sander's hand." She laughed.

"Well, it could be worse," Sander said as they made their way to the elevator, where he put his eye to a scanner to open the door.

As they entered his office, Ramiel was typing on a laptop. He glanced up, raising his eyebrows when he saw Amanda.

"Everything's sorted out as far as the mission," Sander said to Ramiel.

Feeling uneasy, Amanda said, "I'll step out and give you two some privacy."

"No, there's no need for that, Amanda," Ramiel said. "I've been thinking you need to learn more about our organization anyway. If you can't trust your daughter, then who can you trust? Please stay."

"Okay," Amanda said smiling slightly.

"Please continue, Sandriel."

"As long as they take the bait, we shouldn't have too much trouble."

"And if they don't?"

"We have enough air support," Sander said thinking aloud. "I doubt they'll have any Stingers ready to go, since they think we're coming in on the ground. As long as they don't have any Stingers, we'll be fine."

"I was serious when I said you don't need to go on this mission. In fact, I would order you to stay here, if I thought you would listen. Losing you would be a huge blow from which House Ramiel could never recover. It's not just our soldiers who look up to you, you know . . . From my intel, so do a lot of House Lucifer's."

"We just don't have enough fallen angels in House Ramiel that fight anymore."

"That's because soldiers aren't known for their long lives, Sander. You know that. Think of all the friends we've lost in battle over the years. The sad truth is it's usually the cowards and politicians who survive. Not the heroes, not the brave soldiers."

"I didn't realize there was a difference between a coward and a politician," Sander said with a smirk. "Present company excluded, of course."

"I agree with you. You just be careful out there, old friend. Don't take any unnecessary risks."

"I won't."

"I do have some unrelated information you might be interested in, from one of my informants at House Lucifer. Elias, the man who was looking at your Mercedes in Louisville, is having an affair with Carmen."

"Carmen? You mean Kadan's wife?"

"Yes."

"That's interesting," Sander said looking off into the distance as if deep in thought. "You know, I could have sworn I saw Carmen at one of the malls in Louisville when I was shopping with Amanda . . . right before we were shot at."

"Do you think it's related?"

"I don't know." Amanda noticed Sander's furrowed eyebrows. "It doesn't make sense to just casually have a hit put on me, or try to kidnap Amanda, if they were having an affair in my city. That would have just brought attention to themselves . . . We both know Kadan would skin Elias alive if he knew he was with Carmen. I'll have to figure it out sometime after I get back, but thank you for that info. It's going to come in handy, eventually."

"Of course," Ramiel said.

Amanda looked at them, thinking it was interesting to hear her father and Sander talk business like this, but to her they still sounded like gangsters, just almost unimaginably powerful ones. But then again, maybe that's all the leaders of countries are, when it came down to it, very powerful gangsters, each looking out for their individual country's interests.

"What about Zekiel?" Sander asked. "Have you detained him yet?"

"No. We have him under surveillance for the time being. We're waiting until the mission is over before we make any moves. As much as I hate to admit it, it is more than likely that House Lucifer has a few informants around here who we have yet to discover."

Sander nodded.

"That's all I have for you, for the time being. Good luck tonight. I'll be waiting for your safe return."

He turned his attention to Amanda. "It's always a pleasant surprise to see you, Amanda! Please do come by any time. I was serious about you becoming more involved in House Ramiel and its operations, if you are interested."

"Thanks! It was nice to see you, too," Amanda said, still not sure how she felt about her father.

"Later, Ramiel," Sander said, as they left his office to make their way to the lobby.

When they got to the lobby, several people turned their heads, always curious to see who had just met with the head of House Ramiel. Amanda laughed as she grabbed Sander's hand. Sander smiled as he casually looked over the room.

Sander noticed the attractive black-haired girl that had caught his eye earlier that morning was walking toward them. He still couldn't remember why she looked so familiar.

"Hi Sander. Remember me?" the girl asked.

As soon as she spoke he thought he also recognized her voice and then he got a close look at her eyes. She had an accent common to the area, but with a unique high pitch. She had incredibly blue eyes unlike any he had ever seen, in all his years on this earth . . . almost gem-like he thought.

"Tena?" he asked.

"Tina with an 'e!'" she replied.

He laughed. "Corinthus's daughter -- yes, I remember you. It's been a while . . . You grew up quick," he said as he looked her over.

"Yeah. It has been years. I'm working for my dad now . . . administrative stuff."

"Interesting," Sander said, smiling. He noticed Tena quickly glance at Amanda, still holding his hand.

"Where are my manners?" Sander said. "This is Amanda, Ramiel's daughter. Amanda, this is Tena, Corinthus's daughter."

Amanda and Tena shook hands, and Amanda complimented Tena on her dress.

"Thank you," Tena said. "I had heard so much about you, and seen you once. I was just too nervous to introduce myself. I didn't want to look like an idiot, just in case you weren't Ramiel's daughter."

Amanda laughed. "I really wish more people would introduce themselves."

"Have you had a chance to meet anyone else?" Tena asked.

"So far, just you, and two girls named Jessalyn and Dimitra," Amanda replied.

"Oh yeah I know them," Tena said. "We're all good friends, and I'm sure you and I will be, too. We'll have to all get together sometime."

"Definitely," Amanda said.

After they exchanged phone numbers, Tena said, "I have to get back to work, but I'll see y'all around."

Sander nodded, and Amanda said, "Yeah, see you."

"She seems nice," Amanda said.

"Yes, she does. She was like this tall last time I saw her." He held his hand up to his chest. "I'm glad you're making some friends."

"I'll have someone to hang with while you're out shooting people," Amanda said laughing, cracking herself up.

Sander couldn't help but laugh. "That's not all I do, you know." He paused to think. "Wow, I've never really thought about it before. Maybe it is!"

"I was kidding."

"So was I," said Sander, grinning.

"We should probably head back, so you don't get in trouble with Denise."

"Yeah." He glanced at his watch, thinking about the mission that night for a moment. "Let's get out of here."

When Sander and Amanda got to Tabrill and Denise's house, they were sitting in the living room.

"There they are," Denise said.

Sander and Amanda sat on the couch.

"Did you have a nice meeting with Ramiel?" Denise asked.

"Yes," Amanda said.

"Ramiel mentioned Amanda getting more involved with House Ramiel," Sander said.

"That's a good idea," Tabrill said.

"How do you feel about that?" Denise asked, looking at Amanda.

"I'd like to, eventually," Amanda said. "Once I get used to everything. I mean this time last week, I was a waitress with no money, and now I'm surrounded by everything I could ever want, plus there's the whole fact that I found out that fallen angels are real." She laughed. "It's definitely taking some getting used to."

"Yes, I believe it does take time to sink in," Tabrill said.

"I'm still not used to it myself," Denise said, shaking her head.

"If you ever have any questions about the organization, feel free to ask anything you want to know," Tabrill said.

"There is one thing I was thinking about earlier. If my dad, Ramiel, runs House Ramiel, does Lucifer, the devil, run House Lucifer?"

Sander smiled, "That's a complicated one."

"I can try to explain it," Tabrill said.

"Go for it," Sander said.

"Currently the head of House Lucifer is a fallen angel named Draysus. He could be viewed as Lucifer's representative, in a way. Draysus takes orders from Lucifer, following his will.

Now, don't get me wrong, Lucifer is in fact on this earth tempting humans, and us as well, every chance he gets. He is just not the figurehead of the organization that took his name. For instance, if you were at a House Lucifer compound, you couldn't just go take an elevator to see Lucifer, but Draysus, the head of House Lucifer does commune with Lucifer . . ."

"I think I understand," Amanda said.

"I don't know how often you read the Bible," Tabrill said. "But I believe it is Peter 5:8 that states: 'Be alert and of sober mind. Your enemy the devil prowls around like a roaring lion looking for someone to devour.' This is truer than most humans realize. We fallen angels knew Lucifer personally, and that passage describes him perfectly, I think.

Tabrill stopped to think. "I don't know how much Sander explained, but we in House Ramiel remember being deceived by Lucifer. Even though it could be argued, and is argued by some, that we rule the world thanks to him, we still recognize that God is more powerful than Lucifer ever will be. That's something almost all of House Lucifer refuses to believe. I personally think it's because they are so close to Lucifer and continually hear his lies and experience his deceptions. They think Lucifer will come out on top. We in House Ramiel, well most of us, are sober-minded enough to realize God truly is, and will always be, more powerful."

"Then why does House Ramiel still do evil things?" Amanda asked.

"That's what I'm saying! Good question Amanda," Denise said.

"Whoa!" Sander said. "And I thought that last question was complicated. This one's even more complicated. I'm curious, too, actually."

"Yes, where do I begin with that one?" Tabrill asked. "I guess, in comparison to House Lucifer, we like to consider ourselves as being good. But we are still, in spite of having experienced both God and Lucifer, still like humans -- full of lust, vanity, and jealousy. In this world, sometimes evil things must be done to have and maintain power. House Ramiel will do what it must to remain powerful. If House Ramiel didn't, then House Lucifer would completely take over this world, and then you would see absolute unrepentant evil. So I think, to answer your question, we do what we must to combat House Lucifer, even if sometimes it is not considered good."

"Would you agree?" Tabrill asked Sander.

"I think that was a good answer . . . but a very political one," Sander said. "I think we are evil, just not as evil as House Lucifer. There are very few truly good people -- angels or humans -- in this world, as far as I'm concerned. I know quite a few fallen angels who don't care about the good or evil of it, and are just holding a grudge against Lucifer for deceiving us and getting us banished from Heaven."

"That's another way to put it," Tabrill said, thinking. "There is good and evil in all of us . . . Sometimes I even think there's some good left in Sandriel."

Sander smiled.

"I've seen a lot of good in you Sander," Amanda said. "You're not as cold-hearted or evil as you want everyone to believe."

Sander was looking at the ground. "Tabrill, I feel you staring at me."

Tabrill laughed.

"OK," Amanda said, "I have another question."

"Uh-oh," Sander said, grinning.

Amanda punched Sander playfully in the arm.

"This is an easy question. Are your wings all the same color? I was just curious. I've seen Sander's but no one else's."

"That is an easy question," Tabrill said. "I thought you were going to ask me the meaning of life after those last two."

Everyone laughed.

Tabrill stood, letting his wings out. The room lit up with a soft amber glow, bright enough to make Amanda and Denise squint slightly. Amanda was going to ask Sander to show her his again, but she knew it seemed to trouble him when he showed his wings.

"They are all pretty close in color," Tabrill said. "No extreme colors that I've ever seen in all of my time."

"No bright pink or purple wings, thankfully," Sander said, grinning.

"Oh, you know you wish you had some purple wings, Sander," Denise said.

Sander laughed at the idea of having bright purple wings.

A few moments later Craig, Tabrill and Denise's youngest son, walked in. He was carrying what Sander noticed was an HK416 A5 rifle.

"Hello baby," Denise said. "Don't you look handsome! Doesn't our boy look handsome, Tabrill?"

"Very handsome," Tabrill said, standing to give him a hug. "You make me very proud."

"Come on now, Mom. You're embarrassing me," Craig said.

Craig looked over at the couch. "Sir," nodding at Sander, and "Ma'am," nodding toward Amanda.

"Have you met Amanda?" Denise asked.

"No, Ma'am. I haven't had the pleasure," Craig said.

"Hi, I'm Amanda. Nice to meet you," Amanda said as she walked over to shake Craig's hand.

"Hi. Nice to meet you too, Ma'am."

"Amanda, isn't my boy so well mannered?" Denise said. "It's my boy Maurice I've got to work on," she nodded her head.

"Where is Maurice?" Craig asked. "I thought he was coming over for dinner, too, before we head out."

"He's upstairs sleeping."

"Do you want me to go wake him up?" Craig asked.

"Yeah, go ahead. Dinner will be soon."

As she waited for dinner to be ready, Amanda sat on the couch beside Sander and watched him picking at a fingernail, staring off in the distance at nothing in particular, as if lost in thought. She wondered what was going through his head at the moment. She wondered if he was as nervous as she was that something might happen to him tonight.

She touched his hand and he looked at her and smiled, but he still had a look in his eyes like he was looking right through her, still thinking. He shook his head slightly and said, "Sorry, I was in a zone there."

"It's fine," she said softly.

Just then Denise said, "Dinner is ready." Amanda and Sander sat at the table with Denise, as Tabrill went to get their boys.

"They are on their way," Tabrill said, as he sat at the head of the table.

The maids began bringing out their food.

"Tonight, we will be having lasagna," Denise said. "I hope that's okay with everyone. Where are those, boys? I swear they are late for everything."

Maurice and Craig entered the room, already dressed in their black camo fatigues.

"Ooh, I get to sit by the man himself," Maurice said as he sat by Sander.

Craig sat at his chair without comment, looked down, and appeared to Sander to be saying a prayer.

"So, we going to send these boys to Hell tonight or what, Sandriel?" Maurice asked.

Sander nodded. "That's the plan," he said.

"It's been a while since we rolled up on some fools together," Maurice said. "They won't know what hit them."

"Indeed," Sander said.

"You two! What kind of talk is that at the dinner table?" Denise said.

"Sorry, Mama. I'm just excited," Maurice said.

"Sorry, Denise. Maurice is a bad influence on me," Sander said. "I'm usually better behaved."

"Ha ha! This is my boy, right here," Maurice said, laughing.

"You two!" Denise said. "You two are going to end up eating in the living room."

Amanda laughed at the way Denise talked to two men who were probably two of the most dangerous men at this compound.

"Sorry, Ma'am," Sander said, grinning at Amanda who was already smiling at him.

Denise said, "Now that we are all here, I want you all to know how much I love each and every one of you. That includes you, too, Miss Amanda. I feel blessed to have you as the newest member of our household. I also want you to know that I will be saying a prayer for you boys' safe return, whether you like it or not."

She looked at Sander. "Sandriel, I know you'll be looking out for my boys, but you need someone looking out for you, too. I hope God will keep you safe whether you think you deserve it or not."

Sander smiled slightly and nodded.

"Did I ever tell you all about the time me and Sander went to Spain to remind this politician who was running things?" Maurice asked.

"Not at the table," Denise said.

"Yeah, sorry. I'll tell you all some other time," Maurice said, grinning. "Let me at least ask Sander one thing, Mom. It's important for tonight. What weapons are you taking? M27, M4A1, or what?"

"No. I'm thinking an HK like Craig," Sander said. "Pistols of course, and Katana, just in case."

Maurice nodded. "Yeah, just in case. Hopefully you won't need that Katana." Maurice looked unusually serious for a change, Amanda thought.

After dinner Craig and Maurice hugged their mother and father and went to immortal headquarters.

"If you'll excuse me, I should probably get dressed," Sander said, as he looked at his watch.

Sander went upstairs and put on the tactical gear he had brought with him, putting a leg holster with a Glock 19 on his right thigh, and the scabbard, a Saya, on his left-hand side, sliding it under a belt, removing the Katana from it a few times seeing if it would be comfortable with all of the other gear he would be wearing.

When Sander went downstairs, Amanda, Denise and Tabrill were sitting in the living room drinking coffee.

"Handsome Sandriel!" Denise said.

"You look bad ass," Amanda said, looking at the Katana and his black camouflage. He reminded her of a ninja. She walked up to him and said, "Can I see that?" She touched the Katana.

"Sure," Sander said as he gently handed the Katana to her. "Be careful; it's very sharp."

"How old is that Katana?" Tabrill asked.

"16$^{th}$ century," Sander said.

"Very nice," said Tabrill, as he watched Amanda pretend to be slicing things with it. "Hopefully it won't see any blood tonight."

"Hopefully," Sander said seriously.

The reality -- that Sander was getting ready to go use this Katana she held in her hands to kill people -- struck Amanda like a blow to her chest. They will have swords and katanas, too, she thought. She couldn't imagine someone swinging one of these at her with the intention of killing her with it.

"Please don't go," Amanda said.

"We both know I have to," Sander said, taking the Katana from her.

"Please, be careful. You're my guardian angel, remember," Amanda said, feeling like she was getting teary eyed.

"Of course. I'll always be your guardian angel," Sander said.

Amanda hugged him like she'd never see him again, and she wasn't positive that she would. Everything up until now had been so great between them, and now she felt as if it could all come crashing down.

Sander cleared his throat. "I should probably get going."

"I can give you a lift over there if you want, Sander. I need to head to the Main House to meet Ramiel. We'll be listening to communications throughout the mission."

Sander nodded.

Denise walked up to Sander. "You know you weren't walking out this door without a hug from me. Me and Amanda will be up waiting for you and the boys when you get back."

Sander smiled, although thin-lipped, as he removed the Saya with the sheathed Katana, just carrying it now.

"Ready?" Tabrill asked.

Sander nodded and followed him.

As he closed the door to the garage, Sander took one last look at Amanda who was looking at him. She didn't speak, being slightly choked up. She raised her hand as if to wave.

As they drove to the immortal headquarters there was dead silence. Tabrill lit up a cigarette and handed it to Sander who was looking out the window at nothing in particular. Sander took the cigarette, nodded, and said, "Thanks."

When they got to the headquarters, Tabrill said, "Give 'em Hell."

"I intend to," Sander said seriously.

As Sander entered the immortal headquarters, the men cheered.

"Hell yeah!" Maurice said, walking up to him. "It's getting real now!" He punched Sander's fist.

Sander walked back to a room with multiple tables. It looks like a buffet of military gadgets, equipment, and small-arms, he thought. Sander put on his tactical vest and grabbed extra clips and grenades, night-vision goggles, a helmet, and an MK3 Navy knife.

After going to his weapons locker and getting his custom HK416 assault rifle, he headed toward the conference room.

He saw John, McDermott, and Jefe from earlier.

"Everything still good?" Sander asked.

"Yes," Jefe said. "Intel still looks good. We have received a report that at least one fallen angel may be there, however."

Sander nodded. "Any idea who it is?"

"No, unfortunately not."

"All right, explain to your men before we leave: call it in the second they see him. Neutralizing the fallen angels will be my first priority, if there is one or two there. Also, I know almost everyone here has either served in Special Forces or at least gone through special operations training, but explain to them that fighting an angel is different. Remind them to take the angel's legs out. *Speed* is our advantage."

"Roger that, Sir," Jefe said. "I'll go gather up the men."

Sander walked into the room where the men were being given final instructions from John. Sander saw them all look at him as he entered the room. John went over the plan with them, systematically explaining exactly how it should go, if nothing went wrong. Though every man there knew that didn't usually happen.

After a final speech, the men loaded into trucks and made their way up the road to the airfield, loading into their assigned MH-6 Little Bird transport/support helicopters. Each Little Bird had a two-man bench on either side that would allow the soldiers to quickly hop off or rappel from the helicopters. Sander took his seat next to Craig, Denise and Tabrill's boy. He knew Maurice could handle himself, but Craig was much younger and, while a good soldier, wasn't as experienced.

As they took off Sander looked at the four AH-6 Little Bird attack helicopters that would be leading the assault. If everything went according to plan, the AH-6s were pretty much all they would need to wipe out every one of the House Lucifer soldiers, he thought.

Everything went smoothly on the way to their assigned landing zones. The three other men on Sander's helicopter jumped off at the same time he did, as he saw the AH-6 attack helicopters several hundred yards ahead raining Hell on the unsuspecting enemy. So far so good, he thought. He noticed the three men from his helicopter following him, instead of immediately taking cover like they were supposed to, while he sprinted in and searched the barracks in their area for stragglers. Humans had a habit of following the fallen angels when they were in combat, he thought. He heard sporadic gunfire going off all over the compound and could tell there were more soldiers there than they originally thought. "Get down and find some cover," he said to Craig and the two other men, Eugene and Mick. Sander went through five of the barracks at lightning speed, making sure they were clear. When he came to the sixth, he saw a man on a communications device with a sword in his hand. He began to spin around. Sander shot his knees and his sword arm as the man spun, sending the sword sliding across the floor. A fallen angel, Sander thought.

"I know you," the angel said slowly, his voice tight with pain. "You're Sandriel."

The fallen angel was bleeding profusely, Sander noticed as he held his weapon at the fallen angel's forehead, preparing to fire. "My name is Nasriel. Please don't kill me; I beg you. We met once. You met my wife Kelly. I love her so much . . . Please. I just had a daughter. Please Sandriel . . . I will owe you my life . . . I'm begging you . . ."

Sander looked at Nasriel's knees, which were completely shattered. He stopped pointing at Nasriel's forehead. "You might live through this, but you won't be walking anytime soon. If you leave this room, I'll kill you."

Nasriel lay there weeping, covered in blood, repeating, "Thank you, Sandriel." Sander ran out to meet up with the other men.

As Sander ran to where Craig, Eugene, and Mick were supposed to be, he saw they weren't there. He noticed one of the AH-6's fly overhead for another strafing run.

"Man down! Man down! This is McDermott! We have a man down!"

"This is Sandriel. I'm on my way to your position."

On his way to McDermott's position, Sander saw three House Lucifer soldiers trying to flank them. Sander ran up behind them, shooting all three in the back of the head before they had a chance to react.

Sander jumped into a large ditch and saw McDermott holding a bandage on a man's leg. When he looked, he saw Craig, Eugene, and Mick were there, too, firing at a group of men about 100 yards away. They had either gotten confused or scared when he left them and ran to McDermott's position.

"How many are there?" Sander asked John, who was taking careful aim.

"Five," John said. He fired twice. "Three now." He smiled.

Just then, the back of Mick's shoulder seemed to explode in a mass of bone fragments and blood. He dropped back screaming. Sander fired back, hitting a man without a helmet in the head, and watched him through the scope as he fell, lifeless. He heard the crack of a bullet by his ear and then saw Craig fall backwards silently clutching his throat, as blood poured through his fingers. Sander put his hand on the wound, looking at Craig in the eyes, telling him to keep breathing.

"You're going to be all right Craig. We'll get you home."

"Someone come here and keep some pressure on his neck!" Sander yelled. Eugene pressed down on the wound. "Keep talking to him Eugene. Keep him breathing."

John fired. "Got him . . . What the . . . Dammit, we have a fallen angel boys!" John fired again as Sander turned and saw the blur of an angel sprinting in a zigzag pattern across the field at incredible speed. He had a sword in his right hand and his wings out, blazing. A true warrior, Sander thought as he showed his own wings and sprinted toward the advancing fallen angel. The fallen angel turned and headed toward Sander. The men stared awestruck at the sight of the two angels rushing at each other. Even the sporadic gunfire in the distance seemed to stop.

Sander felt a bullet strike his left arm from somewhere in the distance, and he spun around, dropping his pistol. Turning to face the angel Sander parried his first blow with Katana, catching himself on his left leg. Dodging to his right as the enemy angel's longsword swept over his head, Sander came up, slicing through his adversary's stomach and chest. Startled by the cut, the fallen angel stepped back and blocked two of Sander's blows. Wounded, the angel from House Lucifer swung his sword unsteadily as Sander dodged and advanced with a lunge partially decapitating him.

Sander sheathed his katana into the Saya, picked up the other fallen angel's longsword and sprinted back to the ditch. Ignoring his men's cheers, he looked to make sure Craig was still breathing, and asked John if he had shot the man who shot him in the arm.

"Yes, I got him," John said, thinking Sander looked like some kind of evil demon . . . covered in blood, with his wings out, holding that longsword.

McDermott also looked at Sander. "Looks like we're clear here. Jefe and Maurice's groups are still under fire."

"Stay here. Don't let these men die. I'm going to go help the others clean up what's left.

Sander sprinted to Maurice's position.

"You hit?" Maurice asked seeing Sander covered in blood.

"My arm. I'll be fine."

"We could see that fight in the open field. Badass."

"How many are there?"

"Seven, I think."

"Want me to get behind them?"

"No reason. Jefe just called the AH-6 back in. It'll be over in a minute."

"Your brother was hit."

"Is it bad?" Maurice asked tensely.

Sander nodded yes.

"Do you think he'll make it?" Maurice asked softly.

Just then the AH-6 flew over, decimating all of what remained of House Lucifer's soldiers with its GAU-19 heavy, multi-barreled machine gun.

"He can still make it," Sander said. "He was hit in the neck, but he's still breathing, and it doesn't look like it hit any arteries."

"If he doesn't make it, I'm going to kill Zekiel myself," Maurice said.

Sander nodded.

Jefe walked up and looked at Sander. "Are you okay?"

"My left arm's kind of messed up. It feels like it's broken, now that the adrenaline is wearing off. But I'll be fine."

"That was a hell of a fight between you and that House Lucifer angel," Jefe said. "Both sides stopped shooting to watch. I've never seen anything like it."

Sander ignored his praise. "Did you guys have any casualties?"

"Nothing serious," Jefe said.

"Good. Call in the choppers and let's get the hell out of here."

"They're on the way," Jefe said.

"All right, see you back home."

Sander and Maurice flew back with Craig on a medical helicopter. Craig was still breathing and was stable, the medic told them. Sander's arm was broken by the bullet, and even for an angel it would take some time for the bone to heal correctly. Sander heard someone over the radio say the mission was a complete success, but as he looked down at the young man struggling to breath with the bloody bandage wrapped around his neck, it didn't feel like a complete success to him.

As the helicopter landed at the House Ramiel compound hospital, the medical staff came out and wheeled the injured inside. Someone tried to assist Sander, still covered in dried blood, and he shook his head. Maurice followed the stretcher carrying his brother.

Sander saw Ramiel approaching him. "Good job out there," Ramiel said. "I'm sorry about Craig. I'll have my best surgeons looking after him. We will not lose that boy."

Sander nodded.

"Where's Zekiel?" Sander asked.

"He was apprehended when the battle began. He's at the station." Ramiel looked at Sander for a moment. "I know what you're thinking, and I'm not going to stop you. I just don't think you should. Trust me, justice will be served."

"I don't know. I haven't decided." Sander took slow deliberate breaths to calm down. "He better hope Craig lives," he said evenly.

Ramiel lit up a cigarette and handed it to Sander. "Who was it?" Ramiel asked, looking at the extra sword Sander had tucked into his belt.

"Darriel," Sander said. "I didn't recognize him until the fight was almost over," Sander said. "I'm going to go check on Craig and the other soldiers."

Sander walked into the hospital to where he saw a group of immortals standing. "How are they?" he asked.

One of them said, "Mick is in critical condition. Everyone else is stable for now."

"Is this Mick's room?" Sander asked.

"Yes," John said. "They won't let us in, so we're waiting for more news. Craig is down the hall, around the corner there." He nodded.

"Thanks," Sander said.

As Sander walked down the hall, he heard Denise sobbing loudly. As he turned down the corridor he saw Tabrill, Denise, Amanda, Jessalyn and Dimitra looking through a glass window into a room.

Tabrill was the first to notice Sander. He nodded his head, then turned back to the window.

Sander was suddenly self-conscious of how he must look with the dried blood covering him and his arm in a sling.

Amanda saw Sander out of the corner of her eye and ran to him, her eyes wide. She was crying as she hugged him.

Sander wrapped his good arm around her tightly.

He didn't want to let go. "I don't know what to say," Sander said, holding her as he looked at the floor.

"Don't say anything. I was so worried when I heard you were shot . . . We didn't know how bad it was. I felt empty . . . alone."

"I told you I'd be back. I'm your guardian angel, remember."

"Always?"

"I don't break my promises."

Amanda hugged him tightly.

"Is Craig going to be all right?"

"They keep saying he's stable," Amanda said softly.

"How are Denise and Tabrill?" He looked at Tabrill, standing there with his arm around Denise.

"Denise is taking it hard. I feel so sorry for her."

"Where is Maurice?"

Just then Sander's question was answered as he saw Maurice turn the corner. Maurice looked at his mother, and then walked toward Sander. He had a determined look in his eyes, Sander noticed.

As Maurice approached, Amanda let go of Sander and looked Maurice over as he approached.

"I was looking for you," Maurice said. "I ran into Ramiel . . . I'm headed to the station." Maurice looked back at his mother, who had begun crying again.

Sander thought for a moment, looked at the rifle slung over Maurice's arm, and then nodded.

Maurice nodded back at Sander and walked away.

Amanda, having heard the conversation, looked at Sander with a questioning look on her face.

"I think Maurice is going to execute Zekiel," Sander said. "The fallen angel who betrayed us."

Amanda's eyes grew wide.

She looked back at Denise standing there weeping, and thought, "What if it had been Sander laying on the operating table in that room." Even though the thought of executing anyone seemed terrible and wrong to Amanda, part of her understood.

Sander and Amanda walked up to Denise and Tabrill. Sander patted Tabrill on his back, uneasily trying to console him, unsure what to say. He then walked over to Denise, who looked at him sadly.

"I'm sorry," Sander said softly, as he looked down, his eyes unfocused. "I was right there," he said thinking. "I should have told him to stay down . . . I don't know, it happened so fast."

Denise kept looking at Sander, as if she hadn't heard a word he said. She hugged him, and began crying. "He'll be fine," Denise said, as if reassuring herself. "My baby's going to pull through. The good Lord is going to take care of my baby. Just you watch."

Amanda looked at Sander as he said, "Yes, he's going to be fine."

"You all right, honey?" Denise asked, looking at his splint.

"Yes, Ma'am. I'm fine."

"That's good," Denise said, as she turned her attention back to the window. "Yep. Craig is going to be all right. Just you watch."

Sander walked back over to Tabrill and said softly, "Keep me updated."

"I will."

Sander looked around uneasily, "I think I'm going to head out of here."

He turned and walked away.

"Hey Sandriel," Tabrill said. "I'm glad you made it back."

Sander looked at him, and nodded his head slightly, with a saddened look on his face.

Tabrill looked at Amanda, who was nervously biting her bottom lip as she watched Sander.

"You should probably go with him. I don't think he needs to be alone right now."

"Are you sure?" she said looking at Denise.

"Yes sweetie," Denise said. "We'll be all right."

"All right," Amanda said as she went after Sander.

When Amanda caught up with Sander, he was standing outside looking up at the stars.

He glanced at her and smiled slightly. A few moments passed before he said anything. "I hate hospitals. Do you want to get out of here?" he asked, looking at her. "I was going to go to my place, but I forgot my car is at Tabrill's."

"I can drive, if you want."

"All right, yeah, I just don't want to be around here anymore. There's nothing I can do anyway."

At Tabrill's house, Sander went upstairs, got his car keys, and came back down the stairs. He looked at Amanda, who was still standing at the foot of the stairs. "I guess I'll just go to my place."

"What? You're not serious are you? Sander . . . I was worried sick about you. I thought you might be dead!"

"Really?" Sander asked curiously.

"Yes, really. I care about you; don't you see that?"

"I suppose I'm not used to it . . . I care about you, too, Amanda . . . more than you know." He looked at her shoulder, avoiding her eyes. "Did you really think I was dead?"

"Yes! Denise and I stayed here with some of the other wives and got updates from Tabrill, when he had time, and we heard there were casualties. They weren't sure exactly who the casualties were at first, and then names came in and yours was one of them. Tabrill had said there were reports of you fighting another fallen angel, and I thought the worst. When we got to the hospital they kept bringing in the wounded. I looked at everyone they brought in, praying you would be okay. And after they brought them all in, you were nowhere to be seen and no one knew where you were."

Sander watched, transfixed, as a single tear streamed down her cheek.

He hugged her. "I don't know how this sounds, but you were the first person I wanted to see when I got back. I probably shouldn't have told you that, but it's the truth."

"That just made my night, Sander. I just don't know what I would do without you."

She felt tears coming on again, and pulled away, wiping her eyes. "Oh, wow! It's been an emotional night!"

"Yes, it has."

His phone rang.

"Okay . . . Yes, she's here . . . That's good news . . . Okay . . . All right . . . Thanks for letting me know."

Sander looked at Amanda. "That was Tabrill. He said Craig is going to be okay. The bullet didn't hit any arteries . . . If it did strike a nerve, he may have limited movement in his arms for a while. He should be fine, he's going to live."

"That's great news! Thank God."

"I'm glad he's okay." Sander looked relaxed for the first time that night, Amanda noticed.

"Do you have to do missions like this a lot?"

"No, not in the states. This was very rare, but treaties were broken and it had to be done. Our houses can't just go to all-out war against each other openly . . . There would be too many questions, too hard to hide, too many people to bribe. Something like what just occurred could be blamed on a training exercise . . . But if it happened every day or every week, it would eventually leak out. Even then, a lot of people still wouldn't believe it, though. Usually our wars tend to be political and financial."

"Good," Amanda said. "I don't know how much I could take of this."

"Be glad you didn't know me during the Middle Ages."

"That other sword, is it a katana, too? I thought you only took one. Is that the other fallen angel's sword? The one you fought?"

"Yes, it was his. It's a longsword," Sander said. "Here." He handed it to her. "You can see it if you want."

Amanda took the longsword, marveling at the intricate detail on the cross guard, grip, and red jewel-encrusted pommel.

Amanda swung the longsword carefully, back and forth, and Sander parried one of her swings with his Katana. Amanda smiled at Sander, who was grinning at her. They pretended to sword fight as Amanda asked, "What was his name?"

"Darriel."

"Did you kill him?"

"Yes. He could have been the one that shot Craig . . . but I'm not sure. I doubt he would have missed if it was him. But then again, just because you are a fallen angel, that doesn't necessarily make you a perfect shot."

"Nice one," Sander said as Amanda parried one of his slow swings.

Amanda smiled and asked, "Did you know Darriel?"

"Yes. We knew each other before the two houses formed. We were never close, but we knew each other. He was a true warrior. I have seen him on the battlefield before, but never fought him one-on-one. It was over quick, I was expecting him to be better with a sword."

Sander replayed the fight in his head, like he knew he would thousands of times, analyzing every mistake he made.

He playfully parried another of Amanda's swings. "It wasn't even a fair fight," Sander said, grimacing. "Somebody shot me in the arm when I was running at him. As soon as I got hit, between you and me, Amanda, I thought that was the end. I thought I was done for. But I think it just made me angry. Besides, I knew I had to get back and guard my princess." They both smiled at each other.

"That's right," Amanda said blocking a slow swing of Sander's Katana. "Will you teach me to sword fight one day?"

"Of course, I will."

Amanda's phone rang. She lowered the longsword, returning it to Sander.

"Hello, Denise," she said.

As Amanda spoke to Denise, Sander looked at his reflection in the mirror sitting over one of the fireplaces. He realized he still had dried blood on his face and clothing. He looked down at the splint on his arm and would be glad to remove it. He had been told to leave it on for a day, but he had a feeling it was going to come off before then.

His mind wandered to Maurice and what he was going through. He wondered if he had killed Zekiel. He would have called Maurice, but at that moment, Sander wanted nothing to do with anyone or anything that reminded him of that night's battle. He wanted to be left alone, with Amanda. Something about her innocence helped him forget about himself, and what he had become.

"That was Denise," Amanda said. "She and Tabrill are on their way home. Craig is doing fine. He needs to get some rest, the doctors told them."

"I should probably take a shower," Sander said. "Seeing me, covered in blood like this, is just going to remind Denise of the battle. That's probably not best after all she has been through."

"I always say you are more thoughtful and caring than you want others to know," Amanda said.

"Maybe," Sander said, smiling. "But don't tell too many people. I've worked for thousands of years to build up this reputation."

"Your secret's safe with me," Amanda said, winking at him.

After Sander showered he put on the tweed vest and pants he was wearing earlier, after realizing he didn't have anything but suits at Tabrill's house. As he walked toward the stairs he heard Denise talking. He knew Craig would be okay and he also knew it wasn't his fault Craig was shot, but he felt he had let her down, somehow. When he got to the bottom of the stairs he saw Tabrill looking at Darriel's longsword.

"This is some sword," Tabrill said, holding it up to the light.

"Yes, it is. I could have had another one."

"Really?" Tabrill raised an eyebrow. "There weren't any reports of any other fallen angels."

"I know," Sander said. He noticed Amanda sitting on the couch listening to him, intrigued. "I walked in on Nasriel in a bunker, and shot him up. He'll be walking with a limp for a long time. He wasn't a threat anymore, and he started begging and mentioning his wife and kid . . ." Sander thought about the look on Nasriel's face. "I don't know, maybe I do have a sentimental side, but like I said, he was no longer a threat and I didn't see the need to kill him."

"I believe it was honorable of you," Tabrill said.

"Maybe," Sander said, "I just hope I don't regret it one day. I had meant to tell Ramiel about it, but it slipped my mind. I was more worried about Craig and Mick, and everything else going on."

Denise entered the room. She walked up to Sander. "I'm sorry about earlier. I was half out of my mind. But I guess you've heard, my prayers have been answered and Craig is going to be just fine."

"Yes, I heard. I just feel like I let you down."

"I'm not naïve. I know war is unpredictable. You said you would look out for him and you did. There was nothing more you could do. Now give me a hug."

Sander hugged her and Denise went back in the kitchen. Sander then took a seat on the couch by Amanda.

"Have you spoken to Ramiel about Zekiel?" Sander said, curious if Maurice had gone through with the execution, but not wanting to be the one to tell Tabrill about it.

"Yes," Tabrill said looking at Sander and noticing that Amanda, exhausted from the day's events, had rested her head on Sander's shoulder.

Sander glanced at Amanda, then asked Tabrill, "Have you spoken to Maurice?"

"I told you I've known you long enough to know what you're thinking, old friend. And the answer to your question is yes. He did it."

"Good. I know he's your son but it had to be done."

"I almost did it myself after seeing Craig."

Sander nodded.

"Anyway, let's talk about something else for now," Tabrill said. "We'll have plenty of time to go over today's events some other time, plus I believe Miss Amanda is officially out for the night."

Sander looked at her leaning on his shoulder, fast asleep.

"I wonder what she thinks of us, and all of this. To tell you the truth, sometimes *I* don't even know what to think of us or this world we live in."

"Nor do I, my friend. Nor do I."

"I guess I can carry her up to her bedroom. I should get some rest, too."

"You have to be exhausted."

"After fights like that, I have trouble sleeping. I used to drink until I passed out. Now I just deal with it, I suppose."

Sander gently picked up Amanda, being extra careful with his broken arm, and carried her up the stairs.

"You're stronger than you look," Tabrill said.

"Funny," Sander said.

After Sander put Amanda in her bed he went to his room and laid on his bed for an hour going through every detail of the battle, over and over. Unable to sleep, he stared at the ceiling, thinking about the fight against Darriel.

A few hours later Amanda sat up in her bed, looking around, not remembering coming up to her bedroom. She then realized she was still in her dress, and sleeping on top of the covers. Confused, she sat up and sleepily glanced to the right of her bed, smiling as she saw Sander laying there on the floor with his blanket and four pillows sleeping peacefully. "My guardian angel," she said as she laid down and drifted back to sleep.

Chapter Six

When Amanda awoke, she looked over and saw Sander was no longer there. She showered and got ready for the day, picking out a tan cowl-neck sweater dress and black knee-high boots. Looking at herself in the mirror, she realized she was finally feeling self-confident. Since she had come to the compound she felt like a completely different person, she thought she even looked different. She knew it didn't make any sense, but she was beginning to feel pretty, not avoiding mirrors the way she had when she lived with her mom.

As she descended the stairs, she saw Sander sitting on the couch in a light-gray suit, with a light-blue shirt. He was checking his phone; then he looked up at her. "Don't you look pretty this morning, Miss Amanda?"

"Oh, thank you, Mister Sandriel," Amanda said grinning. "I was thinking the same thing about you."

Sander laughed. "Handsome maybe; not pretty." He pretended to be angry.

"I've concluded that the only clothes you own are three-piece suits and military fatigues."

"Well of course . . . those are the only clothes a proper gentleman soldier requires, Ma'am." Sander smiled. "Seriously though, you're pretty close to correct about my wardrobe."

"I knew it!" Amanda said, laughing. "It was nice, seeing my guardian angel protecting me last night."

"Yes, I couldn't sleep . . . I thought being near you might help, and it did. I'm sorry if I woke you."

"You didn't wake me. I thought it was sweet."

Sander smiled, feeling a little shy, he changed the subject. "I was going to stop by the hospital and then by your dad's office if you would like to come with me. Your father said he wanted you to get more involved with House Ramiel. Might as well start now."

Amanda thought for a while, then said, "Yes . . . I'll go."

As Sander drove, Amanda asked, "How is House Lucifer going to retaliate?"

Sander looked at Amanda approvingly, impressed by her question. "That is the question of the day. I think that's what your dad wanted to discuss. We hurt them last night. Nothing they can't recover from, but we definitely sent a message."

Amanda thought for a moment. "Do you think they will attack this compound?"

"No. They wouldn't get close to this compound. They'd be shot down or blown up if they got within 50 miles of this place. We're safe here."

Amanda nodded. "I still have a lot to learn."

"You'll learn it all soon enough," Sander said as he pulled into the hospital parking lot.

As they walked to the entrance Sander saw John, the sniper from the previous night, and his fiancé Dimitra walking toward them.

"Hey Sandriel," John said.

"How are things in there?" Sander said, motioning toward the hospital.

"Better than they were last night," John said. "Everyone is going to live. Mick's shoulder was shot to hell. He won't be going on any missions for a long time, if ever. Craig is finally awake, but he can't talk . . . It could have been worse though, a lot worse."

"Indeed," Sander said, turning his attention to Dimitra. "Hi, Dimitra. Do me a favor and keep John out of trouble."

"I was getting ready to tell Amanda to keep you out of trouble, Sandriel," Dimitra said.

Amanda laughed. "It's good to see you two."

"Good to see you two, also," John said. "I better get out of here. Need to drop Dimitra off and get back to headquarters."

"All right, take care," Sander said.

"See you, Amanda," Dimitra said.

Amanda and Sander walked to the room Craig was in last night, but it was empty. As they continued down the hallway, glancing in the rooms they passed, Amanda said, "Here they are." Denise was standing by a bed.

"Hello, Denise," Amanda said.

Denise hugged her.

Sander looked down at Craig, who was looking up at them.

"He can't talk right now," Denise said.

"Understandable," Sander said. "You're a tough man Craig . . . surviving a shot to the neck like that. I know a lot of men who wouldn't have." Craig blinked his eyes in acknowledgement.

Sander looked at Denise. "Is Tabrill here?"

"No, he just left for the Main House."

Sander looked at his watch. "Yes, I should probably head there, too." He looked back at Craig. "I just wanted to stop by and make sure one of the toughest soldiers I know was recovering properly. Now you get healed up so we can get you back out there. Stay strong, Craig."

Denise hugged Amanda and Sander and they went on their way.

"That was kind of a short visit," Amanda said.

"Yeah, I have a thing with hospitals. They make me feel uneasy. I can't get out of them soon enough."

When they got to the Main House and started to enter the lobby, Amanda looked at Sander and said, "Do you know what time it is, Sander?"

Sander started to look at his watch.

"No, not that kind of time," Amanda said laughing. "Do you know what time it is?"

"What time is it?"

"It's rumor-starting time," Amanda said, smiling and grabbing his hand.

Sander laughed. "Ah, yes. Let's start some rumors."

As they entered the lobby Amanda saw Jessalyn and Tena, Corinthus's daughter, look over at them and wave.

"We should go say hi," Amanda said, pulling Sander with her as she walked toward them.

"Hi, Amanda," Jessalyn said. "I was going to text you later, actually . . . We're having a little get-together tonight for some of the soldiers to celebrate the victory yesterday, and I was going to ask you if you wanted to come."

Amanda looked at Sander, who she noticed was looking around the room. "Sure. That sounds fun."

"Great," Jessalyn said. "You look amazing, by the way."

"Thank you. So do you," Amanda said. "You're both so beautiful."

"Oh, thanks," Tena said.

"You ladies finished giving each other compliments yet?" Sander said, looking at his watch as he smiled.

"Please don't tell me you are bringing Sander as your date," Jessalyn said.

Amanda smiled, "I might if he plays his cards right."

"I guess he's welcome," Jessalyn said, playfully punching Sander's chest.

"It was nice seeing you," Amanda said to Jessalyn and Tena.

Sander nodded to the women and led Amanda to the elevator and then upstairs.

As they made their way to her father's office Amanda asked, "So will you be my date to the party tonight?"

"It would be an honor, Ma'am. I assure you I shall be on my best behavior."

"I'm only asking because I don't know any other fallen angels." Amanda laughed.

"Ouch!" Sander pretended to pull a knife out of his heart.

"I'm kidding," Amanda said, as the elevator door opened.

"Hello, Sander," Ramiel's secretary, Lucy, said smiling. "Hi, Amanda."

Sander looked at her and grinned. "Always a pleasure."

When they got to Ramiel's office, Tabrill, Corinthus and Anthus were standing around her dad's desk.

"Sander and Amanda," Ramiel said, standing up. "Good to see both of you. Great job last night, Sander!" He hugged

Sander. "You guys wiped them out, and I hear you have a trophy to add to your collection. Darriel, I hear it was. It's all the soldiers are talking about today. It was the first time any of them had seen a fight between two of the fallen."

"He was a worthy adversary."

"Don't be humble," Anthus said. "I heard you killed him with one swing of your sword."

"Is that what they are saying?" Sander said, uneasily forcing a smile. "It was a few, and it was a Katana."

Amanda could tell Sander didn't like talking about it.

As could Ramiel, apparently, as he changed the subject. "We were just discussing what happened with Zekiel, and what should happen with his son, Aiden."

Ramiel explained to Amanda that Aiden was in love with one of the daughters of the head of House Lucifer, and Aiden and his father Zekiel had been feeding House Lucifer information.

"So, was Zekiel executed?" Amanda asked.

"Yes," Ramiel said. "Last night once we were informed the battle had begun, we apprehended Zekiel and his son. Maurice shot Zekiel in his holding cell."

"What about Aiden? Did Maurice shoot him, too?" Amanda asked.

"No, we still have Aiden detained," Ramiel said.

"I see," Amanda said.

"I know what these men think of Zekiel's execution. I was curious what a human, like yourself, thought about it," Ramiel said.

Every eye in the room turned to Amanda.

"I think I understand why you feel that executing him was a good idea," Amanda said. "You felt like you needed to make an example. The problem is the way you went about it. There needed to be a trial first. If you are going to make an example, then it needs to be public for everyone to see. Now there are just going to be a bunch of rumors about what happened. Someone should have stopped Maurice. If you were going to let him kill Zekiel, you could have let him do it after a trial, publicly, so everyone would see that this is what happens to traitors.

"I agree with Amanda," Corinthus said. "You have a smart girl there, Ramiel. You would be wise to take more of her advice in the future . . . I mean absolutely no offense by this," Corinthus said, looking at Sander. "But many members of this council react without thinking about making the most of an opportunity. Holding a trial would have been making the most of that opportunity. Instead we allowed anger and revenge to get in the way."

"If it were Tena laying on that operating table, you're telling me you wouldn't have walked in there and killed Zekiel?" Tabrill asked.

"No, I'm not saying that. I would most likely have killed him, too. I'm just saying that Amanda has a good point, and we need more thinkers like her around here."

"Well we have an opening . . . with Zekiel dead," Anthus said laughing slightly.

Ramiel cocked his head in thought for a moment. "A human on the council?"

"She is your daughter," Tabrill said. "We've had humans on the council in the past. It's just been a while."

Amanda felt slightly uncomfortable, listening to them talk about her, as if she wasn't standing right in front of them.

"Why doesn't someone ask Amanda what she thinks?" Sander said.

Everyone looked at Amanda. "I would consider it an honor, but I don't really know your ways. I mean, I'm used to living in a world that doesn't even know you all exist. The world I come from is so different from the one all of you live in. We may live on the same planet, but we come from two completely different worlds."

"That's exactly why she could help us, I think," Corinthus said. "That different perspective she has from the outside world could be beneficial in some of our decision-making. I would suggest one of my own daughters, but even they have been raised in a world where fallen angels are commonplace, and are no different than us in their thinking. Amanda sees the world differently than anyone we know."

"She does carry Ramiel's blood . . . She could go through the blood ritual . . . live forever . . . Yes. I like this idea," Anthos said. "I think Amanda should replace Zekiel."

Sandriel said, "Well, I didn't expect this!" He looked at Amanda and smiled. "What do you think?"

Amanda hesitated momentarily with furrowed brow. "I'll join the council, if that's what everyone wants. If it will help House Ramiel, I'll do it."

"Well then, there you have it. Are we all here in agreement that Amanda should replace Zekiel?" Ramiel asked . . . Everyone agreed as Ramiel looked around.

"An interesting turn of events," Ramiel said. "I'll take it up with the other members immediately following our meeting, but I don't see any of them objecting . . . If Sandriel and Corinthus can agree on something, then I'm sure they will as well.

Corinthus and Sander both laughed.

"Indeed," Sander said.

"Which brings us to Aiden's fate," Ramiel said. "I've decided to keep him detained for the time being until we see what kind of retaliation House Lucifer has in store. I haven't heard from Draysus or his representatives, but that was expected. They are, most likely, still trying to wrap their heads around what just happened. I did send a message to them telling them that if their breeding program doesn't end immediately, there will be more repercussions. Let's see . . . I think that might cover it for the moment. I'll keep in touch with each of you throughout the day. Everyone is free to go if you want. Amanda, I'll be contacting you shortly, after I speak to the members not present."

Corinthus walked by Amanda on his way out, patted her on her back and said, "Congratulations, Amanda."

Tabrill, Anthus and other council members lined up next to Amanda, shaking her hand, congratulating her, and then making their way to the lobby.

Sander smiled at her as she smiled back. "Oh, wow. I get to go to a party later with a council member."

"So, do I," she said, laughing.

Ramiel approached them and said, "I promise you I had no idea that was going to happen. I was going to suggest that you attend our council meetings as an advisor, but apparently, the others like you, and just like that you're on the council."

"Just like that," Amanda said. "I always pictured there would be more formality to it, selecting a new council member."

"No, there's no real formality like there was in the old days. I still make the final decision in most cases. I like to keep a council of people with differing opinions around to see different perspectives before I choose which path to take. After hearing you speak earlier I think you'll make a very good addition to House Ramiel's council. I'm proud of you, Amanda."

"Thank you," Amanda said.

"There was something I was meaning to tell you," Sander said to Ramiel. "There was a second fallen angel at the House Lucifer compound last night. I shot his arms and legs up, but I let him live. He might have bled out, but I doubt it."

"Yes, Tabrill told me. Nasriel, was it?" Ramiel asked.

"Yes, that's him."

"Nasriel was smart. He didn't try to fight you like Darriel."

"I didn't give him a chance. He was bleeding on the floor before he knew who it was. Anyway, I just wanted to make sure you knew."

Ramiel nodded.

Sander looked at Amanda, "Would you allow me to buy you lunch, Miss Councilmember?"

"Yes, I would love to join you, Mr. Councilmember."

Ramiel nodded his head.

"Care to join us, Ramiel?" Sander asked.

"I would like to, but unfortunately, I've got a lot to do, as you can imagine. Thank you, anyway. I'll call the other council members to make it official, Amanda."

"Okay," Amanda said.

Later in the cafeteria after Sander and Amanda took their seats and ordered, Sander asked, "Have you and your father ever really had a chance to talk?"

"Kind of. When he surprised me with the BMW and the other gifts, I called and thanked him. We spoke for about an hour. But that's it."

"He's a busy man. But, even when he's not busy, he's a little difficult to get to know. He's one of those people who keeps a lot to himself."

"Yes, I've noticed."

"But he does care about you dearly. I can tell. I've known him a long time. Anyway, congratulations again on your new seat on the council."

"So there have been other humans on the council besides me?"

"Yes. It's pretty common. Through the years there have been other mortals on the council. I was away for years and your dad decided to put me on the council. Basically, he tries to surround himself with anyone whose input might help him out at the present time, and apparently, he believes your input is important toward the success of House Ramiel."

"Is it unusual for a woman to be on the council?"

"It's been a long time, but I wouldn't say it's unusual in House Ramiel." Sander hesitated, as if in thought. "I don't think House Lucifer has ever had a woman on their council . . . They tend to stick with the old ways when it comes to most things."

"I'm a little nervous about it."

"Don't be. Just tell him what you honestly think about a situation when he asks . . . I get in disagreements all the time with your father and the other council members. Actually, I almost challenged Corinthus to a duel at our last formal meeting." Sander smiled mischievously.

"What? I like Corinthus. He agreed with me about Zekiel's execution."

"Corinthus only looks out for himself in most situations. I've never seen him once set foot on a battlefield. He's your typical politician, always willing to declare war, but not fight in it himself. It's easy to order someone's death when you're not the one pulling the trigger."

"I see." Amanda thought for a moment. "You guys still seriously duel each other?"

"Yes. That is one of the old traditions we have kept. If you insult someone's honor, you better expect to be challenged to a duel."

"With guns?"

"Swords usually. Guns if that is what's decided on . . . or what's handy at the moment."

"Oh, my God! That sounds crazy!"

"Yes. I guess it might seem crazy to you. To us it's just part of life."

"Promise me you'll never challenge me to a duel," Amanda said smiling.

"I would never challenge you to a duel. The last thing I want is people walking around saying: 'Did you hear about Sandriel? He was killed by some pretty little girl in a duel.' That's not the way I want to be remembered." He laughed.

Amanda laughed. "So you think I would win?"

"Yes. I think you're a lot tougher than you realize."

"Aww, you always know the right things to say," Amanda said as Sander looked at her smiling.

As they ate, Amanda looked around the cafeteria at the numerous well-dressed people, and could not believe what her life had become. For once she felt a real sense of importance.

Amanda noticed some young-looking brunette looking at Sander.

"I think you have a fan."

Sander looked at Amanda with a confused expression. She responded with raised eyebrow.

"Some girl at the table on your right keeps checking you out."

"Is she looking at me like she wants to kill me or something?" Sander asked smiling.

"No." Amanda laughed. "She just keeps looking at you."

"Well that's okay, I suppose."

Amanda's phone rang.

"It's my dad," she said.

As Amanda talked on the phone, Sander's curiosity took hold and he glanced to his right, and noticed the girl Amanda had been speaking about. The brunette looked at him and smiled. Sander smiled back, and then looked at Amanda, who had been watching him while she spoke to her father. Amanda grinned and shook her head. Sander smiled slightly and looked off into the distance, trying to make an innocent-looking face. Then he was dismayed to notice that the brunette was approaching their table.

"Sandriel, do you remember me?"

Sander studied her face for a moment but drew a blank. "No. you'll have to forgive me, Ma'am, but I can't say I do."

"Still a gentleman, I see," she said.

"Some might disagree," Sander said.

The brunette laughed. "Still funny, too," she said.

"How do we know each other, Ma'am? You now have peaked my curiosity," Sander said, smiling at her.

"It's me, Nicole, Xanthiel's daughter."

"Oh, wow! You girls grow up fast around here. Of course I remember you. How old are you now?"

"23."

"Well, it's good to see you, Nicole. You look great."

Nicole blushed a little.

"Thank you, so do you . . . Did you know I used to have the biggest childhood crush on you?"

"No. I didn't know that."

"I do . . . I mean I did . . . Sorry, I'm nervous seeing you after all these years." Nicole looked at Amanda, who was still on the phone listening to her father. "Is that your wife?"

"No. I'm not married."

Nicole smiled, "Are you going to be at Jessalyn's house tonight to celebrate yesterday's victory?"

"Yes. I'll be there."

"Good. I'll see you there. It was nice to see you again, Sandriel."

"It was nice to see you as well, Nicole."

After a few moments, Amanda got off the phone, and smiled at him. "When you're finished flirting, we need to go back upstairs and see dad for a minute."

"Flirting?" Sander said, laughing. "I don't think you've ever seen me flirt before."

"You've never flirted with me." Amanda pretended to be hurt, making a sad face.

Sander smiled. "Well, maybe once or twice."

"Good answer. I'll let the flirting with that Nicole girl slide, then."

"Wait! Are you jealous?" Sander asked with a slight smile on his face.

"No comment, but you are *my* guardian angel."

Sander looked at Amanda thoughtfully. "Forever," he said as he left a $100 bill on the table. "Let's go see Ramiel."

As they walked to the elevator, Sander glanced at his phone. "Your father needs to see me in private for a minute. He wants you to wait with Lucy, the secretary.

"Okay."

Sander nodded at Lucy and went into Ramiel's office.

"Hi, Lucy," Amanda said, making small talk.

"Hello, how are you doing today, Amanda?"

"Pretty good, and you?"

"Your dad's keeping me busy, as usual." She looked at the computer. "It looks like your dad will see you now. They're in the conference room."

"Thank you."

As Amanda entered the conference room, she saw Sander and the other council members standing at attention, all with swords hanging from their waists, five of them on one side, six of them on the other, facing each other, as still as statues. Her father was standing between them with a sword laying across his hands.

"Come forward, Amanda," Ramiel said.

Amanda walked toward Ramiel and stood in front of him. "I welcome you to the council of House Ramiel. May your words ring as true as your sword." He handed the sword to her. "I dub thee Lady Amanda of House Ramiel."

Amanda felt goosebumps. She hadn't expected a ceremony and wasn't sure what she was supposed to say next. Finally, Sander broke the silence. "Congratulations, Lady Amanda!"

She looked at him smiling, and he bowed his head. The other members of the council followed Sander's lead, congratulating her and bowing their heads.

"Now it's official," Ramiel said, smiling at her.

The other council members broke out of their formation and started conversing with each other. Sander walked over to Amanda. "Maybe I should have warned you, but I wanted you to be surprised."

"No. It was perfect," Amanda said.

"Is the sword mine?" she asked Ramiel.

"Yes," Ramiel said. "It is. Its name is King Maker. I carried it during the Crusades. It was forged by Wayland himself."

"My sword has a name?"

"Yes, most of the best ones do," Sander said.

"Does your Katana have a name?"

"Yes. Roughly translated, its name is 'cursed wind.' It was forged by a man named Muramasa. It was said that he was cursed and all who wielded his blades would be cursed, as well . . . becoming as bloodthirsty and insane as he was," Sander said, looking at the Katana, as if deep in thought.

"Why do you carry it then, if it's supposed to be cursed?"

"It's served me well. I use other swords and katanas too from time to time. It just depends on the situation . . . Anyway, enough about legends and weapons. Are you happy with the surprise ceremony or would you have rather had me tell you about it earlier? Some people hate surprises."

"I enjoyed the surprise."

"Good. I'm glad, Lady Amanda."

"I love the title "Lady" the most I think. It makes me feel like a princess."

"You more are less are a princess. You're certainly more powerful now than any princess living on this earth. You are, after all, daughter of one of the two most powerful beings on this planet at the moment, lest you forget."

"I guess it hasn't had time to sink in."

"It will take time. I often forget that this is the only compound you have visited. You haven't had a chance to visit the more regal ones in old Europe and the Middle East. This one is more like a small town. The older ones are more like castles and palaces."

"I can't wait to see them."

"I'll have to take you when things settle down between the two Main Houses."

"I look forward to it. I've noticed a few times you call House Ramiel and House Lucifer the Main Houses. So are there other houses?"

"Yes, there are smaller organizations. Where House Ramiel owns dozens of compounds, the smaller houses might own one, or none at all. The smaller houses, or organizations, are almost always allied with either your father or House Lucifer. There are very few neutral organizations, but there are some that want nothing to do with either of us."

"Everyone! While we are all assembled," Ramiel said, "I thought I would let you all know that there is still no word from House Lucifer, as far as them stopping their breeding program, or otherwise. I have also been contacted by Baelis, Tyrus, Cadriel and Tannis. They will be joining our ranks soon."

"Now those are some old names I haven't heard in a while," Xanthiel said.

"Yes, none of us have. I was thinking the worst," Corinthus said.

"I had heard stories of Baelis from time to time, somewhat recently," Ranthiel said. "It seems he needed some time away . . . some time to find himself again, realize what is important, and who our true enemy is."

"Either that or he's out of money," Anthus said.

Everyone laughed.

"That might well be true," Ramiel said. "But we could use them. We need more fallen angels willing to fight in our ranks. Baelis and Tannis will be flying into Nashville in the next day or two. I'll let everyone know when I receive more information."

"It will be good to have Baelis around again," Sander said.

"I agree," said Ramiel. "I think he heard that you were with us, Sandriel. That might have been what swayed him."

"Yeah. We've been through a lot together," Sander said.

"Gentlemen." Ramiel paused. "I mean gentlemen and Lady Amanda. That's all I have. Unless anyone else has anything, you're free to go."

"Want to get out of here?" Sander asked Amanda.

"One minute," Amanda said, as she walked toward Ramiel.

"I just wanted to say thank you," Amanda said.

"Don't thank me," Ramiel said. "It was the council that voted you in."

"Well, thank you anyway," Amanda said, giving him a hug. "I'll see you."

Ramiel looked at her and said, "Take care, Amanda. I'm proud of you."

"Ramiel," Sander said, "If you need someone to pick up Baelis let me know."

"I can send some immortals," Ramiel said.

"I have some business I wanted to take care of down there anyway. Baelis and I were close. Besides, he'd be safer with me."

"I'll consider it."

"All right."

Amanda made her way with Sander to the lobby.

"I feel a little awkward carrying a sword around," Amanda said.

"Well, you wanted to start some rumors," Sander said. "I'd say walking into a busy lobby armed with weapons might do a good job accomplishing that."

Amanda noticed all the people looking at them.

"Yes, I think you are correct. Let's get out of here, or at least put the swords in the car . . . I never thought that was something I would ever say!" She laughed.

"All right." Sander couldn't help but laugh at how uncomfortable Amanda looked walking through the lobby holding her sword.

As they drove back to Tabrill's, Sander said, "I believe I have some extra belts and scabbards for your sword, if you want."

"I don't really think that will be necessary," Amanda said, shaking her head. "I don't exactly plan to use this thing. Besides, if I ever challenge you to a duel, I'm choosing pistols." She grinned.

"I knew you were tougher than you let on," he said as he opened the door for her.

"Hello, you two," Denise said. "How are Sander and Amanda today?"

"It's Lady Amanda now," Sander said.

"Oh, I just love to hear that," Denise said. "Lady Amanda," she repeated. "It suits you perfectly!"

"Thank you. This is my sword. Its name is 'King Maker,'" Amanda said, handing it to Denise.

"I don't know anything about swords," Denise said. "But this looks like a nice one."

Sander liked listening to them. There was something perfect about their innocence. He wished everyone was more like these two. He knew they were everything he wasn't and never would be. Perhaps that's what drew him to Amanda. There was a vulnerability about her that he felt the need to protect.

"How is Craig?" Amanda asked.

"He's doing better," Denise said. "It's just going to take time."

"I hope he gets better soon. I'm just glad he's going to be okay."

"You're too sweet, Amanda. How'd you ever get mixed up with a boy like Sandriel?"

Sander smiled at hearing Denise's comment as he texted some business associates.

"You two have become inseparable," Denise said. "I think it's good for him. He's been a loner for so long. I used to be worried about him, but he seems happier now."

"You know I'm sitting here listening to you, don't you Denise?" Sander said.

"You can listen all you want; it's the truth," Denise said. "You seem happier than you have in years, since you've been running around with Amanda."

"I keep him out of trouble, and he protects me," Amanda, said smiling at Denise. "It's a tradeoff . . . Actually, I have a party to go to tonight, and I'm kind of nervous about it. I don't really know too many people around here."

"Is Sander going with you?" Denise asked.

"Yes," Sander said.

"Yes. He is." Amanda looked at Sander smiling.

Sander glanced up from his phone, grinning back at her.

"You two will have a good time," Denise said.

"What do they wear at these functions?" Amanda asked.

"What you have on is fine," Sander said.

"I want to look better than fine," Amanda said. "I want to make a good first impression. A lot of those people don't know me."

"I like the yellow dress I bought you," Sander said. "Or something black . . . Black always looks good."

"Okay," Amanda said. "What are you wearing?" She thought for a moment. "Never mind. I'm guessing a three-piece suit." She laughed.

"You would be guessing correctly, Lady Amanda," Sander said, as he removed his splint. "I'll probably wear this. Most of the immortals will probably wear their dress uniforms."

Sander looked up as Tabrill walked in.

"Hello, everyone," he said. "Congratulations again, Lady Amanda."

"Thanks, Tabrill," Amanda said. "It's my first step in taking over."

"Oh, really?" Tabrill said, laughing. "What is your second step in taking over going to be?"

Without hesitation, Amanda said, with a grin on her face, "Challenging Sander to a duel."

Tabrill laughed at the thought of her challenging Sandriel to a duel during one of their meetings. "You better watch your back, Sandriel."

"I know," Sander said, pretending to look afraid. "She's power hungry."

"Y'all are too much," Denise said. "If you want, I can do your hair for you tonight, Amanda."

"Yes, I'd love that."

"You know we are invited, Denise," Tabrill said. "Jessalyn invited all of the council members. I hadn't had a chance to say anything . . . I thought we might make a brief appearance."

"Well thank you for the short notice!" Denise said.

"I'm sorry honey," Tabrill said. "Things have been hectic lately."

"I know, baby," Denise said. "It's all right."

What a cute couple, Amanda thought. "I just got a text from Jessalyn. We'll leave in a few hours if that's okay with you, Sander. I better start deciding what to wear."

"Sure, that's fine. We can go whenever you want," Sander said.

"You seem like something's on you mind, Sandriel," Tabrill said.

"Nothing in particular," Sander said, as he watched Amanda go upstairs. "I think I'm just getting restless being cooped up in this compound."

"That's understandable," Tabrill said. "Once we get everything straightened out with House Lucifer, things should return to normal."

"Yeah . . . Draysus, is a horrible leader. House Lucifer needs to get their act together before Draysus angers God enough to wipe out all that remains of our kind. I know some of the fallen angels in House Lucifer have to see that. Someone over there needs to assassinate him."

"I agree," Tabrill said. "Draysus has a lot of enemies in House Lucifer. Things will eventually sort themselves out."

"I was surprised to hear Baelis is coming back," Sander said, smiling. "It will be good to see him again."

"He, Tyrus, Cadriel, and Tannis will be strong additions to our ranks," Tabrill said.

"Is this okay?" Amanda asked as she walked down the stairs in an ivory-colored off-the-shoulder evening dress.

"You look very stunning, Lady Amanda," Tabrill said.

"Thank you, Tabrill," Amanda said. "What do you think Sander? Is it okay?"

"I agree with Tabrill," Sander said.

"I heard Amanda in here," Denise said. She looked at Amanda. "Oh, to be young again! You are a little head-turner."

"Thank you for the compliments, everyone," Amanda said. "I guess this is what I'll wear. Can you help me with my hair, Denise, if you aren't busy?"

"Of course I can, dear."

As Amanda was getting ready, Sander stayed on his phone, taking care of some of the more illicit businesses he was involved in, and had been kept away from since his previous time at the compound. After that was finally taken care of he checked his watch, surprised at how much time had passed. How did I ever find the time to live life and take care of work without these modern conveniences? He could only imagine what the future would hold.

"Oh, wow! You look amazing," Sander said, looking up and seeing Amanda. "How long have you been standing there? People aren't usually good at sneaking up on me like that."

"Not long. So, do you really think I look all right?"

"Yes. I will be honored to be seen with you, Lady Amanda." Sander grinned at her.

"I will be honored to be there with you as well, Lord Sandriel." Amanda smiled.

"Actually, we fallen angels tend to shy away from using the title *Lord* . . . for obvious reason, I suppose. *Sir* is preferable."

"Then, Sir Sandriel, are you almost ready?"

"Yes, whenever you are."

"Let me say 'thank you' to Denise really quick," Amanda said.

As Amanda said her goodbyes, Sander looked at his reflection on the wall mirror, fixed his hair, and straightened his jacket.

"Let's go, my vain guardian angel," Amanda said, watching him look at himself in the mirror.

When they got to Sander's Range Rover, Sander held the door for her. "I want you to know you really do look beautiful tonight, Amanda. There is no one I would rather be with right now."

"Thank you, Sander." She could feel herself blushing slightly.

When they pulled up to Jessalyn's there were already 50 cars there.

"Are we late?" Amanda asked.

"No, not at all," Sander said. "These aren't exactly formal occasions. They are basically just a chance for everyone to blow off some steam after a mission. People will be coming and going, just to make an appearance."

"Her house is huge!" Amanda said as she looked around. "It's beautiful."

"Yes, it is one of the larger houses on the compound. It's belonged to her family for a very long time."

As they got to the door they were greeted by a butler. Amanda shook his hand. The butler smiled, being so accustomed to the guests ignoring his presence.

"They'll be back here," Sander said, motioning to the rear of the mansion.

Amanda took his hand as he led her past a grand stairway and then down a short hallway to a large ballroom. When they entered, a well-dressed servant announced their entrance, "Sandriel and Lady Amanda." Several people applauded. Amanda looked around at all the servers in their white tuxedos carrying silver trays of champagne and *hors d'oeuvres*. She took a glass from a gentleman who approached them. She was looking at the beautiful dresses of all the women in the room when she heard someone say her name.

It was Tena, Corinthus's daughter. "Amanda, how are you doing?" she asked.

"I'm a little nervous."

"Well, that's what the champagne is for!" Tena said, smiling.

Amanda quickly drank down what was left in her glass.

Tena and Sander laughed. "Well, that's one way to get rid of the nerves."

 "Amanda, this is my fiancé, Kris," Tena said.

Amanda shook hands with Tena's fiancé, who she noticed was dressed in a tan suit jacket with various medals on it, tan tie, tan shirt, and black pants, like many of the other immortal soldiers in the room.

"Nice to make your acquaintance, Amanda," Kris said. "Good to see you too, Sandriel."

Kris was noticeably in awe of Sander, Amanda thought, as if he were looking at someone famous.

"Likewise," Sander said, as he looked around the room.

"That was one hell of a fight the other night," Kris continued. "The other immortals have been talking about your fight against Darriel since they got here." He nodded to a similarly dressed group of men standing in a right-side corner of the room.

"It's always interesting to see how much they have embellished the truth by the end of the night," Sander said.

"It is, Sir," Kris said. "I saw it with my own eyes, though. I had never seen anything like it. It was amazing."

Sander wasn't sure what to say, and just nodded.

"Well I hate to say hi and run," Tena said. "But we need to make the rounds and say hello to everyone or we'll be here all night."

"It was nice to see you both," Sander said.

"You, too," said Tena.

As they walked away, Amanda said, "I like her. She's not stuck up like some of these people seem to be."

"Yes, they are both nice people," Sander said. "Very down to earth."

As Amanda was watching the violinist and cellist playing, Dimitra and a girl she didn't recognize approached them.

"Sander and Amanda," Dimitra said. "You two are looking very elegant this evening."

"Hi, Dimitra," Amanda said, admiring her black dress.

"Hello, ladies," Sander said.

"I didn't want to interrupt you two, I just wanted to introduce Amanda to my little sister, Kira," Dimitra said. "She's been wanting to meet you."

"You're not interrupting," Amanda said, as she shook Kira's hand. "Very nice to meet you."

"I've heard so much about you," Kira said.

"Only good things I hope," Amanda said.

"I heard you were very pretty," Kira said. "And that rumor turned out to be true."

"Aww, thank you," Amanda said.

"What other rumors have you heard, Kira?" Sander asked.

"Those are mostly about you," Dimitra said, smiling.

"I can only imagine," Sander said.

"How's your boyfriend John doing, Dimitra?" Sander asked.

"Good. He's around here somewhere, causing trouble with the other immortals," Dimitra said.

"He's a good guy. A good soldier . . . Heck of a good shot," Sander said. "He probably saved a lot of lives the other night."

"I'll tell him you said that. It will mean a lot to him, coming from you," Dimitra said.

"Is this where the cool people are hiding out?" Jessalyn said, as she approached them.

"It is now that you're here," Sander said.

"Always so charming, Sandriel," Jessalyn said, turning her attention to Amanda. "You look amazing. That dress was absolutely made for you."

Amanda smiled, looking a Jessalyn. "You look so perfect every time I see you."

"Thank you, Amanda," Jessalyn said. "There's so many people here! I hate playing hostess. I think I'm going to need something stronger than champagne. Oh well, I better continue making the rounds. I'll talk to you all later."

"See you, Jessalyn," Amanda said. She laughed as she watched Jessalyn gulp down a glass of champagne the same way she had earlier. Good. I'm not the only one who feels uncomfortable at these kinds of events, she thought.

As Sander looked around the room, he saw the brunette from the cafeteria earlier, Nicole, looking at Amanda, and then at him. He continued looking around the room pretending not to have noticed. Apparently, that didn't work, he thought, as he observed her walking toward them.

"Here comes trouble," Dimitra whispered to Amanda.

Amanda looked around and saw the young woman who had been talking to Sander in the cafeteria, noticing her low-cut dress that Amanda thought was slightly inappropriate for the occasion. The men around her, however, didn't seem to mind the cut of her dress, Amanda noticed, as she seemed to have the attention of several soldiers.

"She used to date my fiancé," Dimitra whispered.

"Have she and Sander ever dated?" Amanda asked her quietly.

Dimitra shook her head no as "trouble" approached.

"Hi, Sandriel," Nicole said.

"Hello again, Nicole. How are you doing tonight?"

"Good. I'm getting bored though. Want to dance?"

Sander could just feel Amanda and Dimitra listening in, and for some reason it made him laugh a little.

"No, not right now, but maybe later," Sander said.

"All right. Maybe later then. I'm going out for a smoke. I'll talk to you later," Nicole said, as she pinched his abdominals and headed for the door.

"I wish I had a picture of the faces you ladies are making right now," Sander said.

"I'm not so sure how I feel about that girl," Amanda said.

"I know how I feel about her," Dimitra said. "I don't like her."

Amanda laughed.

I don't like her either, Amanda thought, but didn't say aloud, trying to be polite.

"Sandriel!" Sander turned around and saw Maurice.

"What's up, Sandriel?" Maurice asked.

"Same old thing," Sander said.

"You remember my girl Ellen, don't you?"

"Yes, of course. You are looking very lovely, Ellen." He shook Ellen's hand.

"Come on man, stop hitting on my girl," Maurice said. "Hitting on her right in front of me, too. I thought we were close." Maurice smiled.

Sander laughed. "You know I'd never do such a thing."

"I know man. I was playing. That violin music's growing on me. You probably love that stuff, though."

Sander nodded his head and laughed.

Maurice looked at Amanda and Dimitra talking. "Will it be considered rude if I interrupt them and introduce my girl to Amanda? Ellen wants to meet the boss's daughter."

"Amanda's cool," Sander said. "She won't mind. I'll introduce you if you want, Ellen."

"Yes, I'd like that," Ellen said.

Maurice and Ellen stood beside Sander, who said, "Excuse me, Lady Amanda, but Maurice would like to introduce you to his girlfriend."

"Hi Maurice!" Amanda said. "It's good to see you."

"It's very good to see you too, Amanda. I hope I wasn't bothering you and Dimitra. I just wanted to introduce you to my girl Ellen."

"Oh, no. It's fine. You aren't bothering us," Amanda said. "It's a pleasure to meet you, Ellen."

"It's my pleasure," Ellen said shyly.

"Do you know Dimitra?" Amanda asked.

"Yes. I do," Ellen said.

"I was just checking," Amanda said. "You're one of the five or six people that I actually know in this place now, Ellen."

"Oh really? Well, it's an honor to meet you finally."

"You're too sweet. The honor is mine."

"Well, we don't want to be bothering Ramiel's daughter too much, Ellen," Maurice said.

"You aren't bothering us. You should stay and hang out," Amanda said.

"Actually, I was wondering if I could steal Sandriel for a few minutes," Maurice said. "I want him to go over that epic sword fight with the soldiers that weren't there the other night."

"Yeah, of course," Amanda said. "You don't have to be so formal around me."

"All right," Maurice said. "Sander, let's go tell these fools over here about that sword fight."

Sander laughed. "I'll let you tell them, but I'll head over there with you. You're better at telling stories than I am."

"All right. Well, let's go boss," Maurice said.

"You can hang out with us if you want, Ellen," Amanda said.

"Thanks," Ellen said softly, a big smile on her face.

"How long have you and Maurice been dating?" Amanda asked.

"Almost four years now," Ellen said.

"Uh-oh, he's going to be getting you a ring soon," Dimitra said showing off her own ring. "Four years is a long time."

"He better," Ellen said. "If it hits five years, my eyes might start wandering elsewhere!" She laughed. "I'm just kidding; I love him and I know he'll ask me when he's ready."

"Are you and Sandriel dating?" Ellen asked.

"I was wondering about that, too," Dimitra said.

"No, we aren't boyfriend and girlfriend," Amanda said.

"Really?" Ellen said. "I thought you were. Maurice told me he thought you were Sandriel's girl."

"Did he?" Amanda smiled. "If I am, Sander hasn't told me about it."

"Have you two . . ." Dimitra paused, smiling. "Have you . . . you know?"

"This is getting interesting," Ellen said, smiling.

"No. I mean we haven't even kissed," Amanda said.

"Of course, that's what I meant . . . kissed," Dimitra said, laughing. "Seriously, you haven't even kissed, yet? I see you together all the time. I just assumed."

"No. He hasn't even tried," Amanda said. "He is just very sweet to me, and treats me like a princess . . . Even when he sleeps in my room sometimes, he sleeps on the floor," Amanda said.

"He sleeps on the floor. Wow, I always thought he was a player or something. Who would have guessed Sandriel was such a gentleman?" Dimitra said, watching him across the room, talking to a group of soldiers.

"What? Do you think that means he doesn't like me? Or he's not attracted to me?" Amanda asked.

"No, Amanda. He's with you, constantly. I think he really likes you." Dimitra was still looking at him talk to the soldiers. "Look at Nicole over there with her friend. Those girls can't take their eyes off Sandriel. If he wasn't interested in you, he would be with one of them. I've known Sandriel a long time, and I'm sure he knows he could hook up with that Nicole if he wanted to. Instead, he'd rather spend his time with you."

"Yeah, I guess you're right."

"Sandriel is on his way over here," Ellen said.

"Quick, change the subject, or he'll know we were talking about him," Dimitra said.

"I can't think of anything," Amanda said, laughing.

"Oh, my gosh. Now you're making me laugh. I can't think of anything, either. Ellen, think of something!"

"Don't put it on me," Ellen said, as she cracked up.

"What's so funny over here?" Sander asked suspiciously.

"Oh, nothing," Dimitra said.

"You ladies were talking about me, weren't you?" Sander asked. "Ellen, surely you wouldn't lie to me."

"I plead the fifth," Ellen said, as Amanda and Dimitra laughed.

Jessalyn, her husband Jason, and Maurice walked over to them.

"Well it looks like someone is having fun," Jessalyn said, looking at the three girls laughing. "I'm going to hang out over here with the fun crowd."

"I think they were over here talking about me," Sander said, smiling.

"Get over yourself, Sandriel," Jessalyn said jokingly.

Amanda noticed a mandolin player, guitarist, a drummer, and flutists join the violinist, cellist and piano player.

"What are all the musicians coming out for?" Amanda asked Jessalyn.

"They are going to play some medieval music," Jessalyn said.

As the music played, Tabrill walked up to them. "It appears I have arrived just in time."

Sander looked at Tabrill as several couples went to the center of the room and began to dance.

"Like the old days," Sander said to Tabrill.

"What is that dance?" Amanda asked Sander, watching the couples. "It looks like something out of a movie about knights and princesses."

"It's called the Saltarello," Sander said. "It's how we would dance at court, back when we lived in castles instead of compounds, a very long time ago."

"A very long time ago, indeed," Tabrill said, as he seemed lost in a moment of reflection.

"I love it," Amanda said, watching the couples dance. "It's so proper, and romantic. I feel like I've entered a time machine." She laughed.

Amanda observed the dancers, intrigued. She could almost picture the men in their medieval dress, wearing swords and dancing with their ladies, surrounded by suits of armor. As she looked around the room, she realized for the first time that it was decorated like a castle, in a way. She had been so nervous and focused on the people earlier she hadn't taken a chance to fully take in her surroundings. A castle with modern conveniences, she thought.

The dance was very simple but elegant. The couples lined up with the women on the right of the men, where they would bow and curtsy to each other, then they would skip forward and back several times. The woman would then stop while the man would politely skip and dance around her, followed by the woman doing the same. Then they would skip forward again. Then pause and take turns dancing around one another again. They did this several times and then the couple at the front of the line would make their way to the back. There was such a graceful elegance to it, between the dancers and the music. She felt as if she had entered the days when chivalry wasn't just a word, but was a code some men truly tried to uphold.

"Were you ever a knight?" Amanda asked Sander.

Sandriel looked at her and said, "Yes. I have worn several suits of armor and fought for and against many kings."

"Do you care to dance, Lady Amanda?" Sander asked.

"Oh," Amanda, "I'm afraid I might mess it up."

"You can't mess it up," Sander said. "Look at the soldiers who just joined the line of couples."

Amanda watched as some of the soldiers seemed to be doing modern dances around the women, when it was their time to dance around them.

Amanda laughed. "That's hilarious. I see what you mean."

Maurice asked Sander and Amanda, "Are you two going to dance?"

"We'll go if you go," Ellen said to Amanda, then turned to Maurice. "No twerking, Maurice!"

Everyone around them laughed.

Maurice laughed, as well. "What are you talking about Ellen? You're the one always twerking when you think nobody's looking. I've seen it . . . I've just never said anything about it until now."

Amanda, Jessalyn, and Dimitra were cracking up.

"All right, we'll go if you do," Amanda said to Ellen.

Amanda and Sander entered the line of couples, followed by Maurice and Ellen.

Sander bowed, as Amanda curtsied.

"Two step kicks," Sander whispered to Amanda. "Forward, two, three, kick. Circle, circle, and now turn."

Sander skipped around her, whispering, "Now, your turn."

After Amanda delicately skipped around him, he took her hands and they spun around in a circle four times.

"Perfect," he said as they proceeded up the line of couples. "You're a natural! Just do that same thing, over and over."

After the second sequence, Amanda said, "I've got it."

Amanda had never felt more like a princess in her life as they proceeded up the line of couples.

When they got to the front of the line, Amanda heard the soldiers cheering as Sander danced graciously around her. The party goers clapped along loudly to the drum beat, Amanda noticed, as she skipped around Sander. They seemed to have the attention of the entire room, everyone curious about Ramiel's daughter. Finally, after they spun each other around, everyone applauded as they made their way off the dance floor.

"That was great," Tabrill said to Amanda. "You would have fit in perfectly in our court during the Middle Ages."

"Very beautiful," Jessalyn said.

"Thank you," Amanda said to both of them, as she turned to watch Ellen and Maurice finish their part of the dance.

"Maurice is going to the back of the line again to keep dancing," Sander said to Amanda as he laughed. "Ellen is going to kill him."

Tabrill overheard them and said grinning, "That's my boy. Never knows when to stop."

"Amanda, I heard you are on the council now," Jessalyn said.

"Yes, it just happened."

"Congratulations. Have you decided when you are going to go through the blood ritual?"

"No, I haven't really been told much about it other than what Sander told me. He told me it was a blood transfusion."

"It is. I got mine done when I was 25."

Amanda looked at her curiously. "How old are you? I mean you look young even for 25."

"You're just being nice."

"No, I'm not. You're beautiful."

"Thank you, so are you. I'm 53 years old, actually."

"Oh, my God. That's crazy!" Amanda said, staring at her. "That's amazing . . . So you really do stay the same age as when you have the blood ritual done?"

"Yes. Physically you do."

"Wow. Are there any other benefits? Sander said there weren't."

Jessalyn looked deep in thought. "No, to a fallen angel there wouldn't be any benefits, like speed or strength or whatever. But after I went through it, I noticed some of my blemishes completely disappeared, and my skin became almost perfect. It was the strangest thing. I haven't needed to wear a concealer or anything like that since I had it done. I guess that's a benefit." She laughed.

"Yes." Amanda smiled. "That's definitely a benefit."

Amanda looked around the room at the other women, and realized most of them did look like they were in their twenties and thirties.

"I guess I would have it soon. How old do you think I look?" she asked Jessalyn. "Be honest, please. Don't worry about my feelings."

Jessalyn looked at her for a minute. "I would guess twenty."

"Close. Almost 19."

"I wasn't too far off."

"How about Sander?" Amanda asked smiling.

Jessalyn looked at Sander as he was talking to Dimitra's husband, John. "Well, I've known him for a while, but if I didn't, I would guess he was 28 . . . possibly 30."

"You think? I thought he was 24 or 25, when I met him. You better not tell him how old you think he is. You know how vain he is." She smiled.

"Yes, I know," Jessalyn smiled and said, "I wouldn't want to hurt his delicate feelings." Amanda and Jessalyn laughed together as they watched him.

Amanda looked at the musicians as they stopped playing the medieval music and went back to playing classical, with only the violinist and cellist remaining.

Jessalyn noticed the change in music, and said, "I wish I could stay and hang out with you longer, but I have to play hostess again, and keep up appearances. I'll chat with you later, Amanda."

"Bye, Jessalyn." Amanda began wandering around the room, looking at the large portraits of important-looking men dressed in varying century's fashions - some in uniform and armed with swords, some in business attire.

Sander, seeing Amanda looking at the paintings, approached and said, "Those are Anthus's sons. Anthus is Jessalyn's father."

"There are so many of them."

"Some fallen angels have lots of children, I suppose. Some never have any -- much like humans."

"Do you have any children?"

"No . . ." Sander hesitated. "Not living, no."

Amanda could see a sadness in his eyes, and changed the subject.

"Why are some of the men in the paintings so old-looking? Why would they wait so long to have the blood transfusion?"

"Those are from a time before we knew about the blood ritual. House Lucifer knew about it quite a while before we did. They don't face the same moral dilemma we do when it comes to experimenting on humans, it seems. If anyone discovers how to extend a normal human's lifespan, who doesn't have an ounce of angel blood running through their veins, it will be them. I guarantee they have someone, somewhere running experiments on humans as we speak."

"That's so insane to me. I was thinking about having the blood transfusion soon."

"Oh really," Sander said, surprised. "What made you decide? You're still pretty young. A lot of women seem to wait until they are about 25."

"I'll be 19 soon."

Sander thought about it. "In the end it's a huge decision, and it's your decision to make, no one else's. If you do go through with it, I suppose I really *would* be your guardian angel forever."

"Literally forever. Do you think you would get tired of being around me after a while?"

Sander looked down, thinking. Finally, he spoke, "No, I don't believe so. Honestly, most people in this room that I've spoken to tonight, when you weren't around, seem to be under the impression that we are dating." He laughed. "Do you know why? It's because it's been almost a century since they've seen me around a woman as much as I'm around you. . . They all think it's because I never got over my wife, or I'm still grieving, or something along those lines. But it's not that at all . . . The honest truth is I don't like most people . . . So, I never settled down or remarried." He smiled. "And you *are* different . . . You're special. I actually enjoy your company . . . something I'm not used to."

"I don't know whether you're telling the truth, or you're just a very smooth talker."

"It's a little of both," Sander said, looking in her eyes, smiling at her. "The question is will you ever get tired of having me around as your guardian angel?"

"No, I won't," Amanda said, without hesitating. "I don't have a complex answer like you. Sometimes, a woman just knows."

"Look at you trying to hide out," Tena said, as she and her Kris approached them.

Kris nodded and Sander nodded back.

"We weren't hiding," Amanda said. "We were discussing life and got carried away in the moment."

"This sounds interesting," Tena said. "What about life?" Tena looked at her inquisitively. "Are you two secretly married and not telling anyone?"

"What?" Sander said. "That's not really a rumor, is it?"

"No," Tena said. "I just thought it was funny. Actually, I might start telling people that, just to see how long it takes to catch on."

"No, seriously don't," Sander said, as he laughed. "I'm trying to picture Ramiel's face right now, if he heard that Amanda and I had been secretly married."

"Don't worry. I don't start rumors," Tena said. "I was only kidding. I was getting ready to head home and wanted to say goodbye before I left."

"Aww. Well, it was nice to see you Tena," Amanda said, as she gave her a hug.

"We'll see you two around," Tena said.

"She cracks me up," Amanda said. She looked around, "Oh, a lot of people are leaving."

"Care for one last dance, Lady Amanda?" Sander asked. "I have to warn you. I'm not the best slow dancer in the world." He looked at the other nine couples dancing in the center of the room.

"Neither am I. But I would love to dance with you, Sander."

As they walked to the center of the room, Sander put his right hand on her lower back. He glanced at the people watching him and Amanda and whispered in her ear, "I do believe a majority of the people in this room will be conversing about us while we are on this dance floor."

Amanda laughed. As she looked around, she realized he wasn't joking. She whispered in his ear, "I'm going to just keep whispering in your ear and giggling."

Sander laughed.

"Would you prefer it if no one was paying attention to us?" she asked.

"That's a difficult one to answer. I don't mind the attention. It's when people start rumors that are in poor taste about me, that's what bothers me."

Amanda smiled, and whispered in his ear, "You didn't answer the question."

"I know." Sander laughed. "I'm getting ready to spin you, okay?"

She smiled. "Of course."

Sander spun her around, and many of the people applauded.

"Oh, wow. They applauded."

"You look like a princess. They can't take their eyes off you."

"Tonight, I feel like a princess. Thank you."

"For what?" Sander whispered.

"Everything."

For the rest of the song Amanda and Sander were silent, both lost in their own thoughts, but while that song played, there was no place either of them would rather have been. When the song finished, Sander bowed to Amanda, who curtsied back, and they made their way off the floor.

Amanda noticed some of the couples in the room clapping after she curtsied, and she noticed Tabrill approaching them.

"That was truly magnificent. Well done, you two."

"Thank you, Tabrill," Amanda said shyly.

"Looks like people are clearing out around here," Tabrill said as he looked around the room.

"Yeah," Sander said. "We should say goodbye to the hostess and head back, I suppose."

Amanda nodded in agreement.

Tabrill, Sander, and Amanda saw Jessalyn talking to her husband, Jason, and walked up to them to say their goodbyes.

"Thank you for having us. I had a wonderful time," Amanda said to Jessalyn and Jason.

Jason nodded and smiled.

"Anytime," Jessalyn said. "Really, we need to get together sometime when I don't feel like I have to keep everyone entertained, so we can just hang out. I'm very glad you three could make it this evening. It means a lot to me."

"There wasn't really anything else going on, so we thought we'd show up for a bit," Sander said, smiling at Jessalyn.

Jessalyn ignored his comment and playfully punched Sander in the chest while she turned her attention to Tabrill.

"I do really hope Craig gets better soon," she said. "I will have to have a party to celebrate when he finally recovers."

"Yes," Tabrill said. "I think Craig would like that. Thanks Jessalyn and Jason for a wonderful evening."

"See you," Amanda said as Jessalyn leaned in to hug her.

"Later Jason," Sander said.

"See you around, Sandriel," Jason said.

"You guys ready?" Tabrill asked.

"Um, we didn't drive here together," Sander said smiling.

"Oh, that's right. I'm kind of lost when Denise isn't around," Tabrill said.

"That's okay. Amanda's the same way when I'm not around," Sander said trying to make Tabrill smile. Sander wished Denise could go through the blood ritual.

That made Amanda laugh. "What are you even talking about?"

Sander smiled. "All right, let's get out of here."

When Sander and Amanda got to his Range Rover, Sander opened the door for her. She stopped and looked at him. "I just wanted to say thank you for a perfect night."

"It was an honor. There will be many more perfect nights to come in our future."

She looked at him again, smiled, and then got into the SUV.

"I'm glad you had a good time, Amanda," Sander said as they pulled into the street.

"It was because you were there."

"I feel the same way about you being there."

Sander put his right hand in hers. Amanda just looked at him and smiled, looking at his features - the sharp nose, the strong jaw line. She hoped they really would be together forever, once she went through the blood ritual. No guy had treated her so well and expected nothing in return before. A true gentleman.

"Well, Lady Amanda, we are here."

Sander got out and opened her car door. He took her hand as the butler opened the front door for them. Sander nodded at him as he saw Denise sitting on the couch talking on her phone.

"I'll call you back later," Denise said. "Sandriel and Amanda are here and I want to hear all the gossip."

"What gossip?" Sander asked.

"Honey, there is always gossip," Denise said laughing. "Lady Amanda, did you have a good time?"

"I couldn't have asked for a better time. Everything was so beautifully decorated, everyone was nice, I made some new friends, I learned how to do a medieval dance, and my date was a complete gentleman."

"Well, you did have a good evening."

"I really did. I won't be nervous about going to the next one. I wish you had been there. We saw Tabrill."

"Yes, I wanted to go, but I thought I would run up to the hospital instead."

"Yes, that's understandable."

"I'm glad you kids had a good time."

Sander laughed to himself when she called him a kid. Sometimes he thought about saying, 'You do realize I am older than this earth or any living thing on it?' . . . but he knew he never would. He rather enjoyed being called a kid. He knew it made absolutely no sense, but he looked at her as the mother he never had.

"I got to know Dimitra and Jessalyn a little better, too," Amanda said.

"They are sweet girls," Denise said. "I'm glad you didn't get caught up with some of the other riff-raff around here. When people know they are going to live forever and have all the money they could ever ask for, it has a tendency to change them, for the worse."

"I agree with that last comment," Sander said. "You don't have to worry about that with Amanda." He looked at Amanda. "She has a genuinely good heart. She's not like most humans -- or fallen angels for that matter."

"That was sweet of you," Denise said. "I was expecting you to say something smart-ass."

Sander grinned. "No, I was being serious for once. I can't quite put my finger on it, but she's different." He looked back over at Amanda, who was staring at him. "I'll figure it out eventually."

Tabrill walked in.

"Hey, sweetie. I was getting worried," Denise said.

"Yes, I ran into some old friends on my way to the car," Tabrill said.

"Craig is improving," Denise said. "They still want to keep him at that hospital, though."

"Hopefully not too much longer," Tabrill said, not wanting to think about his son stuck in a hospital. He changed the subject. "You should have seen Sandriel and Amanda on the dance floor, Denise."

"Were you two showing off?" Denise asked

"No," Amanda said as she smiled. "Neither of us are particularly good dancers, honestly."

"They had everyone's attention in the room," Tabrill said. "I hate to say this, because Sandriel might challenge me to a duel, but they looked like they cared very much for each other, and I think everyone else saw it, too."

"All right, Tabrill, go get your sword. Let's get this duel over with," Sandriel said as he laughed. "But that's not too bad." He hesitated. "I do care about her; it doesn't bother me if people know it."

"I was just messing with you, old friend," Tabrill said. "What I should have said was that you both looked very happy together."

"Yep, it's dueling time," Sander said, cracking himself up.

"So, does that mean those people are going to start more rumors about us?" Amanda asked.

"Probably," Tabrill said.

"Good," Amanda said. "Let them talk."

Tabrill laughed, admiring Amanda's boldness. She didn't behave like the insecure girl he first met, he thought.

"It was a good night for all," Tabrill said. "Now if you'll excuse me, I am going to call it a night. Sandriel, Ramiel texted that Baelis and Tannis are arriving in Nashville in the morning."

"Yeah, I got it too," Sander said. "I was going to talk to Ramiel about that. I have some business down there I've been meaning to take care of. I hadn't originally planned on sticking around here for this long." He glanced at Amanda, who was looking at him with a little grin on her face.

"Well, I'm glad you did," Amanda said.

"So am I," Denise agreed.

Tabrill nodded. "We all are, Sandriel. Okay. Well, goodnight everyone."

"Goodnight," Amanda and Denise said.

"Your business in Nashville isn't dangerous, is it?" Amanda asked Sander.

"No, it's nothing to worry about," Sander said. "Actually, I'm going to call your dad now while I'm thinking about it. If you'll excuse me, ladies."

As Sander stepped into the other room, Denise looked at Amanda and said, "It's taken a little time, but he's slowly becoming a gentleman."

"Well, I assure you he was nothing but a gentleman tonight," Amanda said. "You've done a very good job with him, Denise."

"He's a good boy. He just needs to settle down, have a family, and get out of that gangster lifestyle."

"He does seem to have some gangster tendencies," Amanda said, laughing. "He means well, though."

"Yes. I think he does, too."

"I'm seriously considering having the blood transfusion -- the blood ritual -- done soon. Do you think I should go through with it now, or wait until I'm a little older?"

"Now, that is a serious question. A question I'm not sure I can answer for you, honey."

"That's what Sander said," Amanda said, feeling frustrated.

"Sander was right . . . for once." Denise laughed.

"If you could have had the procedure done, what age would you have had it done?"

"Sweetie, you are not going to quit until I give you an answer, are you? Now, this is only for me personally, but I look back to when I was 24, and I think that was how I would like to look if I was going to have to look the same way forever." She thought for a while. "Yes, 24 was a good age."

"Maybe I'll wait. I don't know."

"There's no rush."

"There kind of is, if this is the way I want to look."

Sander entered the room. "Are you ladies talking about me?"

"No, we are not, Mr. Sandriel," Denise said.

Amanda laughed. "I've noticed whenever two women are talking, Sander always thinks it's about him."

"It usually is," Sander said, smiling.

"In your dreams," Amanda said.

"Maybe," Sander replied.

"We were talking about the blood transfusion," Amanda said.

"Yes, that's a huge decision. I'm glad I never had to make it. I've always looked like this: I've been terribly handsome ever since I can remember," Sander said. He tried to keep a straight face, but started laughing.

"I don't know about terribly handsome," Amanda said. "I would say cute, in an odd way." She smiled and looked at him.

"Yeah, whatever," Sander said, pretending to have his feelings hurt.

"Oh, get that sad look off your face," Amanda said. "I know you well enough to know how full of yourself you are."

"That's funny. But anyway, I have to get up early and need to get to bed," Sander said, as he looked at his watch.

"I should probably get some rest too," Amanda said. "Have a good night, Denise."

"Sweet dreams," Sander said. Going up the stairs.

Amanda went over to hug Denise. "Thank you so much for everything you've done for me."

"You are too precious," Denise said. "You're welcome, sugar. Have a good night."

Amanda went upstairs. She peeked in Sander's room and saw him walking out of the bathroom. He had already changed into black pajama bottoms and what looked to her like a brown Army t-shirt.

"Hello there, Lady Amanda," Sander said, seeing her out of the corner of his eye.

"Hello. I was just checking on you."

"That was polite of you." He grinned.

"Seriously, thank you again for tonight. I had the time of my life."

"So did I. It was fun. We'll have to do it again, sometime."

"We will. You know, I've noticed I feel safer when you are sleeping beside my bed."

"Well, I am your guardian angel, so I suppose it's my duty to make sure you feel safe. I'll be over in a minute, with my oddly large number of pillows and my blanket to protect you, if that is your wish, my Lady." He bowed slightly.

"It is."

Amanda went to her room and changed into her yellow nightie. Not too revealing, she thought. I can't have Sander thinking I'm a slut. After removing her makeup, brushing her teeth and then her hair, she laid down on her bed. A few moments later Sander entered carrying five pillows and a comforter.

"Why in the world do you need that many pillows?" Amanda asked, as she laughed.

"Seriously Amanda, you can never have too many pillows," Sander said, as he threw the pillows on the floor, laid down, and covered himself with the comforter. "I'm a fallen angel. I know these kinds of things."

"You're hilarious."

"Thank you, I try. I might not see you in the morning, unfortunately. I'm going to pick up Baelis and Tannis and take care of some things."

"I figured you would. Just promise me you will be careful and come back to me."

"I promise. I will be back to protect you. It really shouldn't take too long, actually."

"I know whatever business you have to take care of is more dangerous than you're letting on, but I'm not going to pry. Just come back. That's all I ask. I need you around."

"I care about you too much not to."

"You just made my night, again."

Sander smiled, looking at her as he turned off the light. "Sweet dreams, Amanda."

"Sweet dreams, Sander."

Amanda closed her eyes and said a silent prayer, asking God to forgive her of her sins and thanking Him for all He did for her. She told God that, while she knew she wasn't worthy enough to ask Him for anything, she would be forever grateful if He would keep Sander safe from any harm.

At the crack of dawn the next day, Sander awoke, went to his room, and dressed in a dark-blue three-piece suit, light-blue shirt and gray tie. He put on his double-shoulder holster over his vest, making sure there was a bullet in the chamber of each Glock 19. He put on his suit jacket and walked to Amanda's room. He looked at her, admiring how peaceful and perfect she appeared. He would do anything he could to protect her from all the evil things and men in this world. Men like myself, he thought.

On his way to his Range Rover Sander called Ramiel. "Did I wake you?"

"No, I've been up," Ramiel said.

"I'm heading down there now."

"Are you sure you don't want to take anyone with you?"

"No, I'll be fine. Besides, all this security around here is making me soft."

"It's called being careful."

"Ah, I'm not very good at that," Sander said, jokingly. "It still makes you soft."

"I'm not going to argue, my friend," Ramiel said, as he laughed a little. "You just make it back here safely."

"I will. I'll be back in a few hours."

"Alright. See you then."

Sander drove through the constant twists and turns of the old country roads, feeling free again. He didn't like staying in one place too long, and it was nice to get out and do his own thing. Before long he was on the interstate and on his way to see his old friend Baelis. He wondered if Baelis still had the thick Irish accent. He noticed there wasn't much traffic on 1-65 this morning, so he sped up. As his mind was wandering, reflecting on yesterday evening's events he looked in the rearview and saw the flashing lights. "You have to be joking," he said, as he glanced at his speedometer. Stupid, Sander.

He could see there were two police officers in the car as he pulled over to the right emergency lane. He put his car in park and rolled down his bullet-resistant window as far as it would go. Sander then pulled out his wallet and double-checked that the "magic" phone number was in front of his license, placing the wallet on his lap. The police officer walked slowly to the driver's side window and said, "License and registration."

Sander handed the officer his wallet and said, "I have weapons in the car, as well as on myself. I am licensed to carry all of them. In my wallet, here, is my license, as well as a phone number you should call."

The police officer took his wallet in his left hand and said, "Registration."

Sander looked at him and said, "I have a pistol in my glove compartment, that I am also licensed to carry." He reached in the glove compartment, grabbing the envelope containing his registration, and saw two unmarked black vans pull in front of his SUV. Out of the corner of his eye he saw the other police officer that had been in the car behind him rushing up carrying an M-4 carbine. Ten men immediately jumped out of the vans in front of him, all equipped with various assault rifles, as several other vans pulled up around his Range Rover. Men jumped out of them, surrounding him. As he turned his head toward the officer at his window, he felt two sharp stings in his neck. Reaching up he felt the darts, and saw the man dressed as a police officer drop a tranquilizer gun and point a .45 Desert Eagle at his head. He was surrounded and he knew it. This is it, he thought, as he heard a helicopter overhead. His vision began to blur.

No way I'm surviving this one. His thoughts turned to Amanda as he passed into unconsciousness.

When Sander awoke he looked around the room curiously, surprised he was still alive. He was sitting on a cold, steel floor. There was nothing else, other than a black wool blanket, in the roughly 20x20 cell. He was wearing all-black clothing that reminded him more of pajamas, or the uniforms the Viet Cong wore during the Vietnam War, than a prison uniform. The more he looked around, the more the room looked like a huge converted safe of some sort. Someone had shot him in each of his hands. He wouldn't be making a fist for a while, he thought. It might take a while to heal correctly, if he lived long enough. There was a lightbulb in the center of the tall ceiling and two cameras in the front two corners, each side of the single door.

He heard the steel door being unlocked. He knew if anyone had gone to so much trouble to capture him alive, they were definitely going to be prepared for him if he rushed the door and killed whoever came through it. Escaping right now would be pointless. He would wind up dead. He needed to stay alive to get back to House Ramiel, back to Amanda like he promised.

When the door finally opened, he saw a well-dressed gray-haired man whose face he recognized. It was Gavriel of

House Lucifer. Sander knew he was the current second-in-command at House Lucifer.

"Hello, Sandriel."

"It's been a while."

"It has, hasn't it?"

"The Battle of Barnet, I think."

"The Wars of the Roses?" Gavriel asked. "No, certainly not. Surely we've seen each other since then."

"I meant the last time we met in battle. I've seen you at various treaty signings since then."

"Yes. Of course."

"So how did you know where I was going to be?"

"We didn't know for sure if it would be you or not picking up Tannis, honestly. I guess you could say we got lucky."

"Who is the traitor in House Ramiel?"

"Since I'm not sure at this time what your fate will be, I think I will keep that information to myself for the present."

Sander looked at the bullet wounds in the center of each of his hands. "So, do you plan to kill me or ransom me?"

"I'll have some bandages brought to you for that, and some pain medication if you so wish. No matter what you may think of House Lucifer, not all of us are heathens. There was a time when you and I fought under the same banner. However, there are several men here that hold grudges against you. You are solely responsible for the deaths of many men in House Lucifer, might I remind you."

"You never answered my question. Are you going to ransom me or kill me"?

"Ah, yes, I apologize. I got distracted. Like I said, we weren't sure it was going to be you picking up Tannis, but we on the council did think the odds were pretty high, considering everyone else in that cursed house is a coward, too afraid to leave the confines without bringing an army with them."

"Yeah, I probably should have done that," Sander said.

Gavriel chuckled. "Yes, it might have been wise, considering what you did to our compound a few nights ago; but, you are a soldier. Your bravery, while rash, is admirable. That is why you are respected in both houses. To answer your question as to whether you will live or die, the truth is we don't know. Now that we have you the council will meet, and we will discuss the various options. Then after House Ramiel is contacted we will argue and debate some more, and then your fate will be decided. Hopefully the entire process won't take too long."

"What do you think they'll do? We've known each other a long time, Gavriel. Tell me the truth," Sander said.

Gavriel pulled at his bottom lip slightly, as he thought. "You are a threat to House Lucifer; there is no arguing that fact. Not so much as when you were off doing your own thing. But now that we've received reports that you have not only rejoined House Ramiel's council but taken a liking to Ramiel's daughter, the danger you potentially pose to our house cannot be denied."

Sander remained silent but felt his heart racing at the mention of Amanda. If he got out of this alive he would find the traitor and make them suffer more than any person he had ever hurt in all of his years on this earth.

"However," Gavriel continued," Like I said earlier, you do have admirers amongst our council, myself included, who think it would be the honorable thing to ransom you. Lucifer himself knows you are worth a fortune to House Ramiel. We could most likely ask for whatever we want and have it given to us in exchange for your safe return to Ramiel. I think if we kill you, then House Ramiel will just kidnap one of us, and kill them, and then we will just start a cycle that will eventually lead to the destruction of both of our houses."

"I wish you were the one making the decision."

"I wish you had joined House Lucifer, all those years ago. Think about it. If you were with us, we would have crushed those weaklings in House Ramiel centuries ago.

"You're a smart man Gavriel. You know if you destroyed House Ramiel, and House Lucifer was free to do whatever they wanted, things would be just like they were before the Great Flood. God may be forgiving but I don't think He is going to give us a second chance. If we go back to our old ways He will make sure none of us survive."

"Lucifer has assured us we will win, eventually. I am confident in this as well."

"Why do you still believe Lucifer after all this time?" Sander asked. "Are you blind? Or are you so close to him that you can't see through his lies anymore?"

"What do you mean, Sandriel?" Gavriel asked. "You cannot deny we live like kings. We run this world, just like Lucifer told us we would."

"We live like kings on this world. This world means nothing in the long run. What happens to us when we die? It's because of Lucifer that we will never step foot in Heaven! Lucifer promised us eternal life, yet we can still die. We lost the war in Heaven, and many of us died in the Great Flood. Lucifer lied to us, he deceived us, and he's still deceiving you."

"You're forgetting why we rebelled in the first place," Gavriel said. "It was so we could have free will. Lucifer promised me I would have free will, and now I have it."

"He also promised me we would win the war in Heaven," Sander said. "Look how that turned out. We lost!"

"We lost the battle, but not the war, Sandriel. Lucifer has promised us eventual victory, and I believe him."

"I suppose we will never agree."

"Most likely not," Gavriel said as he checked his watch. "I shall return later. It's interesting talking to you like this. I wish it were under different circumstances."

Sander nodded. After Gavriel departed, Sander looked around the room. He stared at one of the cameras, wondering who was watching him. He was thinking about who the traitor could be when he heard the locks on the door again.

He glanced up and saw it was Draysus, the current head of House Lucifer, followed by eight heavily armed fallen angels he recognized.

"The great Sandriel doesn't look so intimidating now!" Draysus said. "You were easy enough to catch."

Sander sat on the floor looking at him.

"Tell me. What were you thinking? Traveling alone, right after you raided a compound and killed one of my friends?"

Sander thought about killing him right then and there, but knew he would only be able to get to maybe three of them, at the most, before he was shot. He needed to stay alive, to fulfill his promise to Amanda.

"You're a very brave man to walk in here with eight bodyguards," Sander said.

"You know your life is in my hands."

"Yes, but it makes no sense to kill me."

"Why is that?"

"Ramiel will give you whatever you ask if you let me go."

"Yes, but I also know you. If I let you go I know you will stop at nothing to see me killed."

"If I wanted to kill you so badly I would have done it years ago. Think about it. I'm nothing more than a soldier. I follow orders; I don't make them."

"Yes, but you are a deadly soldier. You've killed countless friends of mine throughout the years."

"If you kill me you know that House Ramiel will come at you with everything they have."

"Yes, that may be true, but I would rather fight against House Ramiel knowing you were dead, than eventually fight against them knowing you would be fighting for them. Anyway, these are things I will take up with my council. I just wanted to see you for myself before I contacted Ramiel."

Draysus turned and left the room, his men following closely behind.

Chapter Seven

Amanda woke up and looked beside her bed, noticing Sander had already left. After she showered and prepared for the day, she put on a light pink midi dress and made her way downstairs.

"Good morning, Denise," Amanda said.

"Well good morning, sweetie," Denise said. "Don't you look pretty!"

"Thank you. So do you."

"Oh, you are a sweet girl," Denise said, smiling.

Amanda's phone beeped. It was a text from Ramiel telling all council members to get to his office immediately.

"That's odd . . . or is it?" Amanda said. "Do you know if Tabrill gets texts from my dad about unscheduled council meetings? Is it normal?"

"Sometimes he does."

"I just got one. I better go over there."

"I hope it's nothing too serious."

"Me, too."

As Amanda drove to her dad's office, she realized how alone she felt without Sander around . . . She did feel strangely empowered, driving to the Main House by herself, but deep down she wished Sander was with her.

As she walked into the lobby she thought it looked unusually busy . . . There were always a lot of people in the lobby, but a lot of times it was groups of people standing around chatting, or looking bored. Everyone seemed to be walking around with a purpose this morning.

After Amanda put her eye to the scanner and entered the elevator, she heard someone behind her say, "Amanda, can you hold that door?" She held the door and saw it was Anthus.

As he entered the elevator, Anthus said, "Thank you. Do you know what this is about?"

"Your guess is as good as mine."

When they got to the office, Lucy, the secretary, looked uncharacteristically serious. "Ramiel is in the council room."

Amanda and Anthus walked back to the council room. Ramiel was on the phone, while he looked at a laptop, surrounded by seven of the other council members. They were either on their phones or speaking intensely to one another.

Anthus and Amanda looked at each other, neither sure what to say. A few moments later the final council members walked into the room.

Ramiel ended his call and everyone was silent as he did a quick headcount. "Now that we are all here" . . . he hesitated for a moment, a look of concern on his face. "They have Sandriel. House Lucifer kidnapped Sandriel this morning. I was just notified."

As the men in the room immediately started talking amongst themselves about the news, Amanda felt herself begin to go weak. Anthus put his hand on her back, fearing she might collapse. "We will get him back, Lady Amanda," he said.

Be strong, Amanda thought. You are on the council now. She took a deep breath to compose herself. She looked at Anthus and said, "Yes. We will get him back."

Anthus nodded. "Indeed we will."

"If you will all have a seat, we need to discuss our options," Ramiel said.

Ramiel had the council's full attention: "Here is what I know. Sandriel was adamant about picking up Baelis and

Tannis in Nashville this morning. He said he had some business to take care of in the area. Sandriel never made it to Baelis or Tannis, and I spoke to Draysus a little over an hour ago. He said they had Sandriel in their custody. I've had one of House Ramiel's contacts in Nashville fly in Baelis and Tannis to our compound." Ramiel looked at his watch. "They should be arriving shortly, so we can see what they know. Any questions?"

Everyone began speaking at once.

"One at a time!" Ramiel said.

Corinthus spoke first. "I hate to say this, but the finger seems to be pointing at Baelis and Tannis. They obviously got to Sandriel on his way to pick them up."

Ramiel said, "I thought about that, but why would they have allowed themselves to be brought to the compound if they were involved in this? And let's be honest; Baelis and Sandriel are basically brothers. Baelis would never betray Sandriel, or vice versa."

"Cain and Abel were the first human brothers," Anthus said. "And we all know Cain killed Abel, eventually. My point is that the brotherly bond, while strong, only goes so far. Perhaps Sandriel upset him somehow. They are close, but they have both been known to make rash decisions at times."

"Yes, this is true," Ramiel said. "I can't really see either Tannis or Baelis betraying Sandriel, but it *is* a possibility, and that is why I had them brought here."

"What do they want?" Amanda asked. "What does House Lucifer want for Sander? They have to want something."

Everyone looked at Ramiel. "Draysus didn't make any specific demands. I think he was trying to feel me out, see how I would react. He still has to discuss the situation with his council. He did, however, mention the possibility of Sandriel's execution . . . I'm not sure what they will do."

Staring down at the table, Maalik said, "How did we let this happen? Sandriel should have known better than to go off by himself, so soon after a raid on one of House Lucifer's compounds."

"There is no stopping Sandriel, once he's made his mind up to do something. We all know that," Ranthiel said.

"Yes, it was unwise of him," Anthus said. "House Lucifer really would be better off executing him when you think about how many of them he has killed in the past, and will potentially kill in the future."

"If they do execute him, which seems like the most likely scenario, what is our next move? We need to start thinking about that," Corinthus said.

"What is wrong with you?" Amanda said. "Sander is your friend, and they have him. The first priority and the only thing we should be talking about right now is how to get him back alive. So what if he's a hothead. What he did *was* stupid. He should have taken some security with him, or not gone at all, but he didn't. The mistakes he made are irrelevant. The one and only thing that should matter to you right now is getting Sander back."

"I've been standing here listening for a few minutes, and this girl here is the only one I hear making any damn sense," said a man with a slight Irish accent.

Everyone turned their attention to the door, where Baelis and Tannis had just entered, followed by six immortals. Amanda noticed Baelis and Tannis both looked about the same age as Sander, and were dressed in the same well-tailored three-piece suits he would have been wearing, had he been here.

Baelis continued, "We need to get Sander back, whatever it takes. If it takes going to full-out war with House Lucifer again, then let's do it. It's bound to happen one day, anyway." He finished in measured emphasis: "Get. Sander. Back!"

Ranthiel said, "For all we know, you were in on all of this, Baelis. Sandriel was on his way to pick up you and Tannis when he was captured."

"Sander's my best friend," Baelis said glaring at him. "If you ever again imply I would do anything to harm him, I will be harming you next, Ranthiel. So, you better watch that tongue of yours or I'll come over there and cut it out."

"Gentlemen!" Ramiel said sternly. "I know emotions are high, but let's be civil. Threatening each other is going to get us nowhere. I do agree, however, that ensuring Sandriel's safe return should be our first priority. None doubt your loyalty to Sandriel, Baelis; we just don't know how they knew Sander would be on his way to pick you up. They had to have had a small army to capture him, which implies they had this planned, and therefore had to have been given information about your arrival in Nashville by someone.

Corinthus said, "Figuring out how House Lucifer knew Sandriel was on his way to pick you up might help us figure out a way to save him."

"I did it," Tannis said.

Every head in the room turned toward Tannis.

"What was that?" Ramiel said, looking fiercely at Tannis.

Tannis cleared his throat as he stared blankly at the floor. "I did it," Tannis repeated. "House Lucifer has my daughter -- my youngest. They told me they would kill her, or worse -- take her to one of their hospitals where they run experiments -- if I didn't give them some useful information."

He paused for a few moments; the room was in stunned silence. "I figured you would send someone to pick up me and Baelis so I gave them a time, and the most likely route . . . I didn't know it would be Sander . . . He is my friend . . . I'm so sorry . . . I had to save my daughter. I will understand if you kill me for what I've done, but I received word that my daughter is safe, so at least I shall die knowing no more harm will come to her."

"You coward!" Baelis said as he grabbed Tannis' throat with his left hand, threw him to the ground and proceeded to hit him in the face.

The immortals looked quickly at Ramiel for orders. Ramiel nodded his head. It took four immortals to pull Baelis off Tannis, who now lay on the floor battered and bleeding but still breathing.

"Have Tannis locked up," Ramiel said to the attendants. "Send someone over to look at his wounds."

"Yes sir," an immortal said, as they dragged Tannis away.

"You're free to go, Baelis. Stay around the building though; I might need you soon."

Ramiel continued with the council, "We now know who the traitor was. We don't have all day to discuss why Tannis did it and whether or not it was justified. We need to discuss all possible options pertaining to Sander's safe return."

Corinthus said, "I look at it as if *we* had kidnapped *their* biggest threat to us -- Kanthius. Kanthius is like Sandriel in many ways, except he fights for House Lucifer, of course. When our soldiers hear Kanthius is somewhere, it makes them nervous, much like their soldiers get nervous when they hear Sandriel has been seen on the battlefield."

"Yes. I agree. Continue," Ramiel said.

"The question is: For what would we ask, if we had Kanthius? I believe the answer is no reasonable amount of money, land, or political interest that they would actually give us would be worth releasing Kanthius. This is because we know that eventually Kanthius has the potential to kill any one or all of us. So we would be better off, overall, executing Kanthius, and they, I believe, will come to the same conclusion about Sandriel."

Tabrill said, "So if we go along with that way of thinking, then we should go ahead and consider Sandriel a dead man . . ." He glanced at Amanda, who met his glance and stared back at him coldly. "If he is going to be killed either way, then maybe we should just attack them."

Amanda noticed that the council seemed to have a hierarchy. The slightly older-looking angels seemed to do most of the talking. So she decided to listen for now, but she wasn't going to let them forget that the only thing that mattered was getting Sander back.

"There might be more to this, though," Ramiel said. "If we attack them, or retaliate in any way, they will undoubtedly kill Sandriel immediately. The ball seems to be in their court, as the saying goes. The only real thing we can do is wait and hope that they offer terms for his release. We don't have any bargaining chips. We have Zekiel's son Aiden -- who Draysus's daughter is in love with -- but Draysus wouldn't trade Sandriel if we had all of his daughters, much less only Aiden.

"Right now, I think what we need to do is to use whatever contacts we have to find out where Sandriel is being held, and go from there. Everyone is dismissed until further notice."

As the men in the room left, Amanda remained seated. Corinthus patted her on her shoulder as he walked by, in a gesture of consolation. She felt numb, as if none of this was really happening. How could they be talking about Sander like he was dead already? The only guy she had ever cared about, the only man who had treated her like a princess, was going to end up beheaded or shot in some terrible cell where no one cared about him. Maybe Sander was right, and God didn't care about him. Would he go to Hell? Would she never see him again? The thought made here want to die, too.

"I'm sorry, Amanda. I should have sent some men with him to protect him," Ramiel said.

"He wouldn't have let you," Amanda said. "I know how he is. I think part of him missed the danger of going out alone. He really should have known better. We just need to get him back."

"I give you my word. I will do everything I can to make that happen," Ramiel said, as he sat down in the chair next to Amanda. "I've always considered Sandriel a good friend . . . a little brother of sorts. I can't imagine a world without him in it. I'll do everything in my power to prevent that. If they harm a hair on his head, I will make sure Draysus is killed, if it's the last thing I ever do."

Amanda had never heard her father speak so coldly before. It sounded more like something Sander would say.

Ramiel said, "We've been through a lot together, Sander and I . . . I remember when we split from House Lucifer, after the Flood. There was some debate as to who would lead our new house, and it came down to Corinthus, Tabrill, or myself, since we had held the highest positions in Heaven amongst those of us who were left. Tabrill wanted no part of leading, so it was between me and Corinthus. We decided to put it to a vote, and it was going to be close, everyone thought. Well before the vote was counted, this scruffy-looking blond-haired soldier named Sandriel, with whom I was familiar but didn't really know, came up to me and said, 'If it's all the same, I just want you to know that if Corinthus wins the vote I'm either going to challenge him to a duel or I'm going back to House Lucifer. I'm not taking orders from Corinthus. I can't stand him.'"

Ramiel laughed a little. "Even back then he was a rebel. I just hope his rebellious nature doesn't result in his death, this time."

"That story sums up Sander perfectly."

"Yes. House Lucifer really has us this time . . . Unless they want an all-out war, they better give us Sander back. I will make it clear that I'm not talking about a battle here or there, or disrupting trade, banking, or political interests. I'm talking the end of us all. Baelis was right: it's bound to happen one day; might as well get on with it. Set up a few false flag operations, pull some strings, and get some governments to attack them. I'll give Draysus and Lucifer the Armageddon they've been waiting for."

"Do you think Corinthus would go along with it?"

"He has no choice. This feud between us has been going on for far too long. They can either let Sandriel go, and we can continue ruling the world, with this uneasy peace between us, or they can kill Sandriel, and we can begin a war that will inevitably lead to the destruction of this world we rule. I'll make that clear to Draysus."

"Good." Amanda nodded.

"If you'll excuse me, Amanda, I have a lot to take care of."

She nodded again, as she arose.

As Amanda walked into the lobby, she saw Baelis walking toward her. "Hi, I'm Bale," he said with a slight Irish accent. "Well, my name's Baelis but my friends call me Bale. So, you are Ramiel's daughter? The one everyone says Sander is always hanging around with?"

"Yes, that's me," Amanda said, as she shook his hand.

"Sander's my mate," Bale said. "We go back a while. Are there any updates? That council needs to stop playing games and start blowing things up. Start using some of that muscle they have and get Sander home. I didn't come back to House Ramiel because of any of them. I came back because I heard my friend Sander was here."

"No, there were no updates."

"All right, then." He looked at the floor. "Well, I'm going to go in here and finish my drink. It was a pleasure to meet you, Amanda."

"You too," Amanda said. She wasn't in the mood to be talkative.

As Amanda walked to her car in the parking lot, she saw Tena walking toward the Main House. When Tena saw her, she walked quickly over to Amanda. "I just heard," Tena said.

Tena hugged Amanda. "I am so sorry, Amanda."

Amanda hugged her back, trying not to cry. "He'll be all right."

"Oh, my God. You poor thing," Tena said. "As soon as I heard, I cried and cried. If there is anything at all that *I* can do, you let me know. If anyone can get through this, it would be Sandriel. He cares about you a lot, and I hope you know that. I'm sure he will do anything he can to get back to you."

Amanda started crying, but quickly tried to stop, not wanting to look weak.

"Everyone here loves you, Amanda, and if there is something you need or if you need someone to talk to, call me or any of the other girls. Okay?"

Amanda nodded. "I should probably get going."

"I understand." Tena said. "Don't forget, you call me if you need someone to talk to."

When Amanda got into her SUV, and saw no one was around, she broke down. It had all been too much. "Please God, get Sander back to me. That is all I ask. That is all I want. Please," she whispered, as she wiped the tears from her face.

She drove to Tabrill's, went upstairs and laid on her bed, wishing there was something, anything she could do. Everything was so out of her control. She felt completely helpless. It was up to God now, she thought.

---

Sander paced back and forth going through drill commands, as he had a habit of doing whenever he was waiting for someone. "Squad will advance, two, three, four; Hup, two, three, four; About turn." He wondered how long it had been since Draysus had been in here. They could have at least put a clock in here, or let him keep his watch, he thought. He heard the locks on the door. He watched as Gavriel entered and lit a cigarette.

"Do you want one?" Gavriel asked, holding up his cigarette.

"No, I'm fine. I was seriously thinking about quitting before all of this happened, actually."

"Yes, you do spend a lot of time in America. Americans don't smoke, anymore. They kind of frown upon it now; it's funny."

"Why is that?" Sander asked curiously. "Why's it funny?"

"Humans quit smoking because they think they are going to live forever. Yet we fallen angels still smoke and we do live forever. Well, we have the *potential* to live forever. A mortal's lifetime is but a blink of an eye to us."

"Has Draysus made his decision?"

"I'll be honest with you. No, he hasn't. We're still debating the pros and cons of keeping you alive."

"Has Ramiel been informed?"

"Yes, he has. He threatened us."

"Really? With what?" He glanced at his hands.

Gavriel saw him looking at the gun wounds that were slowly healing on his hands.

"I forgot something," Gavriel said, leaving as someone opened the door to the cell for him.

Gavriel returned a few minutes later and handed Sander an unlabeled bottle of pills.

"For your hands. Those will help."

Gavriel watched as Sander looked at the pills, seemed to recognize what kind of pain medication it was and swallowed two of them.

"Thank you."

"I believe you were asking about Ramiel's threat."

"Yes. What did he threaten you with?"

"A better way to put it would be what *didn't* he threaten us with."

"Really?"

"Yes. If you come to any harm, he has threatened all-out war -- global war, as in World War III."

"How did it go over with your council?"

"That's difficult to answer. Some think he's bluffing; some don't."

"What do you think?" Sander asked.

"I don't know . . . If it were Corinthus, I would say he's bluffing, but Ramiel is a bit different. I remember Ramiel from the old days. Ramiel was a general who would lead his men into battle. I'll never forget that about him. He seems to have become more of a politician in the last several centuries, but somewhere inside him there is that same general who would lead from the front lines, and wasn't afraid of a good fight. Part of me believes we may have awakened that general."

"What does Draysus think?"

"Draysus's opinion truly is the most important one at the moment. Draysus thinks he's bluffing. He sees what is left of House Ramiel as nothing but politicians, accountants, and bankers. He looks at you as the last of their warriors. Draysus believes that even if Ramiel starts a war we will be triumphant, and that war will be much easier to win if you are not around."

"I see."

Sander saw the door opening again, and Draysus entered with his entourage of immortals. "I knew you were important to Ramiel, but now he is telling me he will throw everything he has at us if I execute you," Draysus said.

"He will," Sander said.

Gavriel and Draysus studied him, trying to read his face, to see if he was lying.

"There aren't many of us left. The fallen angels' numbers are declining rapidly, between the wars, suicides, and killings. I'm one of the last true friends he has on this earth. I think

Ramiel believes that if I am dead, then maybe we should go ahead and get the inevitable final battle over with."

Draysus and Gavriel still stared at him curiously.

"You can take my word for it. If Ramiel intends to go to war, he absolutely intends on winning it. He must have an ace up his sleeve, one that even I don't know about," Sander said, as if thinking aloud.

"If I did let you live, would you swear to me that you would leave House Ramiel?" Draysus asked. "On your honor."

Sander thought for a moment. "No, I can make no such vow. My loyalty lies with House Ramiel."

"Your loyalty will be the death of you. I don't believe Ramiel has the balls to start a world war," Draysus said.

"Believe me when I say he does," Sander said. "I wouldn't follow him if I thought he was a coward, and you know that."

Gavriel kept looking at Sander, while Draysus turned and left with his men.

"You would die and remain loyal to Ramiel, instead of live and be allowed to go off and do your own thing?" Gavriel asked.

"Yes," Sander said.

"Interesting. We could use more men on our side with such devotion."

"If you had the right leader, loyalty wouldn't be a problem."

"Tell me. Is it the girl -- Ramiel's daughter -- that inspires your loyalty?"

"I've always been loyal to House Ramiel."

"I was only curious. Not that I would expect you to tell me, if she was." Gavriel looked at his watch.

"Is there anything else you could use?" he asked, as he looked at Sander's hands.

"A helicopter, leave the door unlocked, and one hell of a disguise might come in handy."

"I'll have them sent immediately." Gavriel grinned, as he looked at his watch again. "I'll return after our meeting to tell you your fate."

Sander watched as Gavriel left. He listened to the locks after the door closed. He looked around the room, wondering how Amanda was doing, hoping she would forgive him if he didn't make it back to protect her as he had promised. How could he have been so stupid? He was beginning to believe he was invincible; he had started to believe the overly embellished stories the soldiers told about him. He had gotten sloppy and he might pay for it with his life. The worst thing was that there was nothing he could do about it.

Sander began pacing the room again, counting to himself, "Hup, two, three four; Hup, two, three, four . . ."

Chapter Eight

Amanda heard a knock at her door as she lay on the bed. "Yes," she said as she sat up. It was Tabrill.

"Hello, Amanda. I can't imagine what this must be like for you. I know Sandriel means a lot to you, and some of the things said during the council meeting must have been painful to hear. We were only trying to be realistic about the situation. Sadly, the possibility of Sander's death at the hands of House Lucifer is very real. However, I did just speak to your father, who told Draysus that if anything at all happens to Sandriel then there will be hell to pay and House Ramiel will throw everything and everyone we have at them."

"How did Draysus take the news?"

"Ramiel said he sounded quite shaken by it."

"Good."

"Yes. That is very good. Draysus has a very nice, comfortable life, and a war with us will end that."

"I want this all to be over with and Sander to be back here. That is all I want," Amanda said. "If Draysus lets Sander go, and terms are agreed upon, will we still go to war with them?

"No. I think if Sandriel is released, then we will give up some political interests and territory, and then a treaty will be signed which will only last until the next time one of us gets caught breaking whatever new treaty we agree upon."

"It's just one continuous cycle."

"It is, Amanda, one deadly, continuous cycle."

The butler came up the stairs, and said, "I beg your pardon, Lady Amanda, but Miss Dimitra and Miss Ellen are here to see you.

"Thank you, Henry."

Amanda walked down to the front door and saw Dimitra and Ellen each holding a very large tray. They both looked at her uncomfortably.

"We heard about Sandriel," Dimitra said. "I wasn't exactly sure what to do. So Ellen suggested we bring over some food."

"Thank you. You didn't have to do that. Come in," Amanda said.

The butler had the maids take the trays of food from Dimitra and Ellen, and they both hugged Amanda. Ellen started crying. "I'm sorry. I'm just very emotional."

"Don't be sorry. Hopefully, he will be back soon . . . If Sander dies, this world is going to burn."

The coldness in Amanda's voice and aggressive look in her eyes caught Dimitra off guard. "I'm sure he will be fine," she said.

"Yes, he will be," Amanda said.

Denise walked out from the kitchen. "Oh, look who it is. Thank you so much for the food."

"We just wanted to do something to help you get through this time until Sandriel got back," Dimitra said.

"Yes, I've been praying ever since I heard about it. I know that boy's done some wrong in his life, but we all have, and the Lord forgives. He's going to get Sandriel home, safe and sound," Denise said.

"I hope He does," Ellen said. "I'll pray for him, too."

"You girls should all get together and pray for him," Denise said. "Matthew 18:20: 'For where two or three are gathered together in my name, there am I in the midst of them.' The more people you girls get to pray for Sandriel, the better. I know Sandriel isn't much for praying, but one day he will see the light again, so the best thing we can do for him in his time of need is to pray that much harder."

"Is Craig home yet?" Ellen asked. "Maurice mentioned that he was getting out of the hospital soon. He said that other than his throat being messed up, he was fine. His arms weren't anywhere as bad as they had originally expected."

"Yes, honey," Denise said. "He stopped by earlier, and his arms are fine, the bullet didn't hit any nerves. He's just going to have a little problem talking for a while, but other than that he is on his way to a full recovery. That's what the power of prayer does!"

"That's good to hear," Dimitra said as she looked at Amanda, standing there expressionless with a cold look in her eyes. It was as if her mind were elsewhere, plotting something. "I guess we should get out of your hair. I just wanted to make sure you were OK, Amanda." She gave her a hug. "Please call me later. It might be good if you had someone to talk to."

Amanda nodded.

Ellen hugged her. "I'll pray for Sandriel."

"Okay," Amanda said.

"That was sweet of them," Denise said as the young women left.

"Yes, it was," Amanda said.

Denise looked at Amanda and could see the pain she was holding in.

"Come here honey," Denise said hugging her. "Don't you be too proud to cry around me, either. I've seen that boy Sandriel cry more times than he will ever admit. Crying doesn't mean you're weak; it just shows you care."

Amanda let the tears flow as she hugged Denise. "I just don't want anything to happen to him. Everything was going so perfect and now they might kill him. He can't die, not like this."

"It's all right, honey. No matter what happens, Sandriel will always be your guardian angel. The only thing we can do now is pray."

"I don't care what we have to do; I just want him to be all right," Amanda said, wiping the tears from her cheeks.

---

Sander wondered how long he had been pacing when he heard the locks at the door. Gavriel entered the room. "How are your hands?"

"Better," Sander said. "All of these years and all of those wars, and would you believe I have never once been shot in my hands until today? I've had a few swords through my left one, just never been shot. I should be healed in a day I think, if I live that long.

"Yes . . . About that, "Gavriel said," I want you to know that I argued on behalf of exchanging you for a substantial amount of territory, banks and other assets that I believe House Ramiel would have eventually agreed to . . . I don't know why I felt the need to tell you that . . . I think it's because after speaking to you I realized that we are similar in many ways. However, because of some decisions, we ended up serving different masters. In a different world, perhaps we could have been friends instead of enemies."

"We still could be," Sander said. "You could join House Ramiel."

Gavriel smiled. "I think Draysus would allow you to join House Lucifer, if I spoke to him about it. He might take some convincing, but I believe he would see how it might be beneficial."

"It looks like we are going to have to remain enemies, apparently," Sander said, smiling slightly.

"Yes, unfortunately that appears to be the case."

"Did the council come to a decision about what to do with me?"

"Yes," Gavriel said, as he pulled a pack of cigarettes out of his suit jacket and lit one. Gavriel took a drag on the cigarette, and said, "Draysus had decided that you are to be executed."

Sander nodded, as he looked down blankly at the ground in front of him. He stood there thinking for what seemed like an eternity.

"How are they going to execute me?"

"Draysus originally wanted you shot here in your cell," Gavriel said. "Some of us on the council argued that because of all you have been through with us before the Great Flood, you at least deserved to be killed in a somewhat honorable fashion -- at least outside somewhere. You don't deserve to die in a cage, after all you've been through. And with this war that's apparently going to be starting soon, some of us are bound to be kidnapped and executed. We would expect to be treated in a similarly respectable fashion . . . After some debate, we all agreed you would be driven out somewhere in the nearby forest and shot."

"When are you going to have it done?"

"Soon. Ramiel gave us a deadline, so we wouldn't have too much time to prepare for his impending attacks . . . if he really does follow through with his threats."

"Draysus seriously believes Ramiel won't go through with it?"

"I believe he still thinks Ramiel is bluffing."

"If Ramiel said he is going to start the final battle between us, trust me, he is. Not only is he a man of his word, but Ramiel has very detailed plans in place."

"It doesn't matter . . . It's out of my hands now."

"I suppose it's out of mine as well, then."

Draysus entered the room with his bodyguards and looked at Sander.

"I take it from the look on your face that you heard the news." Draysus smiled at him. "You didn't really think I would let you live, did you?"

"I thought you would have enough sense to let me go. I was mistaken."

"I don't believe Ramiel will go through with it. When it comes down to it, he's a coward, like all of House Ramiel, and like you."

"If I'm such a coward then duel me. Send out Gavriel and those bodyguards. Lock yourself in here with me and I will show all of House Lucifer who the coward is."

Gavriel looked at Draysus. A challenge to a duel was no small thing among the fallen angels.

"I don't have time for such trivial things," Draysus said pretending the challenge didn't bother him. "I believe Ramiel is bluffing, hoping I will release you. It didn't work. You will die today, Sandriel."

Draysus left the room with his men.

The room was silent as Gavriel looked curiously at Sander.

"Tell me Sandriel: what do you think happens to us when we die? Do you believe we can be forgiven?"

Sander shook his head. "No. There's no forgiving us. Wherever Lucifer goes, so shall we. That's what I believe. We made the mistake of following him, and we will pay for it. We had our chance to stay in Heaven, and instead we rebelled. We were a part of God's plan, but it was our vanity and greed that Lucifer used against us, to convince us that God's plan only served Him . . . Part of me wishes we could be forgiven, but when I think about all the things we . . ." Sander corrected himself. "When I think about all the things *I* have done, all the suffering I am responsible for -- the people I've killed, the suffering I put their loved ones through. No . . . there is no forgiving that."

"I know you in House Ramiel have a tendency to go easy on humans, sometimes, and I was wondering: did you do that because you thought you could be forgiven at some point?"

"I think some of them do believe that there *is* a chance we might be forgiven. I just don't fool myself with such pointless dreams. As far as being easy on humans, just because we don't experiment on them anymore doesn't necessarily mean we are easy on them."

"The experiments *are* necessary though. Without them, we would never have discovered how to prolong the lives of our own children. It's for the greater good."

"Whose greater good?" Sander asked. "Certainly not the humans who aren't our children."

"Perhaps one day we will be able to extend other humans' lives as well."

"That would be a horrible idea. Can you imagine the food shortage if all these humans could live forever?"

"I didn't mean all of them." Gavriel laughed. "Just a select few, a loved one -- perhaps a wife. Besides, as far as the population goes, we would do what we have always done -- introduce a new virus and kill off a large portion of them."

"I almost want to keep you alive, just to have more of these interesting conversations with you." Gavriel said, looking at one of the cameras in the room. "But, alas! I cannot." He looked at his watch. "Tell me, Sandriel: are you afraid? Now that you know that you are about to face God once again for judgement, are you scared at all?"

"No. I accepted my fate thousands of years ago . . . Since then I've only been surviving, waiting for the unavoidable conclusion of my life."

Gavriel looked at his watch. "I'll be right back. It's almost time."

---

Tabrill walked upstairs to Amanda's room. "Your father needs us back at his office."

"Okay," Amanda said. "I'll drive myself."

"All right."

As Amanda walked to her SUV, she stopped as she noticed the long line of military vehicles driving down the road toward the soldiers' barracks. She had never seen so many Humvees and trucks full of troops all at once before. It is impressive to watch, she thought.

She drove down the road, not used to so much traffic on that main street. Apparently her father meant what he had said when he told House Lucifer that he would attack them. To her it looked like the stream of military vehicles went on forever. She hadn't realized how large the compound actually was. Every now and then large groups of helicopters flew overhead. Whatever compound these men were going to attack, it was going to be overwhelmed by sheer numbers alone. She understood that her father was in charge of a large number of people, but this was incredible. When she finally got to the Main House, she parked her BMW and made her way to the lobby. The streets looked barren of everything except soldiers. Soldiers were everywhere. She noticed there was also increased security at the entrance to the Main

House as she entered. Four armed guards she didn't recognize stood at the door.

As Amanda looked around the lobby she observed that people noticeably avoided eye contact with her. Probably because of Sandriel. Amanda went upstairs and saw everyone was already in the council chamber except Tabrill. She took a seat.

"Can I get you anything to drink?" Anthus asked her, trying his best to be polite, feeling bad about all she must be going through emotionally.

"No, thank you."

"You've been holding up very well, Lady Amanda. Under these circumstances, many people wouldn't be. You're a strong person . . ." He seemed slightly nervous, or perhaps not used to consoling people. Amanda couldn't tell which. "I guess I just wanted you to know that."

"Thank you, Anthus."

Tabrill entered and took a seat next to Amanda. "They are really bringing in the soldiers," he said.

"Yes," Anthus said. "They're flying most of them out to different points around the country as soon as they get here and get their orders. House Lucifer wanted to play hardball, and it looks like we are going to give it to them. We're going all-out this time."

Ramiel looked around, and then spoke. "Everyone: now that we are all here, let's begin. As you can see, a large number of our soldiers are in the process of reporting to the compound. I'll speak more about that to my military advisors after the meeting. I did want everyone to know that I have spoken to Draysus, and he believes that our threats are empty. He has decided to follow through with Sandriel's execution, and he will soon find out he has made his last mistake. We are going to crush House Lucifer. This is total war. I have given Draysus three hours to change his mind, and if I do not hear from him in exactly three hours, then we will attack.

"I plan to implement operation Archangel, and have dirty bombs detonated when I receive word that Sandriel has been executed. We have arranged, of course, to make it appear as though House Lucifer was responsible for the dirty bombs, thus gaining the support of even their staunchest human supporters. This, along with bribes, blackmail, and other false-flag operations I have in place, should ensure the governments who were backing them will quickly become our allies. All of our sleeper cells are now on alert and awaiting my word to activate. House Lucifer won't know what hit them."

Amanda stared at her father, watching his lips move, hearing the words he was saying, but understanding nothing. All she could do was picture Sandriel being dragged out and shot somewhere: alone, afraid, with no one to care about him -- no one to say goodbye to him . . . no one to tell him they love him.

Tabrill patted Amanda's back and she snapped out of the trance she had been in. She realized her father had stopped speaking and the other council members were leaving.

Amanda sat motionless at the table, looking down, with eyes unfocused, completely numb and devastated by what she had just heard about Sander. Corinthus leaned over and whispered, "I'm so sorry, Amanda," as he walked by. Tabrill looked up at her, then continue to scroll through his phone, looking through his contacts at the UN.

Tabrill wished there was something he could do for Amanda, but with war looking like it was unavoidable, he didn't have time to sit and talk with her. There was a vast network of tunnels and bunkers under the compound that they would have to relocate to soon, but for now he would let her mourn.

Ramiel ended his call and walked over to Amanda. "I'm sorry, but I did everything I could."

"I know you did. Make them pay."

"I will . . . every last one of them!"

"Good. I'll be at Tabrill's house if you need me."

"Okay, Amanda," Ramiel said, as Amanda stood up and walked to the lobby.

As Amanda exited the elevator, she saw Tena do a double-take when she looked at her. Tena walked over quickly. "Are they going to release Sander? Please tell me they are."

Amanda shook her head no.

"Oh, my God. You poor thing! I don't know what to say."
She hugged Amanda.

Amada felt empty, as if she didn't have the energy to speak,
or see the need to. She felt as if there was no need to do
anything -- nothing seemed to matter anymore. Even revenge
against House Lucifer felt pointless. Everything felt so
meaningless.

"I'll be fine," she said. As soon as Amanda heard herself say
that, it reminded her of Sander, how he was always saying
he'd be fine . . . Maybe he had realized the meaninglessness
of life a long time ago, and that was what he said because he
didn't really care if he would be fine or not. Maybe, when it
came down to it, he didn't really care if he lived or died - the
way she felt at that moment.

"Oh, I know you will be," Tena said. "I have to run these
files to dad's office, but I'll call you later to check up on you.
Okay?"

Amanda nodded and walked to her SUV, ignoring the
countless soldiers, helicopters, and military vehicles around
her.

When she arrived at Tabrill's she tried to force a smile at the
butler, as he opened the door for her, and she walked into
Sander's bedroom and laid on his bed. The entire room
smelled like his cologne, she thought, as she shut her eyes
and fell asleep.

## Chapter Nine

Sander sat down with his back against the cold metal wall, rested his arms on his knees, and pictured Amanda's smile. The way he couldn't help but smile back at her when he saw it . . . Sitting there on the cell floor, he realized how contagious her smile was. Just thinking about it made him happy, even at a time like this -- moments away from his death.

Gavriel entered the room holding a set of thick handcuffs and a heavy black bag.

"I take it those are for me," Sander said.

Gavriel nodded. There was an intense, thoughtful look on his face as he looked at Sander.

Gavriel tossed Sander the cuffs. "Put those on behind your back. Our strongest fallen angels can't break them, so I wouldn't bother trying."

Nine heavily armed men entered the room. Two of the men Sander recognized as fallen angels. They looked at him coldly. Sander turned his back to them, so they could see he had the cuffs on. One of the fallen angels walked up and cruelly tightened them around his wrists.

"We were ordered to give you an honorable death, but if you try anything we'll shoot you where you stand."

"Understood."

So, this was it, Sander thought. Everything he had ever done in his life had led him to this point. Every decision he had ever made, no matter how meaningless it had seemed at the time, led him to where he was right now. Everything seems so pointless. Every worry, every fear. Completely pointless. He should have enjoyed life, he should have spoken his mind, he should have told the ones he loved that he did love them, when he had the chance.

"Sandriel, perhaps we can continue our interesting conversations in the next world."

Sander looked at Gavriel. "Perhaps."

Gavriel saw no fear in his eyes as he put the heavy black bag over Sander's head.

"Give him an honorable death gentlemen," Gavriel said. "If I find out he received otherwise, I can promise you your death will be anything *but* honorable."

"Yes sir!" the men said.

One man grabbed Sanders left arm and guided him down a long hallway. Sander could then feel they were going up in an extremely tall elevator shaft. He was then led down another long hall as he heard the sound of people talking in the distance.

He heard the sound of cars running, as one of the men helped him into what he guessed was a van with benches on the inside. He could feel that the road they were driving down had a lot of twists and turns. He guessed they had driven for about 20 minutes when he heard one of the men ask, "How much farther do we have to go? We should have just shot him once we got out of the parking lot."

"Shut up," another man said. "Just follow the car in front of you. We're almost there."

About five minutes later the van stopped. One of the men helped Sander out and led him through the grass. "Stop there, Sandriel!" the man said, as he turned Sander around. Sander heard the sound of several assault rifles being cocked.

"Let's get this over with," one of the men said.

"Sandriel. Do you have any last words?"

"Yes," Sander said, as all of the men listened curiously. "If you can, will you get a message to Ramiel's daughter Amanda for me?"

"Yeah, I could probably do that," a man said.

"Tell Amanda . . ." Sander hesitated. "Tell Amanda I'm sorry I couldn't keep my promise to return to her."

"Okay," the man said.

Sander shut his eyes. He heard two gun shots and then two more. He couldn't feel anything. Am I dying?

He felt the heavy black bag being pulled off his head, and saw a familiar face. It was Nasriel, the fallen angel he had shot at the raid on the House Lucifer compound several nights ago.

"I'm going to give you a chance to give that message to Amanda yourself," Nasriel said.

"What?" Sander said as he looked at the men, and then at the HK416 assault rifle Nasriel carried slung over his right shoulder as he balanced himself on a cane with his left hand.

"I don't know what you think of House Lucifer, but I am a man of honor. You had a chance to kill me during your attack on our compound, but for some reason you let me live. I am merely returning the favor. My debt to you is now over."

Sander looked around confused, then noticed the two House Lucifer soldiers who lay dead on the ground with bullet holes in the back of their heads, behind Nasriel.

Nasriel turned and looked at the dead bodies. "Those two men were loyal to Draysus; these men are loyal to me."

Sander still had a puzzled look on his face.

"I don't have time to explain," Nasriel said, noticing Sander's confusion.

He unlocked Sander's handcuffs and handed him a set of car keys. "Take that car there and get on that road." He pointed. "Take a right and follow it for about 40 miles and you'll see an interstate exit."

"But why? Why are you helping me?"

"I told you why. You saved my life. Now I've saved yours. We're even. We were both honorable men once, Sandriel. I try my best to remain one. Now we go back to being enemies. Get going."

"How will you explain the dead soldiers?"

"You let me worry about that. I'm sure you'll hear something about it later."

Sander, still shocked by what had just occurred, nodded his head in uncertain farewell to Nasriel, got into the car and drove away.

As Sander drove down the road in the black BMW 5 series 528i, he thought about what the hell just happened. It made no sense to him that they would just let him go like that. He understood the chivalric code, and it was a noble thing for Nasriel to do, but how would he explain it to Draysus? And what had Nasriel meant when he said he would hear about it later? He wondered if Gavriel knew he was going to be released. It didn't matter, right now. Sander knew he had to get to a phone and call Ramiel before he launched his attack.

It took him a while but at the third gas station Sander got lucky and found a pay phone. After several tries, Ramiel finally accepted the collect call. "Ramiel, it's me. Sander."

"Why are you calling me collect? Is this something Draysus is forcing you to do?"

"No, I'm out. Nasriel was supposed to execute me but he let me go, because I didn't kill him at the compound. He owed me a life debt. He's a very honorable person."

"How do I even know this is really Sandriel? We also have voice modification systems."

"*Damn* it, Ramiel! It's *me*. Only you, Tabrill and Amanda knew about me not killing Nasriel."

"That information could have been obtained through torture."

"Yes. Well, any information could be obtained through torture, so I guess there is no way for me to prove this is really me. Anyway, they had me in some underground bunker in Indiana. That elevator took forever," he said, thinking aloud. "I'm about an hour away from the compound . . . maybe a little more. I'll be in a black BMW. I'll be there soon."

"Okay. Be careful," Ramiel said, a bit insincerely. Sander could hear the suspicion in his voice.

I suppose I can't blame Ramiel for being skeptical, Sander thought. He is getting preparing to start what may quickly become a nuclear world war. I hope he doesn't pull the trigger before I get there.

Sander drove toward the compound where Ramiel was without incident. About 20 miles out, he realized a helicopter was following him overhead. He rounded a corner and saw two Humvees parked, forming what looked like a makeshift military checkpoint. He hit the brakes and watched as two armed soldiers approached his car. He squinted his eyes until he made out that one of them was Maurice.

Sander got out of the car, put his hands up, and slowly walked toward them. Finally, Maurice recognized him. "Sander?" He yelled questioningly.

"Maurice, it's me! Sandriel."

Maurice looked at the other soldier. "Go back and tell the others. It's Sandriel." The other soldier sprinted back to the checkpoint.

Maurice ran toward Sander and hugged him, lifting him off of his feet.

"They said you were a dead man!" Maurice said. "Nobody can kill Sandriel. I can't believe it! Oh man, you have no idea. Everyone thinks you're going to be shot! I was crying, man! I never cry! But when they told me about the execution, I lost it. Don't tell anyone, but I was bawling like a baby!"

"There's nothing wrong with crying."

"Man, I'm crying a little bit right now! Nobody's looking, are they?"

"Yes. One guy is staring down here at us . . . Hold on . . . Okay, he looked away."

Maurice quickly wiped the tears from his eyes. "All right, I'm cool now. Damn, it's good to have you back! Right in time, too! We are getting ready to go to war."

"Even though I'm alive?"

"Nobody knows you're alive."

"I called Ramiel earlier."

"Well, none of the soldiers have heard anything about it. We're still getting ready to attack, as far as I know. I even talked to Ramiel a little while ago. He's the one who told me to set up this checkpoint."

"I need to speak to Ramiel. Immediately!"

"All right."

"Can I take one of those Humvees? There might be a tracker on that BMW. It's one of House Lucifer's cars."

"Oh, man! You mean to tell me you stole that sweet BMW from them after you escaped? You are *the man* -- there's no doubt about it!"

Sander could hear the rumors about his escape from House Lucifer starting already, and he smiled a little.

"We'll blow that BMW up for you. You know you can take whatever Humvee you want." Maurice laughed.

"I thought I'd be polite and ask. It's been an odd day." Sander paused. "It's good to see you, Maurice. A few hours ago, I didn't think I was going to see anyone I knew, ever again."

"Sandriel the un*kill*able! That's your new nickname."

Sander smiled as he jogged toward the checkpoint.

When he got to the checkpoint he took a spare M16 from one of the Humvees, threw it in the passenger seat of the second Humvee, which wasn't loaded with weapons, and sped to the compound.

As he approached the gate, Sander immediately noticed the greatly increased military presence as 20 soldiers stood outside of the entrance.

"What the hell," one of the soldiers said. "Is that Sandriel?"

Another soldier yelled back, "It can't be!"

Sander stepped out of the Humvee. "It's me. Sandriel. Open that gate. I need to speak to Ramiel!"

All of the soldiers stared at him in awe, until one of them said, "Hey boy's, it *is* Sandriel! He's alive!"

The soldiers cheered as the gate opened. Even though there wasn't a protocol or command to do so, every soldier stood at attention and saluted him as he drove through the entrance.

Sander passed the various military vehicles on the main road and finally made it to the Main House. He parked in front and slung the M16 over his shoulder as we went up to the front door. Having not been armed for so long, it made him feel safe to be carrying again.

As he walked past security at the front door he heard one of the officers say, "Oh, my God!"

The lobby was bustling with people. As they slowly recognized who had just entered the lobby, one by one the people stopped what they were doing and stared at him as if they were witnessing a miracle.

Sander walked to the elevator and tried the eye scanner. The door didn't open. A nearby security officer ran over. "Sir, they thought you were a dead man." The security officer scanned his eye and Sander entered the elevator. "Thank you."

When Sander entered the office, Lucy looked at him, expressionless, and then suddenly ran over, throwing her arms around him. "I don't know how you did it, Sander. But this is a miracle!"

"I didn't remember saying goodbye. So I figured I'd come back and see you."

"Still the gentleman!"

"Of course," Sander smiled back at her as he entered Ramiel's office.

Sander saw many of the council members looking at him wide-eyed, as Tabrill walked up to Sander and hugged him. "It looks like you've had an interesting day," Tabrill said, stepping back and looking at his black outfit and M16.

Sander smiled. "Is Amanda okay?"

Tabrill shook his head. "No, not really. She thinks you are going to be killed today."

"So did I. I'll go see her immediately after we speak to Ramiel."

Tabrill gave him another hug. "Follow me. Ramiel is back here."

Tabrill and Sander walked back to Ramiel's office.

Tabrill knocked, but instead of waiting Sander opened the door and walked in.

Ramiel was on the phone and ended the call as soon as he saw Sander. Ramiel was speechless as he stared at him.

"You need to call off the attack," Sander said. "Something is going on at House Lucifer. I'm not sure what it is, but Nasriel disobeyed orders and let me escape. He mentioned something about me hearing about it later, when I asked how he would explain the deaths of two House Lucifer guards he shot."

"I know," Ramiel said.

Sander looked at him, confused.

"That was Gavriel on the phone. There has been a *coup d'état*. Gavriel has assassinated Draysus and is now head of House Lucifer. He wants peace between our two houses. I wasn't sure if he was lying until I saw you alive. Now I believe him."

"He's telling the truth, I think. Call him back and let me talk to him."

Ramiel called Gavriel.

"Sandriel is now with us," Ramiel said to him.

"Good," Gavriel said. "I was hoping for his safe return."

Sander motioned for the phone and Ramiel put him on speaker.

"Gavriel, this is Sandriel. Did you play any part in my escape?"

"Ah, Sandriel." Gavriel laughed. "Good to hear from you. I can only tell you that your release was Nasriel's idea. He owed you a life debt. It was his doing."

"The coup you just pulled off. Was that Nasriel's idea, too?"

"No. I saw an opportunity and took it. The council did not agree with his decision to go to war with House Ramiel at the present. I will have to tell you more about it at another time, perhaps. For now I need to get rid of the rest of the men loyal to Draysus and then sort out this peace with Ramiel. Trust me when I say I *do* want peace between us and I am truly happy you made it back to Ramiel and his daughter safely. Nasriel told me what your last words would have been. Now you don't have to disappoint her. Take care, Sandriel. Maybe we'll be able to have more interesting conversations again sometime soon."

"Yes, perhaps we will. Take care, Gavriel," Sander said.

"Ramiel, I know him. If he says he wants peace, then that's what he wants. He's a man of his word."

Ramiel nodded that he understood and continued his conversation with Gavriel.

Sander turned to Tabrill. "Where is Amanda?"

"She is at my house."

"That's where I'll be. Call her if you need me. My phone is still at the House Lucifer compound."

On his way to the elevator, Sander said, "Lucy, can you have a new phone sent to Tabrill's house for me? I seem to have misplaced mine."

"Yes. I'm guessing it's easy to misplace a phone when you are being kidnapped and facing execution. You probably had a few other things on your mind." Lucy smiled whimsically. "Have you had a chance to see Amanda? She looked a tad shaken when she left earlier."

"I'm on my way to see her now."

"She cares about you a lot. I hope you see that."

Sander nodded. "Yes. I care about her, too. I'll see you, Lucy."

"Bye, Sander."

Sander walked through the lobby and once again people stopped and stared at him.

He sped down the main road to Tabrill's house. The butler stared at Sander, the same way everyone else had, as he opened the door for him. Sander looked around downstairs but didn't see anyone except the maids, then he went upstairs to Amanda's room. He was surprised to see she wasn't there, either. He opened the door to the room he had been staying in and saw her sound asleep on his bed. Sander thought Amanda looked beautiful as she lay there, the only human he had cared about in almost a century. He felt his eyes begin welling with tears. I almost lost her forever. He believed there was no way he would be going to the same place as her in the afterlife. She was innocent, while he felt he was the walking personification of everything wrong and evil on this earth. This world was the only place that they would ever have to be together.

"Amanda," Sander said softly as he gently patted her arm. "Amanda, it's me . . . It's Sander."

Amanda opened her eyes when she heard his name.

She looked up at him, and then started, looked around the room, and then back at him.

Sander smiled. "It's me."

"Sander!" Amanda said, "How . . ?" She jumped out of bed and grabbed him, not sure if this was real. "Am I dreaming?" she asked. If I am I don't ever want to wake up, she thought.

"No." He smiled. "I got away . . . It's a long story."

"Oh, my God! It's really you!" Amanda screamed for joy and squeezed him as hard as she could. "I can't believe it! How?" she asked again. "What in the world are you wearing? It's really you! Sander, I thought you were dead!" Tears of happiness were streaming down her cheeks. "You're alive!"

"I had to come back. I had a promise to keep," Sander said. Amanda noticed a tear drop from his right eye.

"I didn't think I would see you again," Amanda said.

"I didn't either. I thought they were going to execute me." He hesitated. "When I thought I was going to die, you were the only person on this earth I was thinking of. I realized then how much you mean to me."

"Oh, Sander. You're making me blush. I'm already covered in tears!" She hugged him hard again and laughed. "I have never been this happy in my entire life! It's a miracle."

Sander didn't believe God would perform a miracle on his part, but he did agree that this was the happiest he could remember being, ever. He held her tightly.

"Amanda, are you okay?" Denise yelled as she came down the hall. "I thought I heard you screaming."

"I've never been better!" Amanda yelled.

"Well, I will be damned!" Denise said, as she looked at Sander and Amanda. "Sandriel, how in the world? The Lord truly *does* work in mysterious ways!" Denise closed her eyes, as she looked up and said, "God forgive me for doubting You and Your power, but even *I* wasn't sure You were going to come through for us *this* time. I should have known better, Lord. I should have remembered my scripture: Matthew 19:26 '. . . With man this is impossible, but with God *all* things *are* possible.' You are a great God, indeed! Amen."

"Amen," Amanda said, smiling.

Sander remained silent and smiled at Denise slightly.

"I know you don't pray, Sandriel, but after what you went through today, you need to start. Everybody in this compound thought you were dead, and here you are, looking healthy as can be, a smile on your face, and flirting with Amanda. God helped you today, boy!"

"I'm not flirting!" Sander started laughing at Denise's comment and at what an insane day it had been.

"Yes. He was flirting, Denise!" Amanda started laughing, overcome with joy at having Sander there, alive.

"Maybe I was, but just a little bit," Sander said as he smiled at Denise.

"Come here, Sandriel," Denise said, opening her arms.

Sander hugged her tightly.

"Baby, you gave us all quite a scare," Denise said. "But now you're home, safe and sound. That's all anybody wanted."

"That's all I wanted, too," Sander said. "I was very lucky to get out of that one."

"You can keep believing it's luck if you want," Denise said. "But I know who really got you out of it."

Sander chuckled. "Don't ever change, Denise."

"Don't worry. I won't."

The butler announced: "Pardon, but there are several visitors at the door."

"Tell them to come in and make themselves at home," Denise said.

Denise looked at Sander and asked, "Why are you wearing black pajamas?"

"Long story," Sander said. "I'd like to change, now that I think about it."

"Take your time," Amanda said. "I'm still trying to accept the fact that you are here right now. It feels like your kidnapping was a long nightmare."

"It wasn't really that bad, until the execution." Sander laughed at how ridiculous that sounded. "Anyway, I'll be down in a minute."

When Denise and Amanda went downstairs they saw Jessalyn, Tena, and Dimitra sitting on the couch.

"Is it true?" Tena asked. "Is Sander alive?"

"Yes!" Amanda smiled from cheek to cheek. "He's upstairs; he'll be down in a minute."

"Wow!" Jessalyn said. "That is unbelievable!"

Dimitra said, "Everyone was so convinced he was dead already. No one escapes from House Lucifer by themselves. I'll never doubt the stories I hear about him again."

"I was convinced he was dead already, too," Amanda said. "I feel horrible saying it now, but for a while I was feeling suicidal."

"Oh honey, you should have come to me," Denise said. "Don't ever think like that again, sweetie. You have too much to offer this world."

"I could tell you were kind of losing it," Tena said to Amanda. "I don't mean anything by saying that. I could just tell you were in a dark place when I saw you. I was worried about you."

"Thank you, Tena. I had never been so depressed before. It felt like my entire world had ended; everything I had dreamed of had been taken from me. Please don't mention that to Sander."

"No, we wouldn't," Dimitra said. "Everyone feels like that sometimes. If they had kidnapped John, I would have felt the same way."

"How did he escape?" Jessalyn asked.

"He just got here. He hasn't had a chance to tell me. I was upstairs in bed when he woke me up. He had promised me before he left that he would return to me, and when I saw him, he looked at me and said, 'I had to come back. I had a promise to keep.'"

"Oh my goodness. That's the most romantic thing I've ever heard in my life!" Tena said.

Dimitra started crying a little. "That is so sweet!" she said, as she put her hands on her chest.

"It sounds like you are making Sander soft," Jessalyn said, as she smiled.

"He's always so sweet," Amanda said.

They all turned as they heard Sander walking down the stairs.

"Hello, ladies," he said, as he put the M16 he had been carrying by the door. "Were you talking about me?"

Jessalyn laughed, as she, Tena and Dimitra got up to hug him. "How did I know you were going to ask that?" Jessalyn said, as she wiped the tears from her eyes. "It's like looking at a ghost."

"A very well-dressed ghost," Sander said.

"Well at least your kidnapping didn't humble you at all," Tena said, as she smiled, looking at his dark-gray three-piece suit.

"Were you scared?" Dimitra asked, as she put a handkerchief away in her purse.

"I wasn't scared exactly," Sander said. "I wasn't afraid of dying. I was more afraid that I would break my promise to Amanda and never see her again."

"Oh gracious, time to get the handkerchief back out," Dimitra said, as her eyes teared up. "That is so sweet!"

"This day has gone from one of the saddest days in my life to one of the happiest," Jessalyn said. "I'm so happy for you both."

"It's like fate brought you two together again," Tena said. "It's like it's your destiny to be together and nothing's going to stop it, not even an execution. Oh, my gosh. That is the most romantic thing ever!"

"I have to admit," Jessalyn said. "That is pretty romantic, the way you escaped an execution to get back to Amanda."

Amanda looked at Sander smiling. Sander had an unusually shy look on his face as he glanced back at Amanda.

"For once I don't know what to say . . ." Sander said.

"Oh, I think I know what you can say," Tena said, jokingly. "You can say: 'Oh Amanda, my buttercup, I love you with all of my heart, you sweet little baby doll.'" Tena started laughing, cracking herself up.

Everyone in the room laughed at the idea of Sander saying something like that, even Sander.

"Well, on that note," Sander said, as he smiled. "Amanda and I should probably head to Ramiel's office to make sure there isn't going to be a war this evening. Seriously though, Gavriel assassinated Draysus today, so I have no idea what's going on with House Lucifer. I was too busy trying to get here to really think about it much, until now. A takeover like that is a delicate situation. For all we know, Draysus's allies have killed Gavriel and retaken power. It's probably best if we find out what is going on."

"I know we joke around with you a lot Sandriel, but I think I'm speaking for everyone when I say we are all so glad you're back, and our world is a better place with you in it. We're all so thrilled that you made it back alive," Tena said.

"I agree, and well-said, Tena," Jessalyn said.

Looking at the floor, Sander said, "Thank you."

But he knew the world was anything but a better place with him in it. Try telling the mothers of all the men I've killed on the battlefield that the world is better with me in it, he thought.

"Well, are you ready, baby doll?" Sander said to Amanda.

"Aww, so sweet," Dimitra said.

"Is "baby doll" my new nickname?" Amanda asked.

"You have Tena to thank for it," Sander said, as he smiled at Tena.

"You're welcome, Amanda," Tena said, as she gave Amanda a hug goodbye.

"I might be calling you soon, Amanda," Jessalyn said. "I have to throw another little celebration party to celebrate Sandriel's return."

"I had so much fun at the last one," Amanda said. "Your house is so beautiful."

"Thank you so much," Jessalyn said. "I'll call you later."

After they said their farewells, Sander and Amanda made their way back to Ramiel's office.

When they entered the lobby, everyone stopped what they were doing and looked at Sander and Amanda. This time however a few people started clapping, then the entire lobby was applauding Sander's safe return. Sander felt his face turning red when several people yelled, "Good to have you back, Sandriel," and "Welcome home, Sandriel!"

Amanda took his hand and walked with him to the elevator. Sander tried the eye scanner again, but it still didn't work for him.

"They still have me locked out," Sander said.

"Why?" Amanda asked.

"The council thought I would be killed, so I guess they thought House Lucifer would use my eyes for scanners like these in our various compounds, possibly.

"Oh," she said, as she hugged him again and then scanned her eye to open the elevator door.

As they entered, Lucy looked at them and smiled. "You both look so happy!"

"I am!" Amanda said.

"I'm glad he's with you, Amanda," Lucy said. "Keep him out of trouble; will you, please?"

"He isn't leaving my sight for a long time."

"Very good," Lucy said.

Ramiel looked up at them from the long council table as they walked into the room.

"Your mood seems to have changed rather significantly, Amanda," Ramiel said.

"Yes. I believe it has," Amanda said.

There were six other council members in the room, some on laptops and some on their phones.

"How are things over at House Lucifer?" Sander asked curiously. "Is Gavriel still in charge?"

"As far as I know, yes," Ramiel said.

"Good," Sander said.

Ramiel looked at him curiously. "Do you trust him?"

"No, I don't trust any of the members of House Lucifer completely," Sander said. "Gavriel, however, seems to be a man of his word . . . Whether or not he has plans that he isn't telling us about remains to be seen, but I think we both know he does. He clearly isn't ready to die and neither are any of the men who supported him. The only reason his coup against Draysus was successful was because they were afraid of the inevitable battle that was about to occur the moment you found out I was dead. His fear of death will at least help us keep the peace longer than we ever could have with Draysus. Gavriel seems to be more level-headed. Draysus was a fanatic."

"Yes, I agree," Ramiel said. "But sometimes even level-headed men become irrational once they have complete power. We shall have to wait and see. I have started having the majority of our troops stationed here sent back to the other compounds. But I intend to keep a large showing of force, at least until the new treaties have been signed."

"What have you two agreed on so far?"

"It's the same treaty as the last one we signed 63 years ago, with a few additions. He has agreed to halt their breeding program."

"As long as they stop the kidnappings."

"Yes, I can understand why that would be an important one to you." Ramiel grinned.

"Where is the treaty going to be signed?" Sander asked. "None of this neutral location nonsense, either. We all know there is no such thing as a neutral location, anymore."

"I was thinking we would sign it here. I've already mentioned it to him, but he said he was worried that it might make him look weak to his men, by coming here to sign a treaty, like he was signing it because we were making him."

"Well, we are," Sander said. "He's the one who doesn't want to fight, not us. Some of us don't fear death as much as him. Draysus was considering letting me go, if I would leave House Ramiel and disappear. I refused."

Ramiel looked impressed by the news. "You were going to die, instead of leave our house?"

Sander nodded. "It would have meant never seeing the people I care about again. What kind of life is that?"

Ramiel noticed him glance at Amanda. "I think I understand," Ramiel said.

"If the leader of House Lucifer came here to sign the treaty it would make him look stronger to his men, not weaker," Amanda said. "It would show them that he doesn't fear us."

"That's an excellent point," Ramiel said. "I also think he is worried about his own safety. We have quite a history of betrayals between our houses."

"Tell him I will guarantee no harm will come to him," Sander said. "He trusts me."

"Yes, that might convince him," Ramiel said. "Because, there's no way we are going to one of House Lucifer's compounds with a *coup d'état* occurring so recently. Unless Gavriel is cutting heads off left and right, Draysus undoubtedly still has some supporters."

"Agreed," Sander said. "Gavriel doesn't seem like one to leave anything to chance, though. He's a thinker. Either way, having it signed here is the safest thing for us to do."

"I don't understand why you have to meet in person to sign the thing," Amanda said. "Can't you just agree over the phone, or do it electronically?"

"Tradition is why we have to meet," Ramiel said.

"Amanda, your way makes the most sense, as far as everyone's safety," Sander said. "But you're going to come to realize that fallen angels do a lot of ill-advised things because of tradition."

"At least with Gavriel we will have peace for a while," Ramiel said. "No matter how brief it may turn out to be."

Sander looked at Amanda and said, "It will give me a chance to show you the histories I have been keeping over the years -- miles and miles of stories about the fallen angels carved into the stone floor of a cave. Maybe I'll put our story in there, one day."

"Oh, I'd like that!" Amanda said.

Sander rubbed his chin as he thought. "After the treaties are signed."

"I'm going to call Gavriel right now," Ramiel said. "The sooner we can get him out here to sign the documents, the better."

"I'll see you Ramiel," Sander said.

"Sandriel, I'm glad you're back, and it's not just because we avoided a war," Ramiel said.

"Thanks, Ramiel," Sander said.

They nodded farewell.

Amanda hugged Ramiel, then she and Sander went to the lobby.

As they exited the elevator, Sander looked around the room and saw a familiar face.

"Bale!" Sander yelled.

Bale turned, appearing aggravated.

"Well, I'll be!" Bale said, as his face lit up with recognition.

Bale ran up to Sander and hugged him. "My God, man, I just heard you were back. They haven't exactly kept us well-informed since I arrived. Probably because I showed up with that traitor Tannis."

"What do you mean traitor?" Sander said.

"What? They haven't told you? After all you went through, I thought they would have."

"Haven't told me what?" Sander asked.

"Tannis is a rat. He's the one who told House Lucifer there would be someone heading down to pick us up."

"Where is he?"

"He said he wasn't sure who was going to pick us up, but he still told House Lucifer someone was probably going to pick us up. I couldn't believe it was him."

"Where *is* he?" Sander asked loudly.

Many of the people in the lobby turned and looked at Sander.

"He's at headquarters, I think. Ramiel had him locked up."

"Let's go to headquarters," Sander said to Amanda.

Amanda saw the fury in his bright-blue eyes. She didn't say anything, but nodded and walked to her BMW as Sander and Bale followed.

The three of them made the short drive to immortal headquarters.

"Just park out front," Sander said.

Sander and Bale got out of the car. When they did, Amanda watched Sander remove one of his pistols from his shoulder holster and cock it. The soldier standing at the entrance, smoking a cigarette, watched Sander as well.

Sander glanced at the soldier and asked, "Is Tannis in there?"

"Yes sir." He stared at Sander's pistol. "Do you want me to take you to him?"

"Yes," Sander said. He looked at Amanda.

"I'll stay here," Amanda said, not wanting to watch what was going to happen in there.

Bale followed Sander and the soldier into the headquarters.

As they walked down the long hallway, several soldiers stopped and watched the group as Sander, with his pistol drawn, entered the stairwell to the jail cells. When they reached the bottom of the stairs, they walked through several doors, which were each remotely opened, to a large room with open-air cells blocked off by rows of metal bars.

Tannis saw them coming his way and started yelling," Sander! I didn't know it would be you! Sander stop! Please!"

Sander lowered his pistol and aimed it at Tannis' head. The soldier and Bale watched curiously.

"Shoot the traitor," Bale said.

"Any last words?" Sander asked Tannis, who he noticed began crying.

"They had my daughter!" Tannis said, as he fell to his knees, weeping. "They were going to experiment on her! What the hell would you have done?"

Sander pulled the trigger.

"Dammit!" Tannis said, as he grabbed the arm Sander had just shot. "Sander, please forgive me! I pray one day you have another child. You would have done the same thing."

"I would have died trying to rescue her, before I would ever become a traitor," Sander said. "If you had told me they had your daughter, you know I would have tried to get her back. Instead, I was almost executed today, because of you."

"Not everyone has the same death wish as you, Sander," Tannis said.

Bale pulled out a pistol and began to aim it at Tannis.

"Let him live," Sander said. "We'll give him a show trial, make an example out of him, and then we'll kill him. It's better that way."

Bale nodded okay and re-holstered his pistol.

"Let's get out of here," Sander said.

Bale and the soldier followed Sander back outside.

Amanda looked at them curiously as the soldier and Bale lit up cigarettes. She saw Sander decline a cigarette from Bale and then give him a hug before he got into her SUV.

Sander didn't say anything, but he could feel Amanda looking at him. "Did you kill him?" Amanda asked.

"No. They had his daughter. I don't know, maybe I am getting soft. It's better that they execute him after a public trial anyway. Would you have been disappointed if I had killed him?"

"No," Amanda said after thinking for a few moments. "I would have understood why you did it, but I'm glad you decided to let him live. Showing forgiveness doesn't make you soft. It shows you are strong. You could have killed him, but you didn't. You were strong enough not to let what he did bother you."

"I suppose that's one way to look at it. I'm not sure if it's the right way to look at it, though."

Amanda laughed and punched him playfully in the shoulder. "You know I'm always right."

"Yes, Ma'am. You are . . . I forgot." Sander smiled.

"Is Bale coming with us?"

"No. He's going to hang out here for a while. He's friends with a lot of the immortals. They look up to him, and he likes the attention."

"Like you?" Amanda grinned at him.

Sander smiled back at her and pretended to ignore her comment. "All right, let's head back to Tabrill's if you don't mind, Lady Amanda. It's been a long day."

When they pulled up to Tabrill's house, Amanda parked the car, looked at Sander and said, "You know when you told my dad that Draysus offered you a chance to be released, but you didn't take it because you would have had to leave House Ramiel?"

"Yes," Sander said. "That was part of the deal. I would have had to leave House Ramiel forever. I'm a man of my word. If I had agreed, I would have left."

"I would have left House Ramiel, too, just to be with you. I wanted you to know that."

"The only reason I told him no was because I thought it meant I would never be able to see you again."

"Sander, I would run away with you in a heartbeat. I still would. We could get away from all this death and killing."

"You can never run away from it."

"But you can. You've just never tried," Amanda looked into his eyes. "There are two different Sander's. There is the Sander you believe you are -- the invincible Sandriel that everyone convinces you that you are -- and then there is the Sander I know. The Sander I know is kind, honest, protective, and a gentleman -- the Sander I want to be with forever.

"Maybe we could get away for a while after the treaty is signed," Sander said. "Do some traveling together. Things are usually relatively safe for a few years after a peace treaty. It would be nice to get away from all of this violence."

"Just me and you?"

"Yes. Just us."

Amanda hugged him. "That sounds perfect, Sander."

"How long do you think it will take before they sign the treaty?"

"Ramiel said he wants it done soon. And he doesn't mess around when he wants something done quickly. So I'm guessing in the next day or two."

"Oh wow, that quick?"

"Yes, so start thinking about where you would like to visit."

"This is exciting! You talk about some rumors starting. People are going to be like, 'Oh, Sander and Amanda are traveling the world together!' Nothing strange about that!"

Sander laughed.

"Are you ready to go in?" Amanda asked, looking into his bright-blue eyes.

Sander looked away shyly and grinned. "Yes, I suppose so."

When they walked inside, Denise was standing near the door.

"What were you two doing out there for so long?" Denise asked. "I was getting ready to call all of my friends and start some rumors."

Amanda started laughing. "Denise, we were just talking about rumors. We weren't doing anything improper. Sander is a gentleman and I'm a lady, so call your gossiping friends and tell them that!"

"Tell her, Amanda!" Tabrill said as he walked into the room.

Denise started laughing. "I remember when Amanda got here the first day: she was so shy and meek, and now she's a strong young woman who doesn't take anything from anyone. I'm proud of you Amanda. You remind me of myself in many ways."

"Thank you, Denise. I picked up all of my more admirable qualities from you," Amanda said.

"I am so flattered to have been such a positive influence in your life."

"We were actually out there talking about traveling the world for a while, after the treaty is signed," Amanda said.

"You and Sander?" Denise asked.

"Yes, only us. It will be good for Sander. Maybe he can go out for once without carrying a gun."

"I don't see that ever happening." Sander grinned. "But it would be good for me to get away."

"That sounds like it would be fun," Denise said. "When are they having the treaty signing?"

"Tomorrow, possibly," Tabrill replied. "I'm waiting on a call from Ramiel. Your new phone is in the kitchen, Sander. They dropped it off earlier."

"Thanks," Sander said, as he went to the kitchen.

Maurice, Ellen, and Craig walked in. Amanda noticed Craig still had a bandage around his throat, as he softly said, "Hello."

"Hi," Amanda said as Denise hugged her boys and Ellen.

"Where is the unkillable Sandriel?" Maurice asked.

No wonder Sander thinks he's invincible, Amanda thought, the soldiers around here treat him like he's a god. Constantly being treated like that must mess with your head after a while. She remembered hearing that sometimes on the battlefield the new soldiers would follow Sander around instead of going to their assigned positions, thinking that being close to Sander would somehow protect them.

Sander walked into the room, fiddling with his new phone.

"There he is!" Maurice said. "Amanda, did he tell you about how he pulled up to the checkpoint?"

"No, he hasn't," Amanda said.

"All right, listen. Ellen, you listen, too. I was watching the checkpoint and I see this sweet black BMW 5 series sedan come speeding down the road, and all of a sudden they brake hard, so I'm thinking I'm going to smoke this fool coming up on us like that. So, as we inch closer I see its some guy in black pajamas coming at me. And low and behold, it's the unkillable Sandriel! Risen from the grave! I could not believe my eyes. Not only is he supposed to be dead, but he escapes in a freaking black BMW 5 series sedan, and then comes strolling up to me like it's no big deal. I thought to myself: this has got to be the baddest man on the planet! I'm not going to lie, but I cried a little bit when I saw him, I was so happy. Don't tell anybody."

"I think we all cried, Maurice," Denise said.

"I'll tell you one person who didn't cry. Sandriel didn't cry. Escaping death is an everyday thing for him. No wonder House Lucifer backed down. They didn't want any part of his death. Even if they did execute him, he would have come back from the grave and exacted his revenge."

Sander laughed. "Do you tell all of our soldiers these stories about me?"

"Of course, I do," Maurice said. "But I'm just telling them the truth."

"Well if you want to know the honest truth. I cried a little bit, too," Sander said.

"You're just saying that to make me feel better," Maurice said.

"I was being serious," Sander said.

"I'm so glad you're okay," Ellen said. She hugged him. "You big crybaby."

Everyone laughed.

"See. Ellen knows the truth," Sander said.

"That's right," Ellen said. "I don't believe any of those stories about you."

Tabrill left the room as his phone rang.

"I'll go see if dinner is ready," Denise said. "Is everyone going to stay and eat?"

Everyone answered yes.

"Oh good. We'll have a nice full table tonight."

"Why didn't you kill Tannis?" Maurice asked Sander rather curiously. "I heard you just shot him in the arm."

Amanda looked at Sander. He hadn't told her the part about shooting him.

Sander glanced back at Amanda. "I think I just felt sorry for him. House Lucifer was going to torture his daughter, but I was still furious at him. I wasn't really thinking when I shot him. My anger got the better of me, after all I had been through because of him, and what could have happened to me."

"I would have put one right between his eyes," Maurice said.

"Maybe I should have," Sander said. "Either way, he'll end up being executed at some point. He and Aiden, Zekiel's boy.

"I wonder if Aiden heard Draysus is dead," Maurice said aloud, thinking.

"I was thinking about that, too, when I was at the immortal headquarters."

"Why is that?" Ellen asked.

"Aiden is in love with one of Draysus's daughters, and he was leaking information to House Lucifer," Sander said. "It sounds horrible, but I'm guessing Gavriel will have all of Draysus's children executed."

"That's sad," Ellen said.

"I agree. That is sad," Amanda said.

"Executing Draysus's children?" Sander asked.

"The entire story," Ellen said. "Aiden loved her, so he was giving Draysus information so he could be with his daughter. He wasn't doing it solely to betray House Ramiel. Everything he did, he did for love."

"I hope they don't execute Draysus's children either," Amanda said. "That's just cruel."

"Cruel but necessary," Sander said. "I think a lot of people living on this compound forget that we do things that are just as evil as them. If I had died, House Ramiel was going use false flag operations to kill countless men, women and children, and then make it look like House Lucifer was responsible. It's evil, but would have won the war, so that most of you would live."

"I'm just glad it didn't come to that," Ellen said.

"Is everyone ready to eat?" Denise asked.

"Yes, Mom," Maurice said. "Sandriel is in here making everybody feel guilty about how evil we are."

Everyone laughed.

"Sandriel," Denise said, "you be more joyous. You are alive and well, and if you think you are doing something evil, then you need to remember it's never too late to change your ways."

"Yes, Ma'am!" Sander grinned.

"I love Denise," Amanda said as she smiled at Sander.

After they took their seats at the well-decorated table, Denise noticed Tabrill still wasn't back from his phone call. "Well, we will get started without Tabrill; I'm sure he has important business to take care of."

"Now, if everyone will bow their heads for a moment of prayer," Denise said.

Amanda looked at Sander as everyone else at the table bowed their heads and closed their eyes. Sander was looking at the table, with a bored expression on his face. Noticing Amanda looking at him, he glanced at her and smiled. She shook her head, thinking: always the rebel, even refusing to pray before dinner. She closed her eyes and bowed her head.

"Lord," Denise said, "we would like to thank You for all You have given us today. We know we do not always do what You ask of us, and do not deserve Your grace, and knowing that makes us all the more grateful for Your blessing. I would like to thank You for looking over everyone at this table, and for taking care of my boy Craig. I would also like to thank You for answering our prayers for Sandriel's safe return, and though he might not see it, I know it was You working in Your mysterious ways who got him back home to us."

Amanda glanced quickly at Sander, who was now curiously looking at Denise, with a slight grin on his face.

"Some of our hearts are harder than others, Lord, but just as Saul of Tarsus saw the light, so shall we all. Some of us just take a little more time. Please forgive us of our sins and know we are indebted to You, as we enjoy each other's company and the meal You have blessed us with. Amen."

"Amen," Amanda said, looking at Sander, who remained silent.

Tabrill entered the dining room and sat at the end of the table opposite Denise.

He looked at Amanda and Sander and said, "We have a council meeting in the morning. The treaty will be signed tomorrow night. Did I miss anything?" Tabrill asked, looking at Denise.

"You missed the blessing," Denise said as maids set salads and lasagna in front of each of them, except for Craig, who was having soup, because of the wound to his throat.

Tabrill shrugged.

Amanda asked, "Why are fallen angels so stubborn?"

"Oh, I like where this conversation is going," Denise said laughing.

"I haven't seen one fallen angel pray since I've been here," Amanda said. "You would think you guys would be doing everything you can to be forgiven."

"That's what I say, too, Amanda," Denise said.

"It is strange," Ellen said. "Immortals pray -- most of them, at least -- but not the fallen angels. And they have actually met God."

"Well, Tabrill, answer the young ladies," Denise said. "Or you Sander, you can put your two cents in, too, if you want."

"It's a personal thing with each of us, of course," Tabrill said. "It's not that I see anything wrong with praying -- I just don't see the benefit of it. God has His plan, and me praying isn't going to change His plan. Sander probably doesn't pray because he rebels against everything." Tabrill laughed.

"No," Sander said. "Well, maybe I do." He laughed. "I don't think we can be, or should be, forgiven, so I think praying is pointless, in my case. Some fallen angels pray, though."

"You were right," Denise said, looking at Amanda. "These two are just plain stubborn."

"This lasagna is great, Mom," Maurice said. "I can't believe we have little man Craig and the unkillable Sandriel eating dinner with us tonight. It's been a crazy week."

"Yes," Craig said, as he ate his soup.

"You'll get a medal and a nice paycheck because of that neck wound," Maurice said.

"Yes. I know," Craig said softly.

"Hey, Lady Amanda," Maurice said. "Remember, when I first saw you, I told you whenever Sandriel was around things always got deadly! I was right. All the soldiers know when they see Sandriel that we're going to be bringing the pain to some fool."

Sander smiled.

"Yes. You were right, Maurice, and Sander does have quite the reputation around here among the soldiers," Amanda said. "It's like they worship him."

"Hell yeah, we do," Maurice said.

"Language!" Denise said.

"Sorry," Maurice said. "Heck yes, we do, Lady Amanda. If you'd seen what we've seen, you would, too."

Sander ignored them. "Tabrill," he asked, "is Gavriel really flying in here for the treaty signing?"

"Yes. You need to call him after dinner. He doesn't seem to completely trust anyone on the council, other than you. He wants you to guarantee his and his men's safety."

"Who is he bringing with him?"

"Nasriel and Kanthius," Tabrill said.

"I'll tell him I can't guarantee Kanthius's safety," Sander said, laughing.

"That's fine with me," Tabrill smiled.

"Who is this Kanthius?" Denise asked.

"He's bad news is who he is," Maurice said.

Craig nodded in agreement.

"I'll put it this way," Maurice said. "When it comes to fighting, House Ramiel has Sandriel, and House Lucifer has Kanthius. If you are on the battlefield and either of them come running toward you with a sword in their hand and their wings out, don't even bother running away, because you're already dead. You'll just die tired!"

Sander grinned. "Kanthius is an honorable warrior. I'll call Gavriel later. I'm going to need his number."

"Call Ramiel first," Tabrill said.

"All right," Sander said. "Sorry about talking business at the dinner table. I was just curious about the treaty signing."

"Tonight you can talk about anything you want," Denise said. "I'm just glad to have you here. Just no cussing. That's the only thing I ask."

"Yes, Ma'am."

"Does that boy cuss when he's around you?" Denise asked Amanda.

"You know, I don't think I've heard him cuss once since I've met him."

"You want me to tell you why?" Denise asked.

"Yes, please."

"Well, this was years ago, but one day I'm upstairs, and I hear Maurice and Sandriel come in the door, and I guess they didn't know I was home. So I walk quietly down the stairs and I hear these two little hooligans saying "F" this and "F" that, cussing like a couple of drunken sailors. I swear every other word coming out of their mouths was a four-letter one. So I went back upstairs and came down with a bar of soap."

Amanda looked at Ellen, who had already started laughing.

"I took that bar of soap and held it in front of Sandriel's face and then Maurice's face and I told them, that if I ever heard them curse in my house again, I was going to make each of them keep that bar of soap in their mouth for five minutes before they would be welcomed back. I haven't heard either of them use that nasty "F" word since."

Amanda burst out laughing at the thought of Sander holding a bar of soap in his mouth.

"That was the only time I've ever seen Sandriel scared," Maurice said, laughing.

Sander said, "I've always thought House Lucifer has Kanthius and House Ramiel has Denise! I'll never be as badass as her."

"You watch that language," Denise said. "I'll wash your mouth out with soap, in front of everyone in here." She laughed.

"Yes, Ma'am. I apologize."

"Apology accepted."

"Well, the soap incident seems to have worked, because he's never cussed around me," Amanda said. "You've done well training him to be a gentleman."

"Thank you, Lady Amanda," Denise said.

"We need to be headed back to headquarters," Maurice said to Craig.

"No dessert?" Denise asked.

"No. We need to get back or we'll be late. We need to drop off Ellen," Maurice said.

"Well, give me hugs," Denise said.

After they left, Sander said, "Thank you for dinner, Denise. If you'll excuse me, I need to make some calls."

"You're welcome honey," Denise said. "It's so good to have you here."

"It's good to be here," Sander said as he glanced at Amanda and dialed Ramiel's number.

"Hello, Ramiel," Sander said. "I'm supposed to call Gavriel?"

"Yes," Ramiel said. "I'll text you his number. He wants you to promise him he will be safe."

"Tabrill told me," Sander said. "Gavriel came and talked to me a few times when I was being held captive and we got along pretty well. Had some interesting conversations."

"How much do you trust him?"

"He's very calculating. But, like I said earlier, I think he's a man of his word. If he tells you something, I'd take it as the truth."

"Give him a call and I'll see you, Tabrill and Amanda tomorrow."

"Yep. See you then."

Sander dialed the number Ramiel had sent. "Gavriel, this is Sandriel."

"Alive and well, I see," Gavriel said.

"Yes, it's been an interesting day."

"Indeed, it has, for both of us."

"Hopefully the peace between our houses will last longer than last time."

"That is my hope as well. Our two houses need to speak to each other more often, so petty problems and differences don't escalate like they have a tendency of doing. But I'll discuss more of that with Ramiel."

"Of course."

"What I wanted from you was your word of honor that no harm would come to me and my men, and that this wasn't some trick of Ramiel's that would lead to our deaths or capture."

"You have my word. Nothing will happen to you. Ramiel wants peace just as much as you do."

"That's all I needed to hear. I shall see you tomorrow, and perhaps we can pick up where our last conversation ended. I know we are enemies, Sandriel, but even enemies can show respect and empathy toward one another. And know that I mean it when I say I was happy for you when I heard you made it back to Ramiel's daughter safely. I could tell you care for her."

That caught Sander off guard. "Thank you," Sander said, not sure how to continue. "I assure you that you and your men will be safe at our compound, and I'll see you tomorrow."

"Take care," Gavriel said.

"You too," said Sander.

Sander hung up the phone, wondering if Gavriel was as reasonable as he seemed, or as cunning and deceptive as Lucifer.

"I spoke to him," Sander said to Tabrill. "They'll be here tomorrow."

"Good, we can get that over with. Hopefully the peace will last for a while. It's been a long time since House Lucifer has had a leader who wanted peace as much as Gavriel seems to."

"They have a habit of getting assassinated," Sander said.

"Yes, they do." Tabrill nodded in agreement. "I'm headed for bed," he said to Denise. "Thank you for a lovely dinner, my love; and thank you, Sandriel and Amanda, for joining us."

"Good night, Tabrill," Amanda said as Tabrill kissed Denise good night.

"See you in the morning," Sander said.

"I should get some rest, too. I was thinking about driving down to Nashville again in the morning by myself," Sander said, trying not to laugh.

"No way in hell!" Amanda said. "Sorry about the language, Denise."

Denise laughed. "It okay, Amanda. I agree. There is no way in hell you are going anywhere by yourself, Sandriel."

"I know. I was kidding," Sander said. "Thanks for everything and thank you for praying for me." He grinned.

"You're welcome, baby," Denise said. "You go get some rest."

"I'm coming up, too," Amanda said. "So go get your pillows and your comforter."

"Yes, Ma'am," Sander said as he walked up the stairs.

Denise looked at Amanda curiously.

"He sleeps on the floor by my bed, to protect me," Amanda laughed. "It sounds so immature when I say it out loud like that."

"No, I think it's sweet and innocent. He's like your guardian angel."

"Exactly, and after his kidnapping I'm afraid to let him out of my sight."

"Oh, you are precious!"

"Can I ask you something, Denise, between you and me?"

"Of course you can, sweetie."

"Do you think Sander likes me, or is he just being a gentleman? I know he cares about me, but I can't tell if he's, you know, interested in me -- like, dating me or something. I can never tell, because he doesn't ever hit on me."

Denise laughed. "Girl, I have known that boy a long time. I can read him like a book and I think he has a crush on you like you wouldn't believe."

"Really?" Amanda was surprised.

"Yes, really. Take my word for it, because I know, but you didn't hear it from me."

"Thank you, Denise. I'm going to bed now."

"Good night, sweetie," Denise said, as she gave her a hug.

Sander was already lying on the floor beside her bed looking at his phone when Amanda walked into her bedroom.

"Were you and Denise talking about me?" Sander asked, smiling.

"Maybe," Amanda said, as she smiled back and took her nightie to the bathroom to change.

After she got ready for bed she walked out and saw Sander was already fast asleep with his phone still in his hand. She took his phone and put it on the night stand as Sander woke up. He looked around for a moment like he wasn't sure where he was and then, half asleep, looked at Amanda and said, "Good night, beautiful" as his eyes closed again and he fell back to sleep.

Amanda smiled as she looked at him, so happy to have him back safe with her. Maybe God had answered her prayer, after all. She liked to think He had. "Good night, Sander," Amanda whispered. "I pray, one day, you find the inner peace and happiness that troubled heart of yours has been searching for." Amanda closed her eyes, exhausted from the day's events, drifting off to sleep, thankful her guardian angel had kept his promise.

Chapter Ten

"Good morning, Lady Amanda," Sander said, already dressed in a light-brown three-piece suit, light-blue shirt, and dark-blue striped tie, with black leather dress boots.

"Thank God you're still here," Amanda said. "I kept waking up during the night checking on you, making sure your coming back wasn't a dream."

"Yes, Ma'am. I thought I would stick around today, so you didn't stress too much." Sander grinned.

"I would have come after you."

Sander checked his watch. "Now that you know I'm here, I'll be downstairs while you get ready. We have a meeting pretty soon and then the treaty signing, and I believe Jessalyn might be doing something to celebrate my return."

"Busy day."

"It never stops around this place. It will be nice to get away," Sander said. "Anyway, I'll be downstairs."

When Sander got downstairs, he noticed Tabrill sitting in a chair in the living room drinking a bottled water. Sander sat on the couch. "What's the meeting about? The treaty?"

"The treaty and what to do with Tannis."

"Well, that shouldn't take long. Execute him."

"That will most likely be the outcome. It's almost a shame. You and he were close, once."

"Yes. Back when I was a little wilder."

"Time certainly goes by fast," Tabrill said as he looked sadly at Denise, who was walking by.

"If they found a way to extend normal humans lives with our blood, do you think she would do it?" Sander asked.

'I don't know." He appeared to be deep in thought. "I really don't know if she would or not. Why do you ask?" He looked at Sander suspiciously.

"Just curious," Sander said. "House Lucifer has been experimenting on humans for centuries. They must have discovered something by now."

"We would have heard something from one of our informants by now."

"Not necessarily. They knew about the blood ritual long before we did. And when I was speaking to Gavriel, he mentioned something about how if they did succeed they would only do it on a select few loved ones."

"Really?"

"Yes, and I think he was telling me this under the assumption I was still going to be executed, before he decided to kill Draysus. He seems to trust me. I'll try to find out more about it."

"Yes, please do. Keep me updated."

"Of course," Sander said as he watched Amanda come down the stairs in a wine-colored, ribbed midi dress with black shoes.

"That didn't take long," Sander said.

"A natural beauty like her -- it doesn't take long to look pretty," Tabrill said.

"Thank you, Tabrill," Amanda said.

Denise yelled, "I heard that Tabrill! Stop flirting with Amanda."

Sander and Amanda laughed. Tabrill just shook his head. "Sorry, honey. I think there's some breakfast in the kitchen, if you want any, Amanda."

"No thanks. I'm okay."

"Well, if you want, we can head to the Main House. If everyone gets there early, we can get all this over with before the treaty signing."

"That's fine," Amanda said.

"You heard the lady," Sander said. "We'll meet you over there, unless you want to ride with us."

"I'll drive myself," Tabrill said. "I don't want to be a burden if you decide to go do something."

"It's no problem. Ride with us," Sander said.

"Let me go say goodbye to Denise and I'll meet you at the car, then."

As Amanda and Sander waited in her car, she asked, "How's your arm doing by the way? The one you were shot in during the raid. I haven't heard you mention it."

"It's healed. It's these that hurt, but they are healing faster than I thought they would." He held up his hands showing her each palm, where he was shot.

"Oh no. Did they torture you? How did I not notice that yesterday?"

"They don't look too bad now, I suppose. They didn't really torture me. Someone shot both of my hands while I was unconscious. I guess so I couldn't make a fist, or maybe just payback for something I had done to them in the past. It doesn't matter. I can make a fist again. That's all that's really important. That, and I'm back here with you."

"Aw! Aren't you a charmer?"

Tabrill opened the door and got in the SUV.

As Amanda drove, she noticed the troop presence had already died down considerably since yesterday. "Do you always carry pistols on you, like Sander does, Tabrill?"

"Not always," Tabrill said. "And when I do, it's never as many as Sander." He laughed as Sander opened his jacket, revealing his two Glock 19's and reached down and pulled a small .380 out of his boot. "When I do carry one, it's *just* one. Then again, I'm fairly certain Sander has more enemies than I do."

Sander nodded in agreement.

"Why do you ask, Amanda?" Tabrill asked.

"I was thinking about getting a gun."

"You've been hanging out with Sandriel too much. But then again, if you plan on being around Sandriel a lot, having a way to protect yourself from his enemies is a good idea."

"Then I should probably get one then." Amanda smiled at Sander.

After Amanda parked her BMW, they entered the lobby. It was still as busy as it was the day before. Probably preparing for the treaty signing, Amanda thought.

Jessalyn was walking by them when she noticed Sandriel and Amanda. "Sander, I still can't believe you are alive! You need to start being more careful." She playfully punched him in the chest. "I heard yesterday, and at this point, I don't think anything about you surprises me. She hugged him and Amanda. "I'm in a rush, but celebration at my place tonight. Formal dress, because of the guests. I'll text you the details."

"What guests?" Amanda asked Sander as they went into Ramiel's office.

"I'm guessing House Lucifer, sticking around for her get-together," Sander said. "It's not uncommon after a treaty signing to show a sign of goodwill like that between the houses."

"I see," Amanda said, as they entered the council chamber.

Amanda sat next to Sander. Corinthus approached them.

"I know we've had our differences in the past, but I am truly glad you are back here with us," Corinthus said, patting Sander on the back.

"Thank you, Corinthus," Sander said.

"If it had been anyone else, I would have been shocked. But for some reason, when I heard that Sandriel escaped an execution, there was a part of me that wasn't surprised."

Sander said, "I was very lucky."

"Either way, you are here," Corinthus said. "I know this young lady was happy to see you return. She was ready to massacre everyone in House Lucifer, if that's what it took to get you back."

"Really?" Sander asked, looking at Amanda as his face lit up, smiling from cheek to cheek.

"Yes. I was a little angry yesterday," Amanda said.

Sander laughed. "At least I know you've got my back."

"Always," Amanda said softly.

"If everyone will have a seat we can get on with this meeting," Ramiel said.

After everyone took their seats, Ramiel said, "First of all, welcome back Sandriel! You gave us all a hell of a scare yesterday, but we got through it. And we proved to House Lucifer we were ready for anything they threw at us."

Everyone applauded.

Sander grinned, "I like to keep things interesting around here."

"You do a very good job at that," Ramiel said. "Now to our first order of business: What to do with Tannis. Since you suffered the most by his treason, you may speak first, Sandriel.

"Execution," Sander said. "It's simple. He betrayed us and he must die because of it."

"I have been thinking about this at length," Ramiel said. "While it is true he betrayed us, it wasn't a betrayal for self-gain. He was put in a corner and didn't see any way out. He has also served House Ramiel loyally for an eternity. Something about having him killed seems wrong in his case. He seems truly sorry about what he did; and having my own daughter, I think to myself: what I would do if I found out House Lucifer was going to run their experiments on her?"

"I'll execute him then, if it's going to keep you up at night," Sander said. "Just give me the okay."

"What are the other options besides execution?" Amanda asked.

"We can do whatever we want with him, Amanda," Corinthus said.

"Yes, tell us, as a human, what would you do if the decision was yours to make, Amanda?" Anthus asked.

The council members looked at her curiously. "I think what he did was unforgivable. I mean, I might have been ready to kill him myself, if Sander had died. But by some miracle, Sander didn't die. Plus, what Tannis did, he did for love," she unconsciously put her hand on Sander's. "He was only trying to save his daughter. I don't believe any father should be put to death for trying to save his child, no matter what the crime is. If the decision was mine to make, I would banish him from House Ramiel forever, and also make it clear to House Lucifer that if they took him in, it would be considered an act of war. Banish him for eternity from any contact with fallen angels, but don't kill him. If he can't accept that and chooses to take his own life, then that is between him and God, but House Ramiel's conscience will be clear. We will know we were not the executioners of a man whose only intention was to save his child, no matter the cost to him or others."

"We haven't banished someone since the middle ages," Corinthus said. "But I find myself agreeing with Amanda."

"Does anyone else want to chime in?" Ramiel looked around the table, most people shaking their heads. "Okay then. Let's vote and then I will decide at a later time. All for execution." Four people raised their hands, including Sander. "All for banishment." Eight raised their hands. "Overwhelming majority is for banishment. I will take this into consideration before making my final decision."

"Our next business is the treaty signing. I have spoken to Gavriel. He, Kanthius, and Nasriel will be arriving with two immortals later this afternoon. I don't think we've had anyone from House Lucifer at this compound for over 200 years. Correct me if I'm wrong on that. Anyhow, since this is your first one, Amanda, perhaps someone would care to explain to her how it works. I tend to ramble on at times." He smiled.

"I'll explain," Sander said. "Basically, we get dressed up in formal attire, greet each other, and meet in the council chambers . . ."

Ramiel interrupted. "We'll be meeting in the downstairs office for this one. I don't want them up here."

Sander continued, "We meet downstairs, say hello, everyone pretends to like each other, then Ramiel and Gavriel both sign two identical documents. Then we chat some more and pretend to like each other again, and they go on their way. Actually, Ramiel, Jessalyn mentioned something about wearing formal attire to her party this evening. Are Gavriel and his people going to that, as well?"

"Yes, I thought it would be a nice gesture," Ramiel said. "With Gavriel in charge of House Lucifer, we have a chance to keep the peace longer than we have in centuries."

"Are we going to bet how long it will last?" Anthus asked.

"That's another tradition," Ramiel said to Amanda. "We place bets on how many years the treaty will last. We've been doing it for thousands of years, and I don't recall ever winning, strangely enough."

"That's because you're an optimist," Maalik said.

"Yes," Anthus said to Amanda. "Your father always bets the treaty will last a few hundred years." He laughed. "You're much more likely to win if you bet five or six -- ten years tops."

"I will bet 50 years then," Amanda said. "I'm an optimist too."

"All right, Amanda has already lost then. Go ahead and give us your money now." Anthus laughed.

"I'm going with fifteen years," Sander said. "If no one assassinates Gavriel, I think fifteen years is realistic."

"That's far too long, too," Anthus said. "I'm going with five years, and Sandriel will be the one who breaks the treaty."

Everyone laughed.

"I can't remember the last treaty I broke," Sander said, smiling.

"What about the Treaty of 1813?" Anthus reminded him.

"Well, I forgot about that." He laughed. "That was a misunderstanding, anyway. That one doesn't count."

"Okay, everyone, you can place your bets later, and not in front of House Lucifer," Ramiel smiled. "As, far as the treaty goes, I'll text everyone after I speak to Gavriel. The only big change to the last one was that they will stop their breeding program. Hopefully, everything will go smoothly and we will have a good time tonight. That is all. I'll see everyone later." Ramiel stood, signaling the meeting was over.

As many of the council left the room, Anthus walked over to Amanda. "Good job speaking earlier. I think banishment was a wise choice."

"Thank you."

"Yes, I was impressed, too," Sander said. "You almost convinced me to vote for banishment."

"Thanks, Sander."

"I said almost." He laughed. "Want to get out of here?"

"Yes. I'm kind of hungry."

"Lady Amanda, would you allow me to buy you lunch?"

"Let me buy you lunch, instead. Dad called me this morning and finally set up my bank account. Don't you think the council members are a little overpaid?"

Sander laughed. "You'll soon realize money means nothing to us."

"I noticed that back at the hotel."

"When you have every material thing you could ask for you, you realize the only thing that matters are the people around you, your loved ones. That's why we are constantly kidnapping or killing one another. It's the only way the two houses can really hurt each other, anymore. But to answer your question, I couldn't possibly let a sweet young woman like yourself pay for my lunch. As a gentleman, I simply couldn't live with myself." He smiled.

"I guess I'll let you pay."

She got up and Sander followed her to the office entrance. "Hi, Lucy," Amanda said. "Do you happen to have a bank card for me?"

"Hello, Amanda," Lucy said. "Let me go check."

Lucy returned from a room opposite Ramiel's office with an envelope. "I believe this is it," she said. "Don't spend it all in one place."

"I don't think I could spend it all in one lifetime."

"If you go through with the blood ritual, you will," Sander said.

"I meant a human lifetime."

"Or if you hang out with Sander," Lucy said. "He has expensive tastes. And he's kind of high maintenance, I've heard."

Sander laughed. "I just have nice tastes. Speaking of that, could you have another Range Rover sent to Tabrill's house? Same make and model as the last one. I doubt House Lucifer is going to return my other one."

"Ramiel had me take care of that this morning," Lucy said. "You should get it tomorrow at the latest."

"No rush," Sander said. "Tell Ramiel I said thanks. That was nice of him."

"Will do."

"I'll see you later."

"Stay out of trouble," Lucy said as Sander and Amanda entered the elevator.

Amanda followed Sander into the back room of the cafeteria where they were seated immediately. Sander stood until the host had seated Amanda. When the waiter got there, Amanda ordered the chicken salad and a sweet tea.

"I'll have the same," Sander said.

"You know, it just occurred to me that you have not spent a single night in your house since you've been here," Amanda said.

"I have a duty to protect this young woman, named Amanda." Sander grinned. "I can't very well protect her from my house."

"Oh, is that why?"

"Actually, I've been all alone for the last hundred years, and I've finally met someone I like to be around."

"Oh, that's so sweet," Amanda said, blushing.

Sander smiled shyly, like he often did whenever he was being honest and not attempting to be funny or putting on an act, Amanda thought.

Their food was brought out. "That was fast," Sander said.

"Everyone has heard what you have been through, Sir," the waiter said. "I put your order in front of everyone else's."

"Thank you."

"They probably didn't want to lose their best tipper," Amanda said.

"There is that, too." The waiter laughed. "I'm kidding. It's good to have you back, Sir."

"What should I wear tonight?" Amanda asked.

"Do you have something formal?"

"Yes, I have a black dress that's kind of formal."

"If you need anything you can let Lucy know and she can get it for you fairly quickly."

"Okay, I might. You fallen angels live in a fantasy world; everything you want is at your fingertips."

"You're part of this world now. Aren't you happier? Being here, living with us?" Sander truly looked concerned.

"I'm happier living here with you. But I don't need to have the mansions and cars and endless amounts of money. I would be happy with you even if you were poor, because I can tell you care about me. I've never had anyone care about me before."

"Well get used to it, Amanda, because I'm not going anywhere."

Amanda looked at Sander and wondered if he felt the same way about her as she did for him. She knew Denise thought he had a crush on her, but it was difficult to tell if he really did or if he was simply being a gentleman.

Sander looked at his phone as he saw Baelis approaching their table.

"Well hello, Lady Amanda and Sander."

"Hey, what's up, Bale?" Sander said.

"Where can I get a tux around here?" Bale asked. "What size are you, Sander? We're pretty close. Wouldn't you say so, Amanda?"

"Yes," Amanda said, "You're about the same size."

"I'm a 40 regular," Sander said.

"I'm a little smaller, but it might be close enough. Do you have a tuxedo I can borrow for tonight?" Bale asked. "I brought plenty of suits, but no tux."

"Sure, I should," Sander said. There's a tailor who might be able to adjust one of mine for you, if you want. Just ride with me and Amanda back to Tabrill's."

"All right, I thank you," Bale said, pulling his black shoulder-length hair behind his ears.

"I love your accent," Amanda told Bale.

"Thank you," he said. "That's what happens when you live in Ireland for 500 years."

"I remember when Sander had a British accent, actually," Bale laughed. "Now he sounds like a proper southern gentleman, or redneck, considering on how you want to look at it." He smiled.

"You had a British accent?" Amanda asked Sander.

"I've had many different accents during my time on this earth. I've noticed it takes around 300 years of living in a certain area, for me at least, before I find myself sounding like the area's inhabitants."

"That's crazy," Amanda said. "I never really thought about that. I guess it wouldn't have made sense for me to picture you fighting in the Middle Ages with an American accent."

"I guess most humans don't realize that, to us, it's just common to run into someone you haven't seen for several hundred years. And they sound completely different than the last time you saw them, depending on where they lived and for how long," Sander said.

"Well, after I go through the blood ritual we are moving to England for 500 years, so I can have a British accent. I've always wanted one," Amanda said.

Sander laughed. "All right. If you want to, Amanda, we will."

"Making long-term plans together are you?" Bale asked. "Interesting. That's not like you, Sander."

Sander looked at Bale and said, "Whatever. Let's go get you one of my tuxedos." Sander stood and left $100 on the table.

As the three of them proceeded through the lobby, Tena walked up to Amanda. "Be careful, Amanda. Baelis and Sandriel together equals trouble." She laughed.

"That's kind of true." Bale smiled.

"Indeed," Sander said.

"I'll keep them in line," Amanda said to Tena.

"Amanda's kind of bold for a human," Bale said to Sander. Sander grinned thinking about how much Amanda had changed since he first met her.

"Yes, she is," he said.

"It's so nice to see you, Tena," Amanda said.

"You, too," said Tena.

"Just taking care of some paperwork for dad as usual," Tena said. "But I look forward to seeing y'all tonight."

"You, too, Miss Tena," Bale said as he winked at her.

Tena just looked at him and walked away.

As they walked to Amanda's car, Sander said to Bale, "You know Tena is dating an immortal? I saw you wink at her."

"Ah, I don't care."

Sander laughed. "Well, it's good to see you haven't changed."

"Don't worry my friend. Your girl is probably the only girl on this earth that I wouldn't flirt with."

Amanda, overhearing their conversation, liked that Bale thought of her as Sander's girl. When they got to Tabrill's house, Amanda followed Sander and Bale to Sander's room and sat in a large-backed antique wooden chair as they went through Sander's closet.

"Are you wearing tails tonight?" Bale asked. "Does your tuxedo have tails?"

"Yes. Tonight I am."

"Can I borrow this one with tails?"

"You don't have to wear a tuxedo with tails. Only council members really have to wear the same thing."

"Well, I don't want to look out of place. Let me borrow the one with tails. You aren't wearing a bow tie, are you?"

"No, these are more Victorian-era tailcoats."

Amanda started cracking up, laughing at the way they sounded like a couple of women, discussing what they were going to wear this evening.

"You two don't sound very tough right now," Amanda said.

"Yes, I suppose we don't." Sander laughed.

"Don't tell anyone we were arguing over wearing tails or not. We have reputations to keep up," Bale said, smiling.

"I won't," Amanda said, still laughing at how ridiculous they sounded.

"I think I have everything I need," Bale said.

"Just call Lucy, Ramiel's secretary," Sander said. "She'll find you a tailor on the compound to fix it for you. They shouldn't have to alter it much."

"Can you give me a ride back to the Main House, if you don't mind, Amanda?" Bale asked.

"Sure," Amanda said. "Come on, pretty boys." She laughed as they walked to her SUV.

After they dropped Baelis off at the Main House, Sander looked at his phone. "Did you get that text from Ramiel? Looks like Gavriel and his entourage will be here in two hours."

Amanda glanced at her phone. "Yes, I got it. I need to start getting ready."

"Back to Tabrill's it is."

When they got back to Tabrill's, Denise was sitting in the living room reading a book.

"Hello, busybodies," Denise said.

"Hello. Are you going to Jessalyn's party this evening?" Amanda asked.

"Yes, I am."

"Good! I need to go get ready."

"It's a little early don't you think?"

"The treaty signing," Sander said.

"Oh, that's right," Denise said as Amanda went upstairs.

Tabrill walked in when he heard Sander. "Apparently Gavriel and Nasriel are bringing their wives with them to the treaty signing."

"Why?" Sander asked.

"Ramiel believes it's to show that they trust us. Maybe to signify the beginning of a new relationship between the two houses."

"Well, I doubt they would try anything dishonest with their wives around. They would most definitely be killed if House Lucifer attempted a sneak attack or assassination."

"Unless they just really don't like their wives," Tabrill said, grinning.

Sander laughed. "That's so wrong it's hilarious. They attempt an assassination, so we execute their wives for them." He kept laughing. "I'd never expect you, of all people, to say something like that Tabrill . . . Bale maybe, but not you."

"You two are horrible," Denise said.

"I apologize, but it *was* kind of funny," Tabrill said. "I am a fallen angel too, honey. We aren't exactly known for our sensitive nature."

"I know you are, Tabrill, but I still love you, anyway."

"I'm going to go change before hanging out with Sander gets me into trouble."

"That's a good idea," Denise said.

"Don't blame me. I didn't even say anything. I just laughed," Sander said.

"You're a bad influence." Tabrill laughed as he went to his bedroom.

Sander nodded, smiling.

"It will be nice to have that treaty signed and have some peace around here," Denise said. "I won't have to worry about you so much. I know you think you can take care of yourself, and you do a pretty good job of it, but -- God help me -- I do worry when you disappear for years at a time."

"Do you really worry about me, Denise?" Sander asked curiously.

"I worry about you just as much as I do any of my boys."

"Thank you, Denise."

"Have you and Amanda decided where you are going to run off to after the treaty is signed and the peace is in effect?"

"We haven't really discussed it. But don't worry. I wouldn't let anything bad happen to Amanda . . . ever."

"I know you wouldn't, honey. If anyone could protect her, it would be you. That's why Ramiel sent you to pick her up in the first place. When are you going to tell that girl how you really feel about her?"

"What do you mean?" Sander grinned shyly.

Denise laughed. "See! I can see it on your face right now."

"I don't know. I think she only looks at me as her guardian angel. Just someone to protect her. Either that, or she sees me as a murderous lunatic with a death wish. Besides, she deserves someone better, someone as kind-hearted and innocent as she is. People around me have a habit of dying."

"Sandriel, that girl is head-over-heels for you. You need to tell her how you feel about her and stop being so hard on yourself for everything you've done. Amanda is right about you -- deep down you're a good boy. You just let the devil get ahold of you, sometimes."

"Maybe. You really think she likes me, like that?"

"Let's just say I know she does. Everyone living in this compound knows she does, except for you." She laughed.

Sander smiled. "Thank you, Denise. I better get ready."

I swear that boy is hard-headed sometimes, Denise thought as she watched Sander go upstairs.

Sander dressed quickly in his black pants, white shirt, grey double-breasted vest and black shoes. After tying the black cravat around his neck, he put his double-shoulder holster back on. When he put his black long-tail jacket on, he looked at himself in the mirror, and felt like he was back in the 1800s. All he needed was his old black-top hat and he would be set, he thought. Sander put on an extra belt and grabbed his katana.

When he walked downstairs, he saw Tabrill standing in the hallway off the living room, texting on his phone. It was odd seeing Tabrill dressed as he did 200 years ago, but holding a smart phone.

"Any updates?" Sander asked Tabrill.

"No, looks like everything is going as scheduled for once."

"Has Amanda been down yet?"

"Yes, Denise is helping her with her hair."

Tabrill smiled at Sander.

"What? What's that look mean?"

"You are lost without that young lady. It's good, seeing you like this."

"Like what?"

"Happy. You look happy when you're around her. That's all I'll say."

"What rumors have you heard about me and Amanda? Tell me the truth."

"Oh, I've heard certain things." Tabrill laughed. "I overheard Jessalyn and Dimitra while I was having lunch the other day."

"I knew they talked about me when I wasn't around." Sander smiled. "What'd they say?"

"They were laughing, saying you hadn't even kissed her yet. Don't worry. I know it's just gossip."

"No, it's true."

"What?"

"I don't know. I've been trying to be a gentleman. I wasn't even sure she really liked me as anything more than someone to have around to protect her."

"Sander when you were kidnapped, Amanda cried her eyes out over you, and then when she heard of your execution she laid in bed and refused to eat or even see anyone. Now, I'm not claiming to understand women -- I don't think anyone does -- but I'm pretty sure that's a sign she thinks of you as more than a bodyguard."

Denise walked over. "What are you two talking about over here? You look suspicious."

"We were talking about how horrible Sandriel is at being able to tell when a young woman is interested in him." Tabrill laughed

"Yes, he's pretty bad." Denise laughed.

"Speaking of that," Sander said. "Is Amanda almost ready?"

"She is," Denise said. "She wanted to know if she was supposed to wear her sword, since she is on the council."

Sander looked at Tabrill. "I honestly have no idea," Sander said. "Tabrill, did Lady Emma ever wear her sword? I can't remember."

"Yes. That was a long time ago," Tabrill said. "I think it would be up to Amanda. What color is her dress? I have quite a collection of belts and scabbards that should fit her sword."

"Black," Denise said.

 Tabrill left the room and returned with four black belts and scabbards. "Tell her to try these. I have more, if those don't work."

Several minutes later Denise yelled at Sander and Tabrill, "All right gentlemen, I present to you: Lady Amanda!"

Sander and Tabrill walked into the living room and watched as Amanda confidently walked down the stairs in a black front-slit gown, black shoes, and a black medieval double-wrap belt, with her sword hanging off her left hip.

"Does the sword look okay?" Amanda asked

"Yes. It's perfect," Sander said.

"You really are dressed to kill," Tabrill said.

"That was cheesy," Denise laughed.

"You look truly amazing and the sword only adds to your outfit. Is that better, Denise?" Tabrill asked, smiling.

Denise ignored him and said, "You look so beautiful this evening, Amanda."

"You really do," Sander said.

"Here, let me take some pictures," Denise said. "You all look so nice I can't help it. Sander, you stand next to Amanda." She took several pictures, and then told Tabrill to stand next to them, and took their picture. "OK. That's it."

"If you want, we can head over there," Tabrill said. "You'll want to remove your belt Amanda; it's a hassle trying to drive with one of those things on."

"Yeah, I hadn't thought about that," Amanda said. "Thank you. I'll drive us."

"I'll see you at Jessalyn's later," Tabrill said to Denise as he kissed her goodbye.

As Amanda drove by the front of the Main House, heading to the parking lot, she noticed several soldiers were standing out front with some council members, all dressed the same as Sander and Tabrill.

"There's Corinthus with his sword," Sander said. "I don't think he's ever used that thing in battle."

"You know, I don't think he has either," Tabrill said, rubbing his chin. "Well, maybe once."

"I've never used mine in battle either," Amanda said.

"Well, you have an excuse," Tabrill said. "You, my Lady, have only been alive a little over two decades, and you have Sander to protect you." He smiled, punching Sander's shoulder. "Hopefully your sword will never see any more bloodshed."

"What about mine?" Sander asked.

"The chance of your katana not seeing any more bloodshed is pretty slim." Tabrill laughed. "I would not take that bet. I'm just being honest."

Sander grinned.

Amanda didn't comment, but she didn't like the thought of Sander having to use his katana again. She parked her SUV and they walked to the front of the Main House.

"So, do we wait here?" Amanda asked.

"You are Ramiel's daughter, and everyone at this compound associates you with Sandriel. You could do whatever you wanted and no one would say anything." Tabrill laughed.

"You know what I mean, Tabrill," Amanda said.

"Yes, we are supposed to wait around this area until we get a text from Ramiel, and then the soldiers will line up, and the council members will line up in front of the soldiers. And when Gavriel and your father get here, we follow them into the downstairs conference room," Tabrill said.

"Stick with me and you'll be fine," Sander said.

"You aren't leaving my sight, remember?" Amanda said.

"I don't intend to," Sander replied.

"Good, I'm glad we're clear on that." Amanda smiled.

Amanda noticed the soldiers began lining up. Tabrill noticed, too. "I guess that's our cue."

Sander checked his phone, "I didn't get a text."

Just then Sander's phone went off with a text from Ramiel to get lined up and make sure the soldiers were lined up, as well.

"Never mind," Sander said. "I got it."

The council members not already outside came out from the lobby.

Amanda stood next to Sander and she put her belt and sword back on. A few minutes later three Humvees followed by two black stretch limousines and four more Humvees pulled up in front of the Main House. Ramiel, Gavriel, and Gavriel's wife exited the first limousine, and Nasriel, his wife, and Kanthius exited the second. The soldiers stood at attention as Ramiel, Gavriel, and his wife walked by them into the Main House. Amanda noticed Gavriel greeted Sander with a nod as he walked by. Kanthius, Nasriel and his wife followed.

"Our turn," Sander whispered to Amanda. He took her arm in his and led her through the line of soldiers. As Sander walked by Maurice, who was standing at attention, Sander punched him lightly in the stomach. Maurice remained still and silent, but smiled.

Amanda smiled, too. Guys are immature, no matter what age they are.

They walked down a long hallway that Amanda had never seen before, still surrounded by soldiers on either side of them. It was an impressive show of force, Amanda thought. All of these soldiers were ready to kill every member of House Lucifer who was present at a single word from her father. That thought had to have entered Gavriel's head.

Finally they entered a large conference room with the flags of several nations hanging on the walls. There was a large table in the front of the room with two documents spread out on them. Lucy, Ramiel's secretary, was standing by the table. She was dressed in a formal navy-blue gown and had her hair down. Amanda had never before realized how pretty she was. Lucy saw Amanda looking at her and she smiled and waved. Amanda waved back, then turned her attention to her dad.

Ramiel looked around the room and then spoke. "I believe we all know each other. So there's no need for too much formality. Let's see . . ." He looked around. "Ah, yes . . . The women in the room could use some introduction. I'll allow our guests to go first."

"Hello everyone," Gavriel spoke. "This is my wife, Mikayla."

Mikayla looked around, smiling, and then smiled at Amanda and waved her hand slightly. She had long, straight blonde hair and a dark tan. She reminded Amanda of a beauty pageant contestant in her ivory evening gown. "Nice to meet you all," Mikayla said.

Nasriel then spoke. "This is my wife, Kelly." She had long red hair and appeared slightly older than most of the women around the compound, Amanda thought. She looked stunning in her strapless black gown.

Kelly said, "Hello," and smiled shyly.

"This is my lovely daughter, Amanda," Ramiel said.

"Hello. Nice to meet you," Amanda said.

"Nice to meet you as well, Lady Amanda," Gavriel said.

"And this is my lovely secretary, Lucy," Ramiel said.

Lucy smiled and waved to the members of House Lucifer.

"Nice to make your acquaintance as well, Lucy," Gavriel said.

"Now that that's over, feel free to mingle, while Gavriel and I look over the treaty to make sure everything is in order."

Nasriel and his wife walked over to Sander and Amanda, and Gavriel's wife Mikayla followed them.

"This is him, Kelly. This is Sandriel, the one I told you about," Nasriel said. "You've met before, but I wasn't sure if you remembered him."

"You'll have to forgive me, but I meet so many people I wasn't sure which one you were," Kelly said. "Thank you for sparing my husband's life."

"I should be the one thanking him," Sander said.

"Now we're even." Nasriel grinned.

"Indeed," Sander said.

Amanda looked at Nasriel. "Thank you, Nasriel, for what you did."

"It was the right thing to do," Nasriel said. "You are a very beautiful young woman, Lady Amanda. Now I know why Sandriel was in such a hurry to get back to you."

Mikayla interrupted. "I love your dress, Amanda."

"Oh, thank you. I was thinking the same thing about yours when I saw you," Amanda said.

"You look pretty badass with that sword," Mikayla said.

"I was thinking that same thing when I watched her walk in," said Kelly.

Sander saw Kanthius looking at him, and walked toward him.

"I'll leave you ladies to chat. I'm going to make sure Kanthius and Sandriel are getting along. They have a bit of a history," Nasriel said.

"So, you are on the council?" Kelly asked Amanda.

"Yes, just recently," Amanda said. "Everything is so new to me. I didn't know fallen angels even existed a few weeks ago, and now here I am with the most powerful ones in the world, watching them sign a peace treaty."

"This is the first time I've ever met anyone from House Ramiel," Mikayla said. "So far, I don't see any differences between our houses."

"I didn't know what to expect either," Amanda said. "When I heard Gavriel and Nasriel were bringing their wives, I thought they are going to be the meanest women I'd ever met." She laughed.

"I thought the same about you," Kelly said. "I thought this Amanda girl is going to be some arrogant, pretentions girl, walking around with a crown on her head like she's some kind of princess."

Amanda laughed. "No, I'm not like that at all."

"I know," Kelly said. "You seem very down-to-earth. No pun intended." They laughed.

"Hopefully, this peace will last, and we can all get to know each other better," Mikayla said more seriously. "They need to let us run things, and maybe there wouldn't be so much fighting."

Amanda and Kelly laughed.

"Yes, I agree," Kelly said.

"Ladies and Gentlemen," Ramiel said. "If you would all gather around to bear witness to the signing of the Treaty of 2017 between House Lucifer and House Ramiel, we will commence."

All were quiet as they gathered around the table at the end of the room. Lucy handed out the signing pens, first to Gavriel and then Ramiel, and said, "Gentlemen, if you agree to the terms of the treaty, will you now sign the document before you?"

They each signed the document in front of them and everyone applauded. Lucy then switched the documents between them and they each signed again. Aides for each removed each house's document for safekeeping.

"Though we may never agree on everything, I hope this is the beginning of a lasting peace and a new era between our houses," Gavriel said.

"I agree," Ramiel said. "Let us do our best to ensure this peace will last."

They shook hands and Ramiel said, "Ladies and Gentlemen, that concludes today's proceedings. We will be leaving soon to celebrate today's historic event. That is all."

"Well, that was quick," Mikayla said to Amanda.

"Yes, they didn't waste any time," Amanda said.

"Are you going to the party after this?" Mikayla asked.

"Yes," Amanda said.

"All right, good," Mikayla said. "I don't know any of these House Ramiel people so I might hang out with you, if Gavriel leaves me to talk business, if that's fine."

"I know being the new person is no fun," Amanda said. "Of course you can hang out with me and Sander if Gavriel needs to handle business."

"Yes, I would like that," Mikayla said. "Thank you, Amanda."

Gavriel walked up to Mikayla and Amanda. "So, I see you've met Lady Amanda."

"Yes," Mikayla said.

"I haven't had the pleasure to properly introduce myself," Gavriel said. He took Amanda's hand and kissed it. "I am Gavriel, head of House Lucifer."

She smiled, "It's nice to meet you. Sandriel has told me a little about you."

"Oh really?" Gavriel said. "I like Sandriel. We had a very good talk the other day. The situation was unfortunate, but it was an interesting conversation nonetheless. I look forward to working more with you, Sandriel, and the rest of House Ramiel to make sure this peace lasts. God knows both sides are tired of the kidnappings. What is the point of ruling a kingdom, if you are afraid to leave your castle?"

"Did you help Sander escape or was that all Nasriel's doing?" Amanda asked.

"Direct and to the point." Gavriel laughed. "I like that. I would like to believe my actions played a part in Nasriel's decision to go through with his release of Sandriel."

"Well, thank you, whatever part you played in it," Amanda said.

"We may have been enemies for as long as either of us can remember," Gavriel said, "but I respect Sandriel and I like to think he feels the same way."

"I think he does," Amanda said.

"I hope it remains that way," Gavriel said. "Mikayla, Ramiel and I need to discuss some things in private on the ride over to the party. Do you think you can ride in Nasriel's limousine?"

"With Kanthius?" Mikayla asked. "You know I don't like him when he's been drinking. I'd rather not, but if I have to . . ."

"You can ride with me and Sander if you want, Mikayla," Amanda said.

"Yes, I'll ride with Amanda, if that's okay," Mikayla said.

Gavriel thought about it for a moment . . . "Yes, that will be fine."

"Good," Mikayla said.

"Honey, I will see you there," Gavriel said as Ramiel walked over to them, patted Amanda on her back and headed with Gavriel outside.

Sander said, "Hello, ladies. Are you ready, Amanda?"

"Yes. Mikayla is riding with us."

Sander looked surprised. "Oh, I guess you two are getting along then?"

"Amanda's nice, and I didn't want to ride with Kanthius, since he's been drinking since noon today," Mikayla said. "He's nasty when he's drunk."

"I wondered what was wrong with him. He's usually all right from what I remember. He was being kind of rude to me earlier. I thought it was because of Darriel."

"Darriel?" Mikayla asked. "Wait, you're the one who killed Darriel? You're Sandriel, killer of Darriel. I know who you are now. Amanda kept calling you Sander and I wasn't sure. I thought you said your name was Sandriel, but it didn't click that you were *that* Sandriel. Angels have such strange names, I didn't make the connection. I've heard so many stories about you."

Sander nodded. "Yes, that's me. If you knew Darriel, I want you to know he died an honorable death. He was a true warrior and I respected him."

"I didn't really know him, but I knew his wife," Mikayla said.

"I apologize for the suffering I caused her," Sander said.

"You don't need to apologize," Mikayla said. "He was a soldier. She knew it was only a matter of time before he died in battle."

Sander was a little shocked by Mikayla's coldness. "Yes," he replied. "Eventually, we all do."

Amanda didn't like the sound of that and changed the subject. "Sander, grab Tabrill and let's go to Jessalyn's."

"Yes, Ma'am." Sander got Tabrill's attention and motioned for him to come over.

"Are we leaving?" Tabrill asked.

"Yep," Sander said. "Gavriel's wife is riding with us."

"The more the merrier," Tabrill said as he introduced himself.

When they got to Amanda's BMW, Sander held the door for Amanda and Tabrill held the door for Mikayla, who sat up front. Sander and Tabrill got in behind them after removing their swords.

"Are all the men in House Ramiel such gentlemen?" Mikayla asked.

"No, just me and Tabrill, Ma'am," Sander said.

 Tabrill tried not to laugh.

"Well I guess Amanda and I are lucky to be in the company of two handsome gentlemen," Mikayla said.

Sander glanced at Tabrill and they both grinned.

"So, have you been married to Gavriel very long?" Tabrill asked.

"Twenty-four years."

"So you're an immortal?" Sander asked.

"Yes."

"Would I know you father by any chance?" Sander asked. "I know pretty much all of the fallen angels who are still living."

"My father wasn't a fallen angel," Mikayla said.

Sander and Tabrill looked at each other shocked. Each knowing what the other was thinking. Gavriel and House Lucifer had figured out a way to extend normal human's lives! Their years of experimenting on humans had paid off after all.

Sander quickly changed the subject, hoping Mikayla didn't realize House Ramiel had no idea House Lucifer had figured out how to extend the lives of full-blooded humans. "So, have you ever been to Jessalyn's before?"

"No. This is my first time," Mikayla said.

"You'll like it," Tabrill said. "Everyone is very friendly."

"I'm pleasantly surprised how similar our two houses are," Mikayla said.

"We all come from the same place," Sander said. We will probably end up in the same place, too, he thought.

"Here we are," Amanda said, pulling up into the rear of Jessalyn's driveway.

Tabrill helped Mikayla out, and Sander did the same for Amanda.

When they walked in they saw the party was already in full swing, as many couples danced in the center of the grand ballroom.

Jessalyn spotted Sander and Amanda as they entered the room. She and Tena walked over to them.

"Hello, everyone!" Jessalyn said.

"You look stunning, Jessalyn. You both do," Amanda said as she admired Tena's dark-red gown. She looked around at all of the men in their Victorian-era tail coats. "I feel like I've entered one of those shows on the BBC that I used to watch."

Everyone laughed.

"Yes, it does look like we've entered a time machine in here," Jessalyn said.

Amanda noticed Jessalyn looking at Mikayla curiously.

"Tena and Jessalyn, this is my new friend, Mikayla."

Mikayla smiled. "Nice to meet you."

"I'm Jessalyn. Welcome to my house."

"Hello. I'm Tena, Corinthus's daughter."

"I'm Mikayla, Gavriel's wife."

Tena and Jessalyn looked surprised.

"Oh," Jessalyn said. "Well, make yourself at home. If there's anything you need, just let me know. It's an honor to have you in my house."

"She rode over here with us," Amanda said.

"I see . . . Ramiel and Gavriel were somewhere around here." She looked around. "Over there in the corner, talking," she said, pointing.

A server came by with a silver tray full of champagne glasses. Everyone took one but Sander and Tena.

"Are you still not drinking, Sandriel?" Tena asked.

"Alcohol and women always seem to end up getting me in trouble, one way or the other," Sander said.

Tena laughed. "You're ridiculous."

"Yes I know. But if you will excuse me, ladies, I need to pull Tabrill aside and talk to him about some important business for a few minutes."

"Okay. See you soon, Sander," Amanda said.

Sander smiled at her. "Of course, Lady Amanda."

Denise, Dimitra, and Ellen saw Amanda and walked over.

"Denise!" Amanda said, as she hugged her. "You look so beautiful!"

At 48 years old, Denise was a very attractive woman. Amanda frequently caught soldiers who appeared to be half her age checking Denise out. She had a very sophisticated look about her that was only amplified by the elegant black sequin gown she was wearing. Amanda introduced Mikayla.

"I just spoke to Gavriel," Denise said to Mikayla. "He is a very charming man, and he loves you dearly. He was telling me what a sweet young woman you are."

"That was nice of him," Mikayla said. "Tabrill is also quite the gentleman."

"He should be," Denise said. "I trained him."

Mikayla laughed.

"Well, it looks like this is where the popular people are," Kelly said as she and Nasriel walked up to Mikayla.

They made their introductions, and Jessalyn said, "I think we're all just fascinated with the people from House Lucifer, after all of the stories we've heard."

"We're just as fascinated by you," Nasriel said.

Ellen walked up and greeted everyone.

"Where's Maurice?" Amanda asked.

"Over there with most of the other soldiers." Ellen pointed to the bar area, where there were about 40 soldiers talking and laughing loudly.

"Excuse me, but are you the one who let Sandriel go?" Ellen asked Nasriel.

Everyone standing there stopped speaking and looked at him. "Yes, I am," Nasriel said. "Sandriel spared my life once, so I spared his as well."

"That was kind of you," Ellen said.

"Thank you, but I looked at it more as a debt of honor," Nasriel said. "He would have done the same for me, if the circumstances had been reversed."

"You saved us from a lot of grief," Ellen said.

"You really did," Amanda said.

Kelly hugged Nasriel.

"How long have you and Sandriel been together?" Mikayla asked.

"Uh-oh." Dimitra laughed. "I'm kind of curious how you're going to answer this one."

"So am I," Tena said.

"I think we all are," Jessalyn agreed.

"Well, we aren't officially a couple or anything," Amanda said, shyly.

"Really?" Mikayla asked.

"People in House Lucifer all believe Sandriel is in love with Ramiel's daughter."

"Really, why?" Amanda asked.

"I think because of some of the things Sandriel said about you when he was in captivity, Lady Amanda," Nasriel added. "It was assumed you were a couple."

"This is getting good," Dimitra said.

"Yes, continue!" Ellen laughed.

"He still hasn't kissed me or anything," Amanda said softly.

"Oh, my god! Go over there right now and kiss him," Dimitra said.

"No!" Amanda laughed. "I can't do that. Maybe I'll ask him to dance, though."

"Yes, that sounds like a good idea," Denise said. "Ask him for a dance."

Amanda walked slowly over to Sander and Tabrill.

"She loves that boy," Denise said.

"I know she does," Dimitra agreed. "Amanda is such a little sweetheart."

"She's nervous, I think," Jessalyn said, as they watched her.

When Amanda was halfway across the room, Baelis walked by her and nodded. He was followed by Kanthius, who was carrying two large mugs of beer. Kanthius sloppily bumped into Amanda, knocking her sideways, and he dropped one of his beers on the floor. The sound of the glass mug hitting the floor got the attention of Sander, Tabrill, and many of the people in the room.

"Watch where the hell you're going!" Kanthius said.

"You bumped into me," said Amanda.

Nasriel, seeing the argument, walked over quickly to Kanthius and said, "I'm sorry, Lady Amanda. Kanthius is drunk. Now apologize, Kanthius."

"I'm not apologizing to a human," Kanthius sneered.

"I said apologize. That's an order!" Nasriel said sternly.

By this time the majority of the people in the room were watching the altercation.

"No," Kanthius said. "If you think I'm apologizing to Sandriel's little slut, you've lost your mind."

"Sandriel!" Tabrill said, as Sander walked toward Kanthius, with his right hand gripping his katana.

Kanthius looked at Sander and said, "You don't scare me," as he pulled out his sword.

Nasriel quickly grabbed Amanda and led her back to Denise and the other women.

Gavriel yelled at Kanthius from across the room in a booming voice. "Kanthius stop right now!"

Kanthius showed his wings, and Sander did the same.

The room filled with an amber glow as the two men approached each other, wings ablaze. Kanthius charged Sander, swinging wildly at his head, as Sander dodged and unsheathed his Katana in one clean motion, cutting deep into Kanthius's left thigh. Kanthius swung again, this time Sander blocking his blow, and then swung at Kanthius's shoulder, as the surprisingly swift Kanthius was able to dodge Sander's blade. Sander lunged forward, swinging twice at Kanthius' head, while Kanthius blocked both blows. Kanthius charged Sander, causing Sander to retreat as he parried Kanthius's attack, slipping on the spilt beer. Sander finally regained his footing, parried another one of

Kanthius's swings and then sliced open Kanthius's right shoulder. Kanthius quickly grabbed his sword with his left hand and blocked Sander's barrage of attacks, parrying the last, and swung at Sander's head as Sander dodged to his right, then came up, cutting deep into Kanthius's left arm. Kanthius's sword dropped to the ground as Sander sliced into Kanthius's right arm again. When Kanthius dropped to his knees in defeat, Sander kicked Kanthius's sword across the floor, and put his blade at the nape of Kanthius's neck.

"Now," Sander said, staring coldly at Kanthius. "Apologize."

"I'm sorry. Sandriel, you've won. Please, don't. I beg of you. I'm sorry."

"Apologize to Amanda!" Sander said angrily.

No one in the room spoke as Kanthius said, "I'm sorry, Lady Amanda. I apologize. Please forgive me."

Sander pushed the blade slightly into Kanthius's neck, just enough to draw blood.

"It's your decision, Amanda," Sander said. "You were the one he insulted."

Amanda straightened, walked to them and drew her sword. There were many gasps from people in the room.

"Is she going to do it?" Dimitra looked at Tena.

"I don't know," Tena said.

"Please don't do it, Amanda," Denise whispered.

She put her sword to Kanthius's neck as Sander stepped away slightly, but still in range to make a killing blow if Kanthius made any sudden movements.

"I pray you remember what happened to you tonight, the next time you think about insulting a woman. I believe everyone deserves at least one chance for forgiveness, even you, and because of that, I will let you live.

"Thank you, Lady Amanda," Kanthius said, "for showing me mercy."

She put her sword back into its scabbard and watched him as he slumped to the side, hitting the floor, and closing his eyes.

Sander kneeled over him and whispered in his ear, "Today Amanda showed you mercy, but if you ever insult her again, I will not be so kind."

Sander and Amanda walked back over to Denise.

Gavriel motioned for his immortals to see to Kanthius as Ramiel called a medic to tend to him.

Everyone watched as one of the House Ramiel medics ran over and put some kind of powder over the wounds and gave Kanthius two shots. One of the shots seemed to awaken him.

A House Lucifer soldier said, "He'll probably live. It's going to take a long time to heal, though." Two men ran in with a stretcher and carried Kanthius out. Several maids walked in and cleaned up the blood on the floor, and the attendants of the party started chatting amongst themselves.

Amanda and Sander were silent.

"That was badass, Lady Amanda. I thought you were going to cut his head off," Maurice said, breaking the silence.

Several people laughed at Maurice's comment, still shocked by what had occurred. It had been many years since any of them had witnessed a duel between the two houses at such a public function.

"Well, at least you gave the guests something to talk about," Jessalyn said. "I don't have to worry about them being entertained. You should duel people at all of my events. It takes the pressure off me."

Sander smiled. "Just remind me next time."

"That was so romantic," Dimitra said.

"Thank you, Sander, for protecting my honor," Amanda said.

"Are you okay, Amanda?" Mikayla asked.

"Yes. I'm fine."

"I agree with Dimitra. That was very romantic. Someone insulted you and your faithful knight risked his life to defend your honor. If that doesn't mean he loves you, I don't know what does."

Sander looked away like he hadn't heard her.

"I apologize on behalf of House Lucifer," Gavriel said to Sander and Amanda. "I promise you that, if Kanthius survives, he will be punished."

Ramiel put his arm around Amanda, "I'm proud of you, dear. You handled that with great class and dignity. I'm proud to have you as a part of House Ramiel, and even more proud to call you my daughter."

"Oh, my gosh! I'm going to cry, that was so sweet," Tena said, as she listened in.

Amanda smiled when she heard Tena, "Thank you, Dad."

"You did a good thing by letting that boy live," Denise said.

"And you did a good thing by putting him in his place, Sandriel," Tabrill said.

"You are quite the swordsman," Gavriel, said. "I hope we remain on good terms for a very long time."

Sander looked on as Ramiel, Gavriel and Nasriel were talking.

Kelly, Nasriel's wife, approached Sander, and said, "I want you to know that I thought that was brave of you."

"Thank you, Kelly. I'm sure Nasriel would have done the same for you," Sander smiled slightly.

Amanda hugged Sander. "Thank you so much."

"Anytime." He smiled, hugging her back.

"Aww, look at them," Jessalyn said, nodding her head at Sander and Amanda.

"That's so cute," Dimitra said. "I'm almost out of tissues, already."

Ramiel hit his champagne glass with a spoon several times. "Gavriel would like to speak."

Gavriel stepped forward and said, "This is an example of the kind of altercation that I don't want to disrupt the peace between our two houses. Kanthius behaved with great dishonor tonight, and he will be punished, severely. Many of us in House Lucifer hold a lot of respect for Sandriel, and his actions tonight demonstrated why that is. He is a man of his word, and we consider it an honor to be in his, and everyone else in House Ramiel's, presence tonight. I propose a toast to Sandriel and Lady Amanda of House Ramiel for reminding us all of something that many of us, including myself, seemed to have forgotten after all these years . . . the importance of chivalry and forgiveness."

He raised his glass. "To Sandriel and Amanda!"

"To Sandriel and Amanda!" everyone cheered.

"Thank you Gavriel," Ramiel said. "Now let's continue the festivities!"

The band began to play again, and everyone continued their conversations.

"I was wondering; would you care to dance with me?" Amanda asked Sander.

"There is no one in this world I would rather dance with right now," Sander said smiling.

"Oh, look they are going to dance, finally!" Denise said to Ellen, as she watched Sander and Amanda make their way to the almost-empty dance floor.

"I, too, would like to make a quick announcement if I may," Nasriel said, as he tapped his glass. He looked at Ramiel, who nodded.

"I too hope our peace lasts a long time. At first the idea of signing another treaty with House Ramiel seemed rather pointless to me, considering the number of times we have broken them. I think the moment I realized that perhaps we could work with these people was when Sandriel had several guns pointed at his head and as far as he knew, was about to die. I asked Sandriel if he had any last words, and do you know what his last words were? He did not beg for his life.

He did not try to bribe me, or accept an offer to be a traitor to his house in exchange for his life. Sandriel simply asked me if I could get a message to Ramiel's daughter. Sandriel was about to die, and all he wanted to do was tell Lady Amanda he was sorry that he couldn't keep his promise to return to her."

"Do you have any more tissues, Denise?" Ellen asked as she wiped her eyes.

Nasriel continued, "The selflessness and courage he showed, in the face of death, made me realize: maybe there are some people in House Ramiel worth working with."

Maurice yelled, "Another toast to Sandriel and Amanda!"

"To Sandriel and Amanda!" everyone yelled.

Amanda had tears in her eyes as she looked at Sander and they walked onto the dance floor.

Sander put his hand in hers and his arm around her and danced slowly to the classical music playing.

"So, those were really going to be your last words on this earth?" Amanda whispered.

"Yes, I wanted you to know you were the last thing I was thinking about when I left this world."

A tear dropped down her cheek.

"Sander, do you have any idea how much that means to me?" Amanda asked. "Don't ever leave me again!"

"I don't intend to," Sander said. "I'm your guardian angel, but there is a slight problem."

"What's the problem?"

"I don't know how to say this . . . ." He paused. "I think I have a slight crush on you."

"Is it a problem if I have a slight crush on you, too?" she asked. "Because I do."

He smiled.

"And if I thought I might be falling in love with you?" he asked.

"No problem there, either," she said. "I have a question, too."

Sander looked happier than she thought she had ever seen him. "Yes?" he asked.

"Are you getting ready to kiss me?" she asked as they continued dancing.

He grinned. "I think there are rules against council members kissing one another on dance floors."

She smiled, leaning in closer to him. "Oh, really?"

"Yes . . . but then again, I've always considered myself to be a bit of a rebel," he said as he pulled her closer and put his lips against hers, kissing her softly.

"I think that's their first kiss! It's so perfect!" Dimitra said, louder than she meant to.

Tena and Denise were wiping their eyes.

Maurice looked at Craig and asked, "Is anybody looking at me?"

Craig smiled as he noticed Maurice had a tear rolling down his cheek. "No, nobody is looking at you," he said softly.

Maurice quickly wiped his eyes and said, "I just had something in my eye."

Craig grinned.

When the music stopped playing, Sander and Amanda were still holding each other, oblivious to their surroundings, oblivious to the people applauding, focused solely on one another.

"I hope you are always with me," Amanda said.

"I will be. I promise. I've never broken a promise to you, and I don't intend to start now," Sander said. "It's just me and you from now on . . . Sander and Amanda."

"Forever," Amanda said.

"Forever," Sander said, looking into her eyes.

As Sander kissed Amanda again she realized that she had never been this happy in all of her years on this earth, and that in him she had found someone who would die for her, care for her, protect her, and love her, until the end of time. Truly, and literally, for eternity.

As time passed, there were more rumors about Sander and Amanda -- some true, most embellished. After that night at Jessalyn's, knowing the peace treaty had been signed and with Sander wanting to keep his promise to Amanda to show her the world, they said their goodbyes to their friends and ran away together. Some people would gossip that they had been seen in Europe, where, they had heard, Sander and Amanda were married. Some would swear they heard from a friend that Sander and Amanda were living in a quiet spot in the mountains, far from the violence of the world to which Sander had become so accustomed, where Sander still slept innocently on the floor beside Amanda's bed, protecting her from all the bad things in this world.

No one really knew the truth, and after over a year of no one hearing from them, the story of Sander and Amanda had slowly turned into a fairy tale among all houses of the fallen angels. Sander and Amanda's story became the story of a human girl and House Ramiel's greatest soldier finding, in each other, the peace in life for which they had been searching. For more than a year, not a celebration went by without someone mentioning Sander and Amanda. No one was even sure they would see Sander and Amanda again. That is until the day Maurice was walking to the Main House and noticed a silver Mercedes SUV drive by, windows down and music blaring.

The End

Made in United States
Orlando, FL
27 July 2023

35496728R10255